ALSO BY JUS ACCARDO

IN THIS SERIES

Infinity
Omega

THE DENAZEN SERIES

Touch
Untouched
Toxic
Faceless
Tremble

The Big Bad Wolf

THE DARKER AGENCY SERIES
Darker Days
A Darker Past

FOR NEW ADULT READERS
Ruined
Released
Embraced
Rules of Survival

alpha

JUS ACCARDO

Entangled Publishing, LLC
2614 South Timberline Road
Suite 105, PMB 159
Fort Collins, CO 80525
rights@entangledpublishing.com

Entangled Teen is an imprint of Entangled Publishing, LLC.

Visit our website at www.entangledpublishing.com.

Edited by Stacy Abrams
Cover design by LJ Anderson, Mayhem Cover Creations
Interior design by Toni Kerr

ISBN 978-1-64063-185-4
Ebook ISBN 978-1-64063-186-1

Manufactured in the United States of America

First Edition July 2018

10 9 8 7 6 5 4 3 2 1

entangled teen
an imprint of Entangled Publishing LLC

For my mom

Chapter One

Sera

The rain stopped, and the wind outside had settled, leaving an uncomfortable silence in its wake. I didn't have a problem with the quiet. I liked it, in fact. But this was something a little different. This was uncomfortable. The kind of stillness that came from forced proximity to someone or something that made your skin itch and your stomach roil. The kind of hush that usually set in right before a devastating storm or a natural disaster.

He did this sometimes. Just sat across from me and stared. He usually wouldn't even say anything. I didn't think he expected me to say anything, either. He just *looked*. Sometimes it lasted a few minutes, just long enough to send that chill skittering up and down my spine. Other times it would go on for hours. He'd blink and breathe and fidget, but his eyes…those remained locked on me, his unhealthy mix of sadness and lust and greed and anger crushing me to the point of breathlessness.

We were at it again, and I was just about out of patience. It was one thing to have been ripped away from my home, from my *life*, by that madwoman, Cora Anderson. It was another to have her poke and prod and use me as a science experiment. She'd altered my mind. Made me forget most of my life before the day I woke up a prisoner on the floor of her cold, dank cell. Those things were all bad, but having been "rescued" by this bastard and forced to stay by his side at all times? That was an entirely new level of torture.

"You're thinking about *him* again, aren't you?" His tone was acidic and his jaw tight. He had a temper, this guy. I'd seen it multiple times. He'd never done anything more than scream at me, but it was only a matter of time with people like this. I wasn't sure how I knew that, but I felt it in my bones. Maybe I'd known someone like him at home. Maybe it was just intuition.

"Yes," was all I replied. I found that simple, one-word responses went over the best. Or, more accurately, the worst. When I said too little, he grew agitated. He wanted me to talk to him, yet the things that came out of my mouth weren't ever what he wanted to hear. I didn't act like he'd hoped I would, didn't say the things he longed to hear. Some days he was determined to change me. Others, he was rabid, blaming me for not behaving like *myself* and demanding that I *wake up*.

Forget that I had no idea who I was.

"While it's not okay, I understand." He offered me a smile—a small, tentative twitch of his lips and gentle shrug of his shoulders. He was making an effort to be kinder today, going out of his way to speak softer and move slower.

That made me even angrier.

"You understand? Then my life is complete. All I've ever wanted was the understanding of a *serial killer*." Even if I hadn't been thinking about…someone else, I would have lied. The fact that I wasn't focused on him, and him alone, drove Dylan—my savior, my *captor*—crazy. But the truth was, I was thinking of *him*. That *other* him. How could I not? Even if I didn't find myself missing him every moment of every day in an almost physical way, I wouldn't be able to put him out of my mind because he was technically sitting here across from me.

The only solace to be found during my captivity at the Infinity Division had been a boy named G. Like me, he'd been ripped from his home and experimented on. Like me, he didn't remember who he was or where he'd come from. We'd formed a strong bond. Kept each other sane in the midst of a torturous situation. Just hearing his voice made me feel safer. Knowing he was there—even if I couldn't see or touch him—calmed the terrible churning in my gut and allowed me to drift off to sleep at night. Then Ash, the foster daughter of our captor, and her friends had freed us, and I'd seen him for the very first time. He was beautiful, with dark hair and chocolate brown eyes. I'd gotten to touch him…

It was brief, and it wasn't enough, and I hadn't been able to stop thinking about him.

"I *am* him," Dylan said. There was a hint of impatience in his voice. Under normal circumstances I wouldn't have blamed him. He'd been telling me the same thing, over and over again, for the last three weeks, and that would be enough to drive anyone over the edge. Well, anyone who hadn't already gone over. Dylan had jumped the sanity line years ago, from what I understood. "You don't need to miss him because I'm *right here*."

The most twisted part of this whole mess? He wasn't technically lying. G—whose real name was apparently Dylan—*was* sitting right here. The face was the same, though G's was thinner. The voice was the same, though the pitch was different. G's was lower, while Dylan always sounded angry. G was scruffier, with slightly darker hair that brushed his shoulders. Dylan kept his hair buzzed close to his head. They were different versions of the same person. From different dimensions of the same place.

It made my head spin to think about it, but a scientist named Cora Anderson—most Cora Andersons, apparently—had invented a way to travel between dimensions. As Dylan put it, there were an infinite number of Earths just floating around out there. All different, if only slightly, from the next. Infinite versions of him and me playing at the same song and dance— one I wanted no part of.

"You're *not* him." My only joy in life anymore was pointing that out to him. Over and over, in as many ways as I could come up with. Because it was true. There were infinite versions of Earth, which meant an infinite number of Dylans—but still only one G.

Dylan jumped up, fists balled tight, and began stalking back and forth. All pretenses of his *softer side* evaporated. I was familiar with this. While he made an effort most days, it was always short-lived. His patience was nonexistent.

The motel room was small. Only eight by ten. And every time he passed, the temperature dropped a little. I didn't know if it was from the breeze he created as he moved through the room, or something darker, but it cut me to the bone and left me feeling hollow.

"What's so great about him?" He stopped pacing and stood in front of me, bending to grip the arms of my chair. Leaning in close, he said, "He looks and sounds exactly like I do. What makes him so different from me?"

"For starters, he wouldn't have kidnapped me." If Dylan lost his temper and killed me, then at least this would all be over. I wouldn't be stuck listening to his annoying comparisons. I wouldn't be subjected to his weird *romantic* overtures and attempts to win my heart. He was another version of G, and I was another version of his girlfriend, Ava. He'd lost her to an accident on his Earth, and it had destroyed his mind. Since then, he'd cut a bloody swath across the multiverse in search of another version of her—me. One he could claim as his own. "He wouldn't blackmail me into staying with him."

Dylan straightened and made a sweeping gesture toward the door. The corner of his lip pulled up and created the smallest hint of a dimple. On anyone other than this madman, it would have been adorable. I'd swoon hard if G had flashed it my way. On Dylan, though, it seemed almost sinister. "Go ahead, then. Leave. Get up and walk away right now if you feel inclined. I won't stop you."

I'd tried leaving once in the beginning, a few days after he'd taken me away from my new friends. He kept me tied up for the next four days, watched me like a hawk, stealing away whatever tiny shreds of dignity I had left. Now, though, the shackles were off because he'd found a much more effective way to keep me in line.

If I left him, I would be stuck. Stranded in whatever world we were in at the time. The chip that allowed him to move between dimensions, the one buried beneath his skin, worked on both of us if we were touching, but I hadn't gotten one of my own. If I ran from him, then I would never find my way home—wherever that was—and I would never find G... He could track Dylan because of the chip, but if I wasn't with him... That wasn't a scenario I could live with, so by his side I stayed until G found me—and I knew he would.

Plus, there was a good chance I'd end up back in one of Cora Anderson's cells if I left.

She'd put some kind of tracking device in me. Property. That's how she'd referred to me. The specifics were unclear, but she'd claimed that on top of being vital to her research, I owed her my life thanks to the tech she'd created, and without her, I would eventually die.

My life was hers.

Of course, if you asked Dylan, my life was *his*. Sometimes I wondered if anyone else would step up and put in a claim. If they did? Fine. I'd enjoy showing them—all of them—that my life belonged to *me*. I just had to bide my time. Wait for my moment.

"Do you think they'll ever stop looking?" It was a legitimate question. I didn't know Cade and Noah very well. Only what Dylan had told me about them— which was colorfully bad. Despite the horrible things

I already knew about him, he'd painted *them* as the villains. They'd been chasing him since he left home, determined to make him suffer. Determined to keep him from finding me.

As for Cora? As surely as I knew G would never rest until he found me, I knew *she'd* never stop, either. She would hunt me until the day one of us died. If I went first, she'd probably cart my carcass back to her lab and do, well, whatever it was she did with her *property*. Maybe I'd end up in some weird science museum. Or maybe they'd stash me away in a freezer to be used at a later date. Dissected and diced to bits. Whatever her plan, I had no intention of making it easy on her.

"Do you wish they would stop looking?" he challenged. The set of his jaw was stiff, and his shoulders were rigid. He was barely controlling his temper.

"Of course not."

"So you can be with *him*?" It was more an accusation than a question. His tone was light, but his eyes...his eyes brimmed with fury. At his sides, both fists were balled tight, the muscles in his arms coiled and taut. Ready to strike. Always ready...

He and G had that in common.

"So they can put an end to you." I stood. "So they can make you pay for all the horrible things you've done."

He pushed me back into the chair. "The horrible things I've done? You mean all the things I did for *you*?"

I stood again, and this time, I pushed him harder. It was one thing to leave him to his delusions, but to allow him to essentially lay the blame at my feet? Not a damn chance. I wasn't responsible for the devastation he'd caused, for the blood on his hands. Every drop he'd spilled coated his own conscience—not mine. "You've done nothing for *me*. Everything you've done, every single selfish action, was for you and you alone. Even now, hiding away in this rat-infested place so you can keep me *safe* from Cora is so that you aren't denied the one thing you feel the universe *owes* you. *Me!*"

I watched it come—the subtle twitch of his left eye and the pull of his lips as he ground his teeth. Rage swirled behind his eyes and I knew… Somehow, I was sure that I'd taken this too far. This could be it. I might have finally pushed him hard enough.

I thought about the twin scars on the insides of each of my wrists. I had no recollection of how they'd gotten there, but every day I spent with Dylan was one day closer to convincing me that I'd had a death wish in my old life. One that had carried through the memory loss and was fighting its way to the surface.

He grabbed two handfuls of my shirt and hauled me away from the chair. Whipping me around as though I weighed nothing more than a feather, he flung me at the bed. I crashed into the mattress and bounced, rolling off the side and hitting the floor with enough force to jar my hip. A jolt of pain shot through me, and I winced, lifting my head to glare at him in defiance. "That's it? All you've got?"

He clenched his fists and closed his eyes for a moment. When he opened them, the anger had gone. Mostly. "You'd like that, right? If I killed you? Then you'd feel justified in believing I'm a monster."

"You don't need to do anything to justify to me that you're a monster." I grabbed the edge of the bed and climbed to my feet. I'd traded one captivity for another, and I'd be damned if I let him bully me into silence. "I've told you repeatedly that I want to leave. That I don't want to be here with you. The fact that you refuse to set me free, to let me find G, proves it in spades."

"For three weeks I've done nothing but keep you safe." He had a point. A small one. Cade and Noah and G weren't the only ones chasing us. Cora's main man, Yancy, and his crew had been nipping at our heels for weeks now. Sometimes we burned the cooldown on his chip, skipping and waiting out in the open until they found us, only to skip again. After the fourth and final skip, we hunkered down in some out of the way hole, like we were now, a brief twenty-four hours of reprieve granted while the chip reset before we had to do it all again.

That was, of course, assuming they didn't land right on top of us when they followed. The way the chip worked, you could track someone's frequency, but the individual landing spot was a bit random. It could put you anywhere from one foot to half a mile away from your target. We'd had a couple of close calls but had gotten lucky this last time. "If it wasn't for me, you'd be back rotting in that cage."

"I think I would prefer that to spending another second with you." It was a lie. I hated Dylan, but even all his staring and misplaced lovesick actions weren't as bad as the things Cora had done to me. All in the name of science, she'd say. Over and over. She told me that I was special. That I would herald a new generation to change the world. I was going to be instrumental in making it a better place—though, I had no idea how.

Dylan flew at me, eyes wild, but stopped when our faces were mere inches apart. I held my breath and waited, but the blow never came. "You're lying. I know because of the way you scream at night. Like the devil himself was standing at your back."

His voice was low and, even though I refused to acknowledge it, held a hint of compassion. He'd been sweet in the beginning. Each word had been carefully chosen to make me comfortable. Every action was played out with the sole purpose of wooing me. In the beginning, I almost fell for it. Not for him, but for the show. For the mask he donned to sway me. He'd been kind, and I'd returned the favor. But when I'd asked him to return me to G, to let me go so that I could find the place I belonged, the mask had slipped to reveal the monster beneath. I screamed at night over the things Cora had done to me, but Dylan was right. The devil *was* standing at my back.

And he had Dylan's face.

"Get your crap together. We need to leave in five." He turned and stalked out the door, slamming it behind him so hard that the small vase on the table beside the bed wobbled then teetered off the edge. It hit the stained carpet, a piece of the rim cracking off and bouncing across to land at my feet.

I picked it up and turned, then spun in a slow circle as I rubbed my left wrist, the raised scars on the inside that could be from only one thing. I didn't remember my old life, but those scars told me that I'd tried to escape it. I had the feeling that I was always trying to escape *something*. That just like now, I'd been trapped. Caged. But whatever it was that I'd been running from back then, I'd changed. I might not know the true extent of that change, but I wasn't about to take the easy way out. I wasn't going down without a fight.

I went to the window and peeled back the curtains. Dylan was just outside the door, pacing back and forth like a caged animal. He did this when I frustrated him—which was at least ten times a day. It was the one small pleasure I was able to squeeze from the current situation.

He was so focused on his irritation that he didn't notice the man approaching from the far side of the building. Tall, with a five o'clock shadow and a wicked gleam in his eyes, the man was dressed in a dark purple suit and walked with a kind of confidence you didn't see often.

"Yancy." I threw myself at the door, fumbled with the knob, and propelled myself outside just in time to see someone else round the corner of the building not far behind him. Several others, actually. Cade and Noah and their friends, and…

…G.

Maybe I should have been shocked, but I wasn't. It was the first time I'd seen him in almost a month, but I knew he'd come for me. There was never a sliver of doubt in my mind.

Our eyes met, and my heart waged war with my brain. We outnumbered Yancy, so logic said that I could simply step back, wait for him to take out Dylan, then let the rest of them take *him* down. In the short time we'd been together, I'd seen G in action, and he was brutal, full of raw strength and graceful power that I was confident could hold its own against the most formidable enemies. Unfortunately, Yancy wasn't just formidable—he was lethal, with moves like an otherworldly cat. The rumor was that Cora had altered him somehow. Made him stronger, faster, smarter… In some ways, I was more afraid of him than her. The fact that Dylan and I had avoided him this long was nothing short of a miracle.

G must have realized the impossibility of the predicament at the same time I did. He was even better acquainted with Yancy than I was, Cora having used the bastard to try and break him. He pulled up short and thrust his hands out on either side to keep the others back. Eyes locked on mine, his lips parted just a hair, and rage flashed across his features. We were so close…

One second passed.

Then two.

"Go!" he roared. Dylan's head snapped up and he noticed Yancy—and G. Yancy let out a string of curses and dove for us. I grabbed my captor's arm as G charged our common enemy, and a second later, they both disappeared.

Chapter Two

So close.

We'd been so damn close. Again.

"You okay?" Kori was at my back, but I didn't turn around. Instead, I focused on breathing. In—out—in—out—in—out—counting each breath as I went until I reached forty. It didn't do much to calm my nerves, but it did keep me from whirling around and snapping her neck like a damn twig.

She meant well. They all did. At least, I assumed they did. Sometimes I wondered about Noah. Cade was obviously uncomfortable around me, but Noah... That guy hated me. I saw it in his eyes every time he looked at me, like he was mentally cataloging all the ways he could think of to skin me alive. Not that I really blamed him. If I were in his position, I would feel the same way. I had, after all, killed his sister.

At least, another *version* of me had.

"Yancy's closing in." Noah folded his arms and grunted.

Yeah. He was. I'd sprinted for the bastard to give Sera the opportunity to get away. I never got the chance to tackle him, unfortunately. The instant they disappeared, Yancy sidestepped me and skipped out as well.

Cade came up beside me and shook his head. I didn't necessarily *like* the guy, but he was a solider through and through, and I respected that. His eyes flickered to Ashlyn, Noah's girl, then back to me as Kori came and slipped her hand into his. "You're sure you don't know anything else that might help?"

I bit down hard on the inside of my cheek. If they asked me one more time, there was a good chance I'd start swinging. Then again, there was a good chance I'd do it anyway. They'd messed me up at Infinity. Force-fed me drugs and tortured me in ways I couldn't have even imagined. I wasn't right in the head anymore.

"I can only tell you what Cora's people did to me—and even that's hazy in places," I said. "I have no idea why she's obsessed with getting Ashlyn and Sera back." While not technically a lie, I wasn't telling them the whole truth. As far as I was concerned, the whole truth didn't matter. Not right now. It would. Eventually. But right now, the only thing that mattered was finding Sera and dealing with Cora once and for all.

"Ava," Noah said. He stalked past Cade and positioned himself in front of me, so close that I could smell the burger he'd crammed down his throat as we skipped from the last world. "Her name isn't Sera, it's *Ava*. Kinda think we've been through this before. And we know what her deal with Ash is. It's the rest that's foggy."

I leaned forward, stopping when our faces were inches apart. My fists curled tight, and a familiar feeling washed over me. A total body itch, like there were a trillion tiny bugs stomping around beneath my skin, just out of reach. How many nights had Cora pushed me to the brink just so that I'd chase that itch? She'd done unthinkable things to get me to scratch. So that I'd let go... I hadn't then, and I had no intention of giving in now—no matter how tempting it might be. With a deep breath, I said, "Ava is the ghost you're chasing. I'm looking for Sera."

Noah's eyes narrowed, and his lips twisted into a scowl. "They're the same—"

Ash wedged herself between us. Cade could usually rein the guy in, but when it came to me, that didn't always work. They had to bring out the big—or little when you thought about it—guns. She rested a hand against his chest and nudged him back a few inches. "Better things to do than argue over something so petty. Agreed?"

Noah hesitated, then nodded once. Their eyes met, and the rigid set of his shoulders relaxed just a little. The anger in his expression didn't dissipate completely, but it did calm to a light simmer. "Agreed."

I didn't say anything, just gave a short nod of my own. The memories I had of my time at Infinity were excruciating in their detail. Smells, tastes, sensations... I remembered, and I *hated*. Cora had remarked once that my temper was a side effect of the formula she'd given me. She had no idea how wrong she was—especially when I listened to the stories about Cade's brother, the other version of me. The kind of darkness that lived in him lived in me as well. It had been there long before Cora came into my life.

"I think we should move forward with the plan." Cade came around to stand beside Noah—probably to make sure we didn't go for each other's throats. Kori followed, but she didn't look thrilled. She exchanged a worried glance with Ash. Cade pretended not to see it, but I knew he had. He put his arm around her shoulders and drew her closer, then glanced in my direction. "You good?"

I nodded again, even though it wasn't true. Since my first moments with these people, I'd been fighting an increasingly hard war. Every time someone said something I didn't like, each time they planned a move I didn't agree with, I inched closer and closer to that edge Cora had tried so hard to shove me over. It wasn't their fault. They were solid people trying to do something good. Trying to look out for the ones they loved. They were trying to help *me*. I respected that and, deep down, hated myself for the unprovoked animosity I felt toward them. But each day that passed, the anger grew hotter. I was living with this nuclear core inside me, and all it would take was just the right kind of push and I'd destroy everything in sight.

They'd gotten a small glimpse. I'd let my control slip twice so far. No one had gotten hurt. Not badly, at least. Cade, who seemed like the leader and peacekeeper of the group, had intervened in time. He'd gotten a fat lip and a few bruises for his trouble, and my guilt had been festering ever since.

"I'm not sure we should move on the plan so soon." Kori dislodged herself from Cade and kept looking between him and Noah—who was technically her brother. "Splitting up might not be the best idea right now. We have a better shot at finding them if we work together."

Cade had been pushing his *plan* for more than two weeks now. Personally, I didn't care one way or the other, but Kori had been doing her best to stall.

Noah snorted. "Are you nervous about splitting up, or are you freaking out about seeing *her*?"

Kori shifted from one foot to the other, head down. Cade wanted to split up. Since they now had more freedom in their movements—before landing on Ashlyn's Earth, they were forced to skip when Dylan did—he'd proposed a side trip for everyone other than us. Cora Anderson was after Sera. Something to do with what she'd done to her during our time at Infinity, but she was also after Ash. She was the key to getting some nefarious project off the ground and rolling full speed ahead. I didn't know the details. Didn't care.

I had one goal and one goal alone.

Find Sera.

"What if she's disappointed?" Kori lifted her head. "What if she's angry that you brought another me? She might think you're trying to replace her daughter..."

Where Kori was from, her mother had died, but where Cade and Noah were from, Cora was alive—and not a sadistic bitch—and Kori was the one who had died. If you asked me, the whole thing was too much of a drama-fest, but Cade thought it'd be good for both of them. His idea was to have Noah bring her—which I think had more to do with Noah's growing animosity toward me, or more specifically, my face—and Ash.

Supposedly they'd be safe on their world and out of evil Cora's reach.

He grasped her hands and smiled. "Cora will be overjoyed to meet you. I promise."

She hesitated for another moment, then nodded.

"Good." Cade grabbed Noah's shoulder and gave him a shake. "Spend a few days, then come find us—but be careful and keep your eyes open. I still say Dylan will circle back home again now that he's got Ava. And remember, Cora can track Ash, so keep your eyes open."

Kori's face paled. "Good? Go? As in right *now*?"

He steered her off to the side, and the two of them talked quietly for a moment while Noah pulled Ash close and wrapped his arms around her. She leaned into him, resting her head against his chest, and shivered just a little. In response, he tugged at his jacket and tucked it around so that it enveloped them both.

I looked away, remembering the promises I'd made to Sera...

"What's the first thing you plan on doing when we get out of here?"

"Food. Obviously." I kicked my feet over the edge of the cot and went to sit on the floor against the wall closest to her cell. We were next to each other, yet far enough away that we couldn't see each other or touch. "What about you?"

"The hottest shower I can find."

I'd never seen this girl. I had no idea what she looked

like. Yet the thought of her naked in the shower sent a spike of warmth through me. "Yeah. That'd be a close second on my list."

"My second would be to spend the day with you."

"Me? You don't think you'll have gotten enough of me by the time we leave this place in the dust?"

She snickered. It was a soft sound that reminded me of a blanket I'd had once. Weird, but true. That blanket was the one thing in the world that brought me peace. It gave me comfort. That blanket was mine.

"You'd like to think so, but get used to it, G. It's you and me. Against this place and against the world."

Screw the food and shower. Screw an entire day. There wasn't much I wouldn't have given to spend even an hour with this girl. To see her smile and watch her move. To feel her hand in mine... "You'll have your shower, Sera. And that day. I promise, if it's the last thing I do, I'll make it all happen."

"I know you will."

When Cade and Kori returned, there was an odd sort of resolution in her eyes. She faced him, and he touched her cheek. They stayed like that for a moment, just *looking* at each other. It was ridiculous, but I was jealous. Of such a stupid, simple little thing. "I'll be fine. I swear."

Kori rolled her eyes. "I'd feel more confident about that statement if we stuck together. Maybe Noah and Ash could go. I'd stay with—"

He took her hand and placed it on his chest, over his heart. "I need you to stay with Noah. If I'm not around, God knows what stupid shit he'll get into."

"You better make sure nothing happens to G." Her gaze flickered to me for a half second, then she took Noah's hand. His chip, the small device buried beneath the skin allowing us to travel between dimensions, had been damaged last month, so he needed to rely on contact from one of us to skip. "Or you."

Ash positioned herself on Noah's other side, threading her fingers through his. A moment later, they were gone, leaving Cade and me alone in the dark outside the hotel Sera and Dylan had fled.

"I think this will work better. It was easier when we first started out," Cade said. He pulled his jacket tighter and thrust both hands into its pockets. "It was just Noah and me. Two people chasing someone down are a hell of a lot less conspicuous than five."

"Makes sense," I said. We'd lost them a few times because Dylan had seen us coming. At one point I contemplated going it alone. They were more invested in bringing down Dylan than finding Sera. I felt like to them she would just be a convenient side benefit of getting what they were after.

But I didn't know jack about the guy, despite being his double. Cade and Noah's insight had proven useful on multiple occasions. I'd give it a little more time before I cut and run. "So, what now?"

Cade started walking, and I followed. "Yancy almost had them this time, so I don't want to wait too long, but I think we need to let Dylan breathe a bit. If I've been keeping track correctly, their skip timer just recharged. Maybe—"

I grabbed his arm and jerked him to a stop. *"Let

him breathe?"

He regarded me with something like the pity I saw in Kori's eyes. "He won't hurt her, G." Same song, another day—but I still wasn't convinced.

People were seven different kinds of messed up—myself included. *Dylan* included. There was no guarantee that he wouldn't lose his shit. That she wouldn't be a target for his rage. And aside from that, knowing what I did about Sera, she was probably ready to crawl out of her own skin by now. She might not realize where it was coming from, or even understand it completely, but being trapped, being *forced* to stay with Dylan, would freak her out on an almost inhumane level...

"He needs to think we've backed off a bit. Or, at the very least, slowed down. Otherwise he'll keep skipping and we'll never catch him. We can land anywhere from one foot away from them to half a mile. That—"

"Yeah. I get it." And I did. *Mostly*. But there was a small part of me, the bits and pieces created when Cora screwed with my head, that wanted nothing more than blood. That part didn't care about Cade and his mission for vengeance, or even about Sera. It fed on an anger festering inside, one rooted deeper than anyone realized. I'd resisted it for the most part, but I didn't know how much longer I could hold out. "So then, like I said, what's next?"

"I guess we should find a place to crash, then skip out in the morning. That should give Dylan a false sense of security. You okay with that?"

"Sure. As long as Yancy doesn't get to them first." We had a history, Cora's personal psycho and me. A violent and bloody history. Not long ago, during one of our last encounters, I'd promised him he'd pay for every bruise, every ache he'd ever inflicted. He'd laughed—and why shouldn't he? I was a rat in a cage at the time. No more a danger to him than a simple cold. But now that I was out, now that he was hunting Sera, all bets were off. The promise I'd made him was fresh on my mind.

"He won't. We'll get to her first." Cade frowned and lifted his head, but he didn't look directly at me.

He never did.

We hadn't spoken much after checking into the hotel. Cade offered to grab something for me when he went in search of food, but as usual I declined. While things weren't as tense as they were with Noah, he didn't like me, either. Every once in a while, when he thought I didn't notice, I'd catch him scowling at me, the venom he normally buried so deep exposed and raw. I got it, though. I wore the face of the guy who killed his girl. Brother or not, that leaves a mark. I didn't blame him. I didn't like it, but I didn't blame him.

I was wide awake when he returned, but I didn't roll over. Still, he knew.

"Sure you don't want anything to eat? I brought back extra." The paper bags crackled as he set them down. "In case you'd changed your mind."

I surrendered the illusion and sat upright. "I'm fine."

"When was the last time you ate?" He dipped his hand into the first sack and pulled out what looked like a sandwich. It had an odd smell, like a mix between tuna and egg. It turned my stomach, while at the same time making my mouth water.

The truth was, I couldn't be sure. It must have been yesterday. Right? Maybe I'd eaten something the day before? Sometimes my mind raced so fast that I lost track of the basic things. Eating, sleeping... I was used to going without. Sometimes, as punishment, Cora would let me sit for days with a heaping plate of food set on the other side of the bars, just out of reach.

Cade pulled off a chunk of his sandwich and popped it into his mouth, then leaned across and set the other on the end of my bed. "You're no good to her if you starve yourself."

His point was logical. Logical, I could do. Still, I couldn't bring myself to grab the food. Sometimes, for a change of pace, Cora would wait days to bring food. Then, when she did, it would make me violently ill. Spoiled, lightly poisoned—I had no idea what she'd done to it.

"Shit," Cade said. He held out the sandwich and twisted his lips in disgust. "I grabbed the wrong one. This has mayo. Mind if I swap 'em?"

A part of me knew why he'd swapped the food. Condiments had nothing to do with it. I'd made my distrust of them—of everyone—crystal clear. Still, in the deepest recesses of my mind, I was grateful, and the second he drew his hand away, I was on it.

He sighed and sank into the chair by the door. "This whole situation sucks for both of us. Being here is...hard."

"One way to put it," I mumbled through a mouthful

of food. Turkey. Possibly chicken. The bread was starting to go stale, and the mayo was warm, but it didn't matter. "If you're about to apologize for the fact that you can't stand the sight of me, don't."

He was quiet for a minute. "Tell me how you would feel if you had to stare at the face of the guy who killed someone you loved? If you had to stand beside the spitting image of someone who you'd watched spill innocent blood for no good reason?"

"Probably wouldn't be a fan." If he only knew the truth, that I was more than just the *spitting image* of a killer, then he would gut me where I sat.

"Think about what it might be like if that person, that *monster*, was also your brother. Your own flesh and blood. Think about how you would feel if you let him slip through your fingers countless times."

"Hey." I threw up my hands and gave a short nod. "No judgment. We're not here to be friends. You don't need to like me. You just have to help me get Sera back, and then we can go our own ways. Like I said, no need to apologize. I get it. But just so we're clear—I *wasn't* the one who killed your girl. You can stop glaring at me like I'm guilty."

"Thought it didn't bother you."

"It doesn't," I lied. It might have bothered me a *little*. I was a bastard, but if I'd had a brother on my Earth, I sure as shit wouldn't have taken away the girl he'd loved. If Cade had done something to slight Dylan, then he should have gone for his brother. Hurting someone innocent to harm your target? That was weak. It was cowardly.

He sank onto the bed across from me. "I wonder if

you had an Ava of your own. Where you come from, I mean."

All I wanted was to go to sleep, but the guy seemed intent on talking. I hoped if I indulged him for a few minutes, he'd leave me the hell alone. "I didn't."

"But your memory—"

"Is all screwed up," I finished for him. "But not like you think. What's wrong with my head isn't the same as Sera's memory loss." It was the most I'd ever said on the matter. The most I'd ever say. If Sera knew the truth about me...

He waited for more and, when I didn't continue, said, "It must be hard for you. For Av—Sera, too. Not knowing where you came from..."

I shrugged. "Not sure 'hard' is the word I'd use. I mean, it is for Sera. Not being able to remember almost destroyed her. She was there a few days longer than I was. Those first nights I remember hearing her cry..."

I still heard the sound, so vivid, in my head. If I closed my eyes and took a deep breath, I'd still be able to smell the bleach and mothball-scented air of that place. Some nights I still tasted the blood in my mouth and felt the sting of the needles as they pierced sensitive skin. She didn't know that I remembered those early days—she couldn't. I'd never told her, because really, what the hell good would it have done? That knowledge would have only led to questions I couldn't answer. To things that would hurt her.

"She had it ten times harder than me, and if it's the last thing I do on this Earth, I'm going to make Cora Anderson pay for every second Sera suffered."

"You guys got close, huh," Cade said. It was a

statement, not a question.

"Yeah. We did. At first it was about survival. We kept each other anchored, ya know?" I lifted my head and found him watching me intently. Waiting for me to spill out all my messy insides. What the hell was I doing? My feelings for Sera, what she meant to me, were my business. The fewer people who knew she was my weakness, the better. Cora had known. She'd used it against me at every turn. All it'd taken was a single veiled threat about a girl I'd never seen before, and I was compliant in ways that made me hate myself. "Yeah. It was survival, and then it wasn't. She's important to me."

There. End of conversation.

"So you remember when you were first there, but not your life before?"

Or not.

"Whatever the stuff was that they gave me, it targeted a certain part of the brain." Another lie. Lies were all that came from my mouth these days.

"Like, long term memory?"

I shrugged. It was as good an explanation as any. "Sounds right."

"So you don't care? About not being able to remember anything?"

The question wasn't did I care—but *would* I? My memories were all intact. Every single, miserable last one of them. Not being able to remember? That would have been a fucking blessing. One the universe obviously didn't think I deserved.

"I care more about the side effects of what they did to me than the result." It wasn't a lie. The serum I'd been given had other side effects, but memory loss, no matter how much I would have welcomed it, wasn't one. But no one knew that—and it was going to stay that way.

"Your temper, you mean?"

I shook my head. He still didn't get it—despite my multiple attempts at explanation. "You can't classify it as a temper. They didn't make me angry." Well, they had, but that wasn't the point here. "They made me *unstable*. A temper is something you can control. What I am…isn't."

Cade shrugged. "I haven't seen that. You've flown off the handle a couple of times, but you're under a lot of stress, man. That's bound to take a toll."

I'd overheard Noah say once that Cade had an overly optimistic way of looking at things. He wasn't kidding. I thought back to all those days in lockup at Infinity. All those tests and experiments. I remembered the moments I was locked inside myself, unable to move or speak, and the times I had no control, my limbs thrashing and fists swinging as if they had a brain of their own. Those were the times that scared me most. The utter clarity of what was happening around me with no way to stop it. I couldn't count the number of Cora's men I'd injured—or even killed in those moments. There was no way to shrug off the feeling of joy it'd given me to see them lying there, broken and bloodied, even though the guilt of it was like a noose around my neck. Those were the moments I'd come close to the breaking point, to the line Cora had tried so hard to nudge me across. Somehow I knew that if I crossed that line, there would be no coming back. What little humanity I had left in me would be gone, and the person I wanted to be would die. The person I wanted to be for Sera.

I didn't much care for Cade, but he'd never done me wrong. I had no reason to want him harmed.

At least not yet.

"Pray that you don't."

Chapter Three

Sera

The scenery changed. I hadn't been skipping long, but so far, the differences had been subtle. This time, though, it was a shock to the system. All the foliage was gone. The trees that loomed overhead only moments ago now gave way to a wide open, angry-looking sky as thunder rumbled in the distance. Instead of lush grass, there were pebbles, a mix of smooth dark brown and jagged light gray, and the wind that whipped around us was icy. It sliced through me like a blade, leaving an all-over chill that made my teeth chatter.

"This isn't creepy at all," I said, more to myself than to Dylan. The buildings were all the same. Brick-faced and boxy with round tinted windows that each had a single horizontal bar across the middle. Every rooftop ended in a vicious-looking point and had an assortment of metal rods poking upward. Some were simple and smooth, while others had intricate designs and spindly protrusions. "Please tell me you don't plan on staying here long."

On the sidewalk across the street, a couple walked hand in hand. The man wore a suit in the most obnoxiously bright yellow I'd ever seen, making him stand out against the dankness of his surroundings. His companion, however, matched the building and sky in their bleakness. Her long skirt was charcoal gray, and her oversize jacket flat black. On her head was a large hat—also black—that hid most of her face.

Dylan turned in a slow circle and let out a whistle. "Wonder what the deal is."

"Does it matter?" I folded my arms. "Are we staying or not? I'm hungry, and I'd like to get some sleep."

He faced me, and no matter how hard I tried not to see it, it was impossible to ignore the hope in his eyes. His expression softened, lips relaxing. "Do you want to stay? Or would you rather we move on? We can do whatever—"

"I don't *care* what you do." I owed this guy no civility. He was a monster and a thief. Playing nice would only feed into his delusion that one day I would accept him. That maybe we'd skip off into the sunset together and live behind a white picket fence. "I'm your prisoner, Dylan. Nothing more. *Never* more. Don't pretend like my opinion matters. If it did, you'd take me back to my friends."

The light in his eyes drained away, replaced by fury. "I'm getting sick and tired of hearing this shit. How about a solution? I wait for G to show up, then just kill him. Sound good? Then you'll have no reason to want to leave. There'll be no one to go back to."

My fingers curled tight, desperate to wrap themselves around his neck. I imagined myself choking him, watching the life slip from his body as he took his last breath. "What the hell do you want from me?"

"I want you back!"

"You can't have me *back*. You never had me. You had *Ava*." I positioned myself directly in front of him, so close that the brown of his eyes was all I saw. I smelled the cheap motel shampoo he'd used this morning and the slight minty scent of the complimentary mouthwash. It wasn't foul but sickened me all the same. "Ava. Is. Dead."

His reaction was swift and harsh. He pushed me. Not hard, but enough to send me off balance. I stumbled, landing on the ground with jarring force. My palm scraped the surface, grating the skin against the uneven rock. "Ava isn't dead," he seethed. "You are Ava."

"My name is Sera," I fired back. I didn't scramble away as he came to stand over me, and I didn't try to stand. Normally, he would never act this way where someone might see us, but he'd been growing careless lately. My resistance was wearing him down. "*Sera*. Say it. Remember it."

He towered over me, blotting out the bleakness of the sky. He was very still, very silent, and the fire in his eyes was all-consuming. In those first few days, despite what I'd heard, I felt sorry for him. I knew what loss felt like—even if I didn't know exactly *what* I'd lost. It could drive you to madness. It could make you question reality. But with each passing day, it became more and more clear that Dylan's loss had destroyed him. It had damaged him irreparably and transformed him into a creature incapable of reason.

"I have all the time in the world," he said. There was ice in his tone beneath the barely contained anger. "I can wait you out. You will realize that you love me."

I picked myself off the ground and stood in front of him. I didn't slouch or flinch. I looked him dead in the eye. "Why?"

His brows rose. "Why, what?"

"Why do you think that? What makes you believe that I'll love you?" I kept my tone even and my expression as neutral as possible. Maybe I could make him see that this whole thing was impossible. At some point, he must have been a reasonable person. Maybe there was a sliver of that still buried inside. "I say this without judgment, but look at all the things you've done. All the people you've hurt and the lives you've destroyed. How would you expect me—*anyone*—to get past that?"

His expression softened. The anger wasn't gone, but he'd come down a notch or two. It was the best I could hope for. "Because it's always that way," he said. "I've got my flaws, but you always see past them. You always find the best version of me."

"Dylan, there are some lines that, once crossed, you just can't come back from. If your Ava were here, if she knew what you'd done, do you really believe she'd still be able to move past it all?"

"Absolutely." There was no hesitation.

I threw my hands into the air. "How can you possibly say that?"

"Because that's just what Ava does. What she always does. All of you. You're all the same. You all love me."

"All?"

"Whenever we're there." There was a flash of vulnerability in his voice. "Whenever we're both around. The other Avas. The other Dylans…"

"And how often is *that*?"

There was a flash of something dark in his eyes. His fists clenched at his sides. He was at war with himself, that much was obvious. But there was pain there, as well. "Can't you see that I'm doing all this for your own good? That I'm trying to save you?"

For the first time, I got the feeling that he wasn't referring to Cora. For some reason, it sent a chill skittering across my skin. "Save me from what?"

"I'm sick of watching it happen." He pulled away and started to pace with quick, jerky movements that made me flinch. "Time after time, I find you. Sometimes I'm too late. Sometimes you're already gone. Other times—" He froze, back facing me, and shuddered violently. "Other times I actually see it happen." He laughed. It was a harsh sound. Like something shattering into a million tiny pieces. "It's funny, when you consider what I've been doing to my brother."

A knot of dread formed deep in the pit of my stomach. Despite the cold, dismal surroundings, a wave of uncomfortable warmth overcame me. "See what happen?"

"The universe keeps ripping you away from me."

"Ripping—"

"You die, Ava!" he shouted. "You *always* die. Accidents, disease, natural disasters… Your life is always cut short."

"If that's what's meant to be, then that's what's meant to be." He looked horrified, and the agony in his eyes overrode some of my anger. Obviously I didn't *want* to die. Not really. "Look, I'm sorry. That you've had to go through all this, to see it happen—that had to be horrible. But you can't save me. You picked me off the shelf with an expiration date. Keeping me tucked away somewhere isn't going to change the outcome of all this."

"And that outcome would be?"

"You just said it yourself. I'm going to die."

"You're not," he said with a resolute shake of his head. "Not this time. I have you, and I know. I intend to keep you safe. I'm going to prove that I can protect you."

"You can't," I insisted. With each day that passed, it was like an expanding cloud over my head, an encompassing black thing that haunted every move I made. "Unless you let me go, I'm going to die."

"Do you plan on running back to Cora?"

"Of course not!"

"Then what good would letting you run off be?" He narrowed his eyes. "She's the only one who can save you. Isn't that what she said?"

"Just let me go. Let me go back to—"

"No!" he roared. "That's all you care about. Getting back to *him*."

"He was there with me. If anyone other than Cora can help—"

"*No!*"

This was getting me nowhere. I'd need a different approach—but what? Reason didn't work, and I was pretty sure I didn't have the stomach—or the acting chops—to pretend to fall for him. Besides the fact that I hated him almost as much as I hated Cora, I didn't think I'd have the time. No. I'd need something that appealed to a weakness. The problem was, I seemed to be the only crack in his armor.

But maybe that was just what I needed.

"How about we make a deal?" I felt dirty even suggesting it, but I was desperate.

He regarded me silently, but the slight upturn of his head told me he was interested. Good. It was a start.

"Tell me. Tell me exactly what it is you want from me. You keep saying you want me back, but logically, you have to know that isn't possible. Not the way you need. No matter what you do or say, Dylan, I'm never going to wake up one day and just love you. So tell me exactly what it is you hope to gain from all this."

He inhaled, never taking his eyes off me. "I want you to give me a chance. I want you to give *us* a chance." He blew out slowly and ran a hand through his dark hair. "I'm not an idiot. I know I've done some pretty fucked-up things. I know there's no coming back from it—with the rest of the world. But you… You always have the ability to see me for the person I *could* be."

"And that's what you want me to do? See you for what you could be—and not what you've become?"

"That's exactly what I want."

There was a hint of desperation in his voice, and I almost felt sorry for him. What he was asking was impossible, though. I'd never see him as anything other than a monster. He'd slaughtered innocent people simply because he was angry with their doubles on another world. He'd killed the same girl again and again to hurt his own brother. "Because you want Ava back."

"Yes."

I couldn't get past those things—but maybe someone else could. More specifically, maybe I could get him to *think* someone else would. "Then here's my offer. I'll help you find another Ava, and you'll let me go."

He opened his mouth, but I wasn't finished yet. G and the others had come close to reaching us a few times. If Dylan had been distracted, if they'd just had a bit more time… Maybe I could give them that. I had no intention of offering up another version of myself to him, but if he thought I would…

"There are other conditions." I rushed on. "You will not hurt G or any of the others. Actually, you won't hurt *anyone*. Kori? Those people you told me about? The Tribunal? Off-limits from here on out. No more bloodshed."

He thought about it for a minute. "I already found an Ava." He inclined his head toward me. "Why keep looking?"

"Because I'm *not* Ava. I'm never going to *be* Ava. My name is Sera—and no matter what you say or do, no matter what threats you make, I will never love you."

He didn't respond right away. Instead he stared. He didn't blink or drop his gaze, but then he did smile. "I'll agree to those terms, but I have terms of my own."

How much worse than being forced to stay with this sicko could it be? "What exactly are your terms?"

"You won't try to leave. I'll give you free rein. Come and go as you please—as long as you continue to hold up your end of the deal and meet my conditions." He came a step closer, his entire demeanor one of menace and fury. "You stop treating me as though I'm a monster, and when I talk to you, you will have a civil conversation with me. I don't care if we chat about nuclear war or the price of tea in China. You will also eat one meal with me every day."

I snorted. Eat with him? He was still holding out hope that I could be swayed. That he could convince me, and not some other version of Ava, that he was the boy of my dreams, like the world's most twisted case of Stockholm syndrome.

Still, I could work with it. I only needed a little time. "So, I have to help you find another me and stroke your ego or you'll, what, kill me? Do I understand that right?"

He clutched his chest and shot me a look of mock horror. If it hadn't been for the fact that I knew him—better than I wanted to—it would have been funny. "You absolutely do *not* have that right, *Sera*. You have to help me find another you and stroke my ego or I'll make it my life's mission to kill *G*."

Chapter Four

Thankfully Cade hadn't wanted to wait until morning to leave. He'd gotten a few hours of sleep, then announced he was ready to skip after Dylan and Sera if I was—which I had been. I'd been ready to go the moment we'd gotten there. Staying in one place too long made me antsy.

Cade glanced down at his wrist one last time before yanking the sleeve of his coat over his forearm to hide the fading blue glow. "Well, we're on the right Earth. Dylan's PATH line is green, so that means they're here, but no way to tell where, exactly."

"Then the obvious move is to start looking."

"Yeah." He took a step forward and stopped. "But that's not going to get us anywhere."

"What's that supposed to mean?" Did he think standing on the sidewalk and waiting for them to walk past us was a feasible plan? What the hell kind of logic was that?

"Think about it." He had that look again; I'd seen it a few times now, the expression he got when he thought he had it all figured out. "We're just skipping from place to place, following their frequency and hoping that it puts us in their general vicinity. When it doesn't—which is more times than not—we're just wandering around aimlessly in hopes that we'll get lucky."

"Yeah," I responded through clenched teeth. "And it would have worked last time if Yancy hadn't been there." That was the first real break we'd gotten. We landed close to visual distance. We'd had them in our sights, and still they'd slipped through our fingers.

"That's my point exactly. We've been at this for what, almost a month now? And that was the first time we got a lucky break."

"You call that a lucky break?" The guy was insane.

He rolled his eyes. "Lucky as in we didn't have to turn the town upside down looking for them. Dylan is smart. He knows how to hide. If he doesn't want to be found, it's like looking for a hair in a vat of pudding."

"A hair… What?"

"Oh. Yeah. Sorry. Expression on my world. Basically means—"

"Hard to find. Yeah. I get it. So? What's your point?"

"My point is, we need to change tactics. What we're doing isn't working."

"We can agree there." We needed a new plan—but what? Our options were limited. "Ideas?"

He leaned back against the brick building and tugged at the leather cuff on his wrist. Kori had given it to him a week ago…something about colors and infinity. "Was hoping you'd have one."

I scanned the area. This version of Wells was dreary. The sky was dark and clouded, and as far as I could tell, it wasn't the most fertile land. The area was void of foliage; even the grass was scant. We'd ended up in an alley, beside a tall brick building. I pushed off the wall and stalked to the corner. When I peered around the side, it was more of the same, all impossibly tall brick buildings with wickedly pointed roofs. Several cars passed on the road, but aside from that, there wasn't much activity. "Well, they're here *somewhere*."

He spread his arms out. "Yeah. Somewhere. As in, anywhere within a half mile. We just talked about this. It's not work—"

"Don't." A growl rose in the back of my throat. What Cade said was 100 percent logical. This *wasn't* working. We weren't going to find Sera this way. Beating feet was just a waste of time and energy. But a larger, more dominant part of my brain heard, *Give up. Pack it in. I can't be bothered. We'll never find her...* "I get it. This isn't a big deal for you anymore. You have your girl back. If this bastard slips through your fingers, no harm, right?"

His expression darkened, and I saw the fight in his eyes, a brewing war between keeping his cool and lashing out at me. He might have been the most held-together of the group, but right from day one it'd been obvious that Cade Granger was sporting some serious anger-baggage. "You're way off base, man. And I think if you step back and take a deep breath, you'll realize that."

You'll realize that...

. . .

"He's in rare form tonight, eh?" the guy latched on to my right side said. He snickered. I thought I heard the guy on my left laugh, too. It was hard to tell through all the screaming.

I thrashed and flailed against their grip. "I'm going to fucking kill you! You hear me?"

"He's— Hold him tighter, Paul!"

I let out a roar and yanked as hard as I could. Paul, the asshole on my right, let go for a second. "Guy is a goddamned lunatic!" he said with a grunt.

They wrestled me into the elevator, then off, and down the hall. I fought like a demon every step of the way. And by the time they managed to drag me back to my cage, I'd given them a split lip, what was sure to be multiple facial bruises, and, if I had to guess, several broken fingers.

The bodily damage and looks of pure hatred should have satisfied me, but when they slammed the door closed and latched the cell, I found that I was still wound up. Still hungry for more.

It was like this, sometimes, when I returned "home" from a day in the lab. The anger was so potent, so unquenchable, that I felt like I could break the world apart. It was like a pressure inside me. One that, if not released, would rip me to shreds.

I inhaled, then let it out in the form of a yell. The sound reverberated in the small space and echoed down the corridor.

"That's not going to help, you know…"

I ignored the sound of her voice and slammed one fist against the wall and then the other. Right. Left. Right. Left.

"*Try taking a deep breath,*" *she tried again.* "*Close your eyes, count to twenty.*"

I threw my body at the bars and gripped until I lost the feeling in both hands. "*Count? You really think* fucking counting *is going to fix this?*"

"*It will save your sanity,*" *she said. As usual, she hadn't been bothered by my tone. She was never dissuaded, this girl. Never gave up.* "*You're better than this, G. You have a disease. Cora? She infected you with something, and you need to fight it.*"

Her sentiment was nice, but it wasn't true. Not 100 percent. Yes, Cora had warped me, but she'd only made what was already there darker and more volatile. If I were a grenade with the pin slipping out before coming to Infinity, then I was now a nuclear bomb with someone's twitching finger hovering right above the red button.

"*Trust me, G. The sooner you get a handle on this, the less they'll be able to provoke you. Just take a breath and think about it. You'll realize I'm right.*"

It took a while, but in my darkest moments, Sera's whole spiel had worked. Not because of the counting or the breathing or any of that crap—but because of her. Because I knew Sera was there, only a few feet away. Because I heard her voice. Because I didn't want to let go of it…

But Sera wasn't here right now.

I let out an enraged howl and launched myself at Cade. For some reason he looked surprised—which made me wonder if he was an idiot. I'd been warning him about this for weeks. Had been telling him that a snap like this was inevitable.

We collided with a jarring crash, and I took us to the ground. But Cade wasn't a pushover. The guy knew how to throw down. I swung, then he did. We traded blows, and even through the haze of red clouding my brain, I knew he was trying more to restrain than harm me. That was fine because in the back of my mind, I was desperately trying to do the same thing.

"You have to chill, man." He latched on to my left wrist and pinned it to the ground just as I struck out hard with my right. The blow caught him across the bottom chunk of his chin, but he took it like a trouper, remaining mostly upright. "This isn't doing Sera any good!"

At the mention of her name, my entire body went rigid.

He took it as a sign that he'd gotten through to me and loosened his hold.

It was the wrong thing to do.

I roared and struck out, putting everything I had into the strike. I didn't see Cade or the alley. I didn't hear him still trying to talk me down. I didn't smell the dumpster only several feet away and stinking to high hell.

I saw Cora. I smelled mothballs and bleach. I heard Sera screaming and crying and calling my name. I saw a battlefield full of bloody corpses and hands stained with fading life…

My fist struck his face, and he went sprawling backward.

If it weren't for the slight rise and fall of his chest, I'd have figured I'd killed him. But Cade was alive and as well as one could be after getting knocked out cold in a grimy alley.

I'd hauled him around the back corner of the building and propped him up against the wall in the cleanest spot I could find, then I settled across from him to wait. And think.

It was more self-loathing than thought, my brain hashing out all the fuzzy details now that I'd come down off the serum high. *Serum.* That's what Cora had called it. The thick, almost gel-like black substance she'd force-fed me once a week for six months. The highlight of the Alpha program. The project was something she'd worked on for the government of her world. They wanted the perfect soldier. Stronger, faster, with total obedience and less emotion.

Obviously, they'd failed—in more ways than one.

Cade groaned and forced open his eyes. Well, eye. The left one was swollen shut. Along with that, his bottom lip was split, and there was already a deep bluish-purple bruise blooming across the entire right side of his face. "Least you didn't kill me…"

The apology I wanted to offer died before I could push it past my lips.

"Do you feel better now?" he prodded, struggling to

move into a more upright position.

I raked a hand through my hair and exhaled. "No." I dropped my gaze, but I still felt his eyes on me.

"What did they do to you?"

I didn't want him to give a shit about what had happened to me. I didn't need his sympathy or concern. Then again, I *had* kicked the crap out of him. I owed him at least some small explanation. "Like I said before, I'm not sure exactly how it works. I was part of an experimental program called Alpha." I had no intention of getting into all the gory specifics, but a little bit of information wouldn't hurt. It wasn't like he could do anything with it. "They gave me something—a drug. But it needed to be triggered. Activated. After that, Cora was always pushing me. Trying to get me to break."

"Break how?"

"Lose control. She pushed my buttons, tried to bust through my pain threshold—anything that might cause me to lose it and lash out. That's what's supposed to activate the serum."

"Lash out?" There was a spark of understanding in his eyes, of sympathy. It made me sick. "Like you just did with me?"

"Not even close." I bit back the urge to tell him to screw off. "That was me holding back."

He snorted. "Remind me to stay on your good side."

It wasn't possible, since I was sure I didn't have a good side, but I didn't say anything. "Think you can stand? We should try looking for them. At the very least, get the hell out of this alley. Sitting here makes us look suspicious."

I climbed to my feet and held out my hand to help him up. He hesitated for a tense moment before accepting.

We walked for a while in silence. This world was one of the weirder ones I'd seen. The men were all dressed like circus attractions—obnoxiously bright colors and outlandish styles—while the women all wore drab, lifeless clothing. Several passersby gave us horrified looks. I guessed it was Cade's red T-shirt and worn combat boots, and my ragged sneakers and bleach-stained shirt. The fact that he looked like he'd gone ten rounds with a meat grinder probably didn't help, either.

Cade laughed. "Man, am I glad Noah isn't here."

"Not a fan of fancy duds?"

"All this side-eye?" Cade gave a friendly nod to an elderly man dressed in a bright purple suit as he passed. The man grimaced and sped up his shuffle. "He'd be shooting his mouth off like crazy. Probably get us into a boatload of shit."

His words were heavy, but his tone was light as a feather. "Seems like you'd be better off without the guy."

We stepped off the curb and made our way across the street. The clothing wasn't the only weird thing about this place. The roads were paved on either side, but the middle four feet or so was a series of bars embedded into the pavement. There were six total and they ran parallel, spaced about a foot apart. "Noah? God, no. We—" The moment Cade's foot touched the bars, there was a loud snap. "Shit."

"What's wrong?"

He jerked to the right, then to the left, and cursed

again. "My foot is caught."

"How the hell did you—" A metallic squeal filled the air. In the distance, some kind of vehicle barreled down the center of the road.

Cade dropped to the ground and yanked at his boot laces. But the more he tugged at them, the more knotted they became. He cursed and tried to shove me aside. "Get away!"

I ignored him and went to work trying to pry his boot from between the two bars. Somehow, he'd managed to wedge his toe beneath one of them, and when they'd moved, they'd locked it in place.

Cade grabbed a handful of my shirt and shoved me away from him. *"Go!"* The car-train-whatever the hell it was trucked closer by the second.

My hair whipped from the breeze stirred by the oncoming vehicle. I pulled harder against his boot. "Not gonna happen."

Chapter Five

Sera

Dylan had been laughing on and off for the last hour. Maybe he found my expression amusing. I imagined it was somewhere between fury and horror. Or maybe it was the fact that, once again, he had me between a rock and an impossible place. Completely at his mercy and a slave to his demands.

Of all the things he'd said, all the things he'd done, his threat about G had to be the most despicable. "You're a sick shit…"

"I'm sick because I'm covering my ass?" He shook his head. "Nope. That's called smart. It's called survival."

"Fine," I snapped. If there was the smallest chance that he could take G out, then what choice did I have? "Terms accepted."

He looked pleased. "Good. Then how about we grab a bite? The food on that last world was horrible."

My first instinct was to tell him exactly where he could go to grab a bite, but I caught myself just in time. The food *had* been bad. Bland and colorless, it had tasted like cardboard and smelled like roadkill. My stomach still churned when I thought about it. *Civil.* I had to be civil. Fists curled tight and jaw clenched, I said, "Sure." Hopefully the food was better than the clothing on this world.

"See? Was that so hard?" He laughed and made a point of bumping into a tall man in a florescent pink shirt and neon orange jeans as he passed, then nodded a silent apology. Obviously when you tallied up all the bad things Dylan had done during his rampage, picking pockets wasn't even in the top ten, but it still made me hate him just a little bit more. "What are you in the mood for?"

"Don't care." Getting off the street might not be the worst idea. We hadn't seen that many people, but the ones we had encountered seemed horrified by the sight of us. For all I knew, it was a crime or something to dress the way we were. It wasn't as noticeable with me. I wore dark jeans and a gray hoodie. But since the men here all wore clothes in every color of the rainbow, Dylan stood out like a sore thumb.

And I was hungry, so…

He huffed, but his annoyance was fake. He was over the moon. Knowing him, he saw it as once again getting his way. But he was in for a rude surprise. I had no intention of hitching myself, or any other version of me, onto his brand of crazy. I could play the game for a while. Wait for my chance, then jump.

Pointing to a smaller brick building across the street, he said, "How about there? Looks Italian. You've always been a sucker for Italian food."

I didn't bother correcting him. There was really no point. And really, the truth was, I had no idea if I liked Italian food. We hadn't exactly gotten five-star cuisine during our stint at Infinity. I found that when he started meshing his Ava and me together, he entered into a delusional cloud.

We pushed through the door of the restaurant and were promptly seated at a small table in the back right corner of the room. The place was empty, and soft jazz music drifted through the dining room.

Seconds after our butts hit the chairs, there was a waiter standing beside the table. He was tall, with dark hair and eyes and a lopsided grin, and wore a bright red shirt with orange fringe across the front. "Something to drink?"

Dylan beamed up at the guy. "I'll have water. My lady here will, as well."

I glared at him through a wall of my hair, and when the waiter nodded and stepped away, I leaned forward on the table. The silverware sat a few inches to my left, and I had to force myself not to grab the butter knife and impale him with it. "Maybe I didn't *want* water. Maybe I wanted a soda."

He wasn't intimidated by my stare. "Never order food until you've taken a look at the menu." He tapped the elegant looking sheet of paper on the table in front of him. "How do you know soda exists here? Maybe this is Health Food World. Or Orange Juice World."

"*Orange juice world?* Seriously?"

He shrugged and leaned back in the chair. They were heavy wooden things decorated with ornate pink tapestries. "I landed in a version of Wells where people only drank variations of seaweed cocktails. Another time it was this stuff they called Ketchy. It was blue and thick and trust me—it smelled like dead rat's ass." He flipped open the menu and skimmed it. One page, two… By the time he got to the end, he looked relieved. "All looks fairly normal."

The waiter came back with our water and took the order. Dylan was kind enough to choose my food for me. I didn't know if Ava got off on that crap, but me? I wanted to bash him over the head. Of course, I had a feeling he wouldn't consider that being *civil*. No, I simply had to suck it up and get through this. For my sake—and G's.

"So where should we start?" I asked. He was the expert in tracking me down, after all. "How do you normally find me?"

"Depends. It's different all the time."

While I didn't want to talk to him, I'd agreed—and I was actually curious. "What do you say? When you find her? Me?"

He lost his grin and sat up a little straighter. "I tell her the truth—exactly like I did you."

I snorted. I couldn't help it. "Well, maybe there's your problem! What kind of idiot tries to win a girl over by admitting he's a killer?"

The muscles in his jaw flexed and darkness flashed in his eyes. "I've never lied to you. *Any* of you." He took a deep breath. His shoulders sagged a little before his entire body went rigid. "I tell you the truth because I know you, of all people, can handle it. You can handle *me*."

I leaned forward and set my elbows on the table.

"Oh, I can *handle* the fact that you're a psychopath—I'd just have no intention of dating you."

"Marrying," he said.

"Huh?"

"You—her—we were getting married. I asked her the night before she died." He pulled something from his right pocket and set it on the table between us. As he drew his hand away, I noticed a subtle shake.

I stared at the ring. A perfect heart-shaped diamond set in what appeared to be white gold with two small emeralds on either side. The band had an engraved swirling design that wrapped around the entire thing. It was breathtaking. "You... Oh. I had no idea."

"Of course you didn't." All traces of anger were gone from his voice. He snatched the ring and tucked it back into the safety of his pocket. "Because you only see me as a monster. You can't reconcile the fact that I'm a person dealing with the worst thing that ever happened to him. I'm trying to get through each day without breaking."

"Dylan, everyone on every Earth is breaking at some point or another." I looked him dead in the eye. "Bad things happen to all of us. Horrible, life-altering things. It's how we choose to deal with them that defines us."

"And how should I have dealt with it?" he snapped. "Just let her go without a fight?"

"That's the only choice you have. She died."

"But it *wasn't* my only choice." The conviction in his tone told me he believed every single word. "I had an opportunity—a way to be with her again—until my own brother sold me out."

I'd heard it all before. He'd been part of the early testing for his world's Infinity project. Dylan had been the first person to travel successfully — and survive. Of course, once he returned home and realized that another Ava might be out there somewhere, he couldn't let the idea go. He wanted to go back out into the multiverse and find her. His government hadn't agreed.

"You broke the rules," I said.

"Everyone breaks the rules at one point or another." The venom in his voice made me cringe a little. "I would have been long gone before anyone ever noticed if Cade hadn't run to the general to *tattle*. I wouldn't have hurt anyone. I would have found you and lived out the rest of my life the way I was supposed to. With the girl I was *supposed to*."

Cade had turned him in, but when they sentenced Dylan to death for treason, Cade had second thoughts and broke him out. It was the biggest mistake of his life. It led to the death of his girlfriend, Kori, and had ultimately created our current situation — not that I should complain. If Cade and his friends hadn't come along, G and I would probably still be rotting away in Cora's cells.

"You—"

"Please, spare us all the speech," a woman's voice cooed. An odd cross between lilacs and roses with an underlying hint of lavender filtered through the room. I fought back a gag. I'd know that putrid smell anywhere.

I pushed away from the table and stood so fast that I sent the chair toppling backward. My nightmare version of Cora Anderson stood a few feet away, blocking the only way out.

"And you," she said, steely gaze focused on me, "spare us the dramatics. Sit."

I didn't know why, but I did. I wasn't locked in her basement anymore, not living under her cruel thumb, yet when she commanded something, my body seemed eager to obey.

"I assume this seat isn't taken." She pulled out the chair between Dylan and me, shrugged out of her white coat and gently draped it over the back, then made a show of settling in.

"If you lay a hand on her—"

"Please. I could have her out of that seat and back in my lab before you even blinked if that's what I wanted. That's not what I'm here for. I'm actually here to make you an offer," she said, looking at me.

"An offer?" No way. This was a ploy. A trick to disarm us long enough for Yancy to sweep through the door and steal away what little freedom I'd found. "What could you possibly have to offer?"

She smiled at me, a grin full of barely veiled contempt and fury. "I can offer you a chance at survival."

The mysterious death sentence. Part of me was ready to jump at whatever it was she had to say. But the more cautious parts, the ones all too familiar with the mind games she liked to play, held back.

Dylan, on the other hand, wasn't so reserved. "What do we have to do?"

She laughed. "Aren't we the eager little beaver?"

I sighed. "Just tell us what you want, Cora." I didn't believe she was here to offer us some great hope, but it didn't seem like we had any other choice but to hear her out.

"Ashlyn's little stunt ensured the Omega project was dead in the water—then she fled beyond my reach."

I couldn't help it. I laughed. "You can't get to her? My day is looking better already."

Cora glared but maintained her composure. "The information she supplied the authorities spurred President Gotti to order a warrant for my arrest. They came for me—with handcuffs." Her face was ashen. "I was forced to flee my own world."

Dylan snorted. "Sounds to me like you got some of what you deserved."

Cora ignored him. "I'm in need of redemption. I have a plan that will earn back my place at home, but it's not something I can do alone. That's where you will come in."

"Redeem yourself," Dylan said with a growl. "What the hell do you think I'm gonna do about it? Better yet, *why* do you think I'd do something about it? You're catshit crazy, lady."

"I would complete the task *myself*, but I'm a bit tied up with something right now."

I had no idea what she was trying to get at. "Still not seeing what this has to do with me."

"Us," Dylan corrected.

"I had a database. It had all my notes, my research, my progress… On it is something I can offer to Gotti that will have him welcoming me back with open arms. Begging, even."

"Let me guess." Dylan slapped the table and let out a hoot. "Someone stole it?"

"Karl."

I hated Dylan. I despised pretty much everything about him, from the way he chortled to the things he'd done. But in that moment, we let out a chorus of laughs that nearly sent us both toppling from our chairs.

I hadn't gotten a bird's-eye view of the relationship, but Cora never failed to bring up her *perfect* husband, Karl. Loving, doting—and apparently, not so loyal.

"When Gotti came after me, Karl skipped out and took all my work with him. He won't be able to understand what's in those files, but if I know my husband, he'll go searching for someone who does. Another version of me, I assume."

"So track him." She had a way to track Ash and me. Why not her husband?

"I can't—but you can." She narrowed her eyes at Dylan. "The chips Phil MaKaden stole from my office were part of a special set I designed specifically for my family. They would have allowed us to track one another across the multiverse. They were in the last phase of testing when it all fell apart."

This whole situation just kept getting better and better. "And you want us to use them to, what? Find Karl? Then ask him nicely to hand over your work?"

"Apprehend him." She slid a small slip of paper with a number written on it—6256—across the table. "With this code, you can access a secret menu. You can track him, and I can track you, as well as show you how to summon me. I will come and collect him."

Dylan snorted. "So, we do your dirty work and you keep tabs on us? What the hell do we get out of it?"

"For starters, I will call off Yancy." She gave a not-so-subtle glance over her shoulder. The monster must be waiting somewhere just outside the building. Wherever Cora went, he was never far behind. "I'll also stop the deterioration."

Dylan looked from Cora to me. "Deterioration?"

She laughed and kept her attention focused on me. "Tell me you don't feel it, Ava—Sera—whatever you'd like to call yourself these days. Maybe it's still subtle. A lost moment here, a second or two of confusion there. The neuroimplant I used to aid the serum in suppressing your memories is failing. In time, it will essentially lobotomize you—unless it's disabled."

"And let me guess. You can do that, right?" I hadn't felt any of the things she'd mentioned, but that didn't mean it wouldn't happen. Would it be a slow slide into oblivion, or would it happen before I knew what was going on? *Boom.* Here and functioning one minute, a nonresponsive vegetable the next? The air turned icy, and I swallowed back a sudden lump in my throat.

No. I couldn't go out like that. Not now. Not before finding G. Not before finding my home...

"I can, and I will—if you find Karl."

"Too easy," I said. This was Cora Anderson, the queen of manipulation. She couldn't be trusted. This was a trick and nothing more. "How can I possibly trust you?"

"That implant—"

"I've got no doubt the implant is messed up. What I don't believe is that you'll fix it. And what about chasing me? I'm supposed to believe you'll give that up, too?"

Cora shrugged. "Dear, right now there are bigger things at stake than my plans for you."

I glared at Dylan, who was seated across from me. "Even if you did keep your word—which I don't believe—I'm still stuck with him. He won't let me go."

"But what if he would?"

Dylan laughed. "I just found her. I'm fairly confident that I can make her see that she loves me."

Apparently he'd already forgotten about the deal we'd made to find another Ava.

Cora laughed. "That is the same on every world. That signature Dylan Granger confidence." She waggled a perfectly painted finger between us. "She doesn't want you. Chances are she won't ever want you. But what would you say if I could promise you something better than her?"

She had his attention. "You can't buy me with money or power. I just want Ava back. That's not something you can give me."

"And what if I said it was? That you have the means to get her back. To get *your* Ava back?" She tapped her own wrist and grinned.

"I'd say you smoked a bad batch. Dead is dead. I'm not stupid enough to buy a spiel about you finding a way to bring back the dead." He stood and hitched his thumb toward the door. "Let's go."

For once he and I were on the same page. I made a move to stand, but Cora grabbed Dylan's arm and dragged him back to his seat. "Of course you can't bring her back from the dead. But as I said, those chips Phil stole were special. *Very special.* With the master code, they can do much more than their predecessors."

Now she *really* had his attention. He sank back into the chair. There was hope in his eyes—hope and desperation. I might not remember my name or where I was from, but I knew damn well desperate people were easier to manipulate. "How much more?"

Cora knew she had him. With a wicked gleam in her eyes, she leaned forward and propped herself against the tabletop. "If you agree to help me, then I will give you Ava back. I will give you a code that will allow you to go back to your world—before the accident happened."

"I don't believe you," Dylan said. He leaned back in the chair and folded his arms, resembling a five-year-old who refused to eat his broccoli.

Cora smiled. "I assure you, it's true. I'll make this simple for you—you have two paths to take. On one, you track down Karl and recover my research. I get what I want, and you get what you want. On the other, I stand and walk out that door. Yancy and my men come in. They take Ava, and you're left with nothing once again." She leaned back and lifted a hand, waggling her ring and middle fingers. "Seems like a no brainer to me…"

Seconds ticked by. Any minute he'd stand. Maybe flip her off and try to drag me from the building. Call her an array of colorful words and spout a handful of threats. But instead, he sighed. "Even if I wanted to, my brother and that lab rat of yours are always nipping at my heels. I don't have time to stop long enough to breathe, much less run your errands."

"What if I could offer a partial solution to that?"

My pulse spiked, and Dylan's attention perked. "Oh?"

She fished into her pocket and placed a small black

box in the center of the table. "Your brother is your baggage, but this might help with G."

I had no idea what it was, but I tried to grab it first—and failed. Dylan shot me a look of pure contempt and rolled the thing around in his palm. "What is it?"

"Like Sera, G was another rarity. The perfect addition to a pet project of mine." She chuckled and kind of rolled her eyes. "We overloaded him on shock therapy and serum to a point where it nearly shut down his brain. Granted, it has a few unwanted side effects on the limbic system—but all worth it in the name of research. However, the nature of the project demands measures be taken to ensure control over the test subjects." She tapped the small box three times. "Measures such as that. With the press of a button, it will begin the disintegration of an implanted pod in G's chest. The contents of that pod are toxic. They'll kill him."

"Bitch!" I lashed out and smacked her hard across the face. I would have hit her again if Dylan hadn't jumped out of his seat and tackled me to the ground. I wondered for a minute where the staff was, then remembered this was Cora we were dealing with. She probably had them out of here before she'd even walked into the building.

Cora laughed at my reaction and said, "To prove to you that I'm not heartless, I'll also give you this."

Dylan helped me off the floor but held tight to my arm. With his free hand, he grabbed the new item. "What is it?"

"It's the antidote for the poison inside the pod. Do with the device what you wish. If you choose to use it, it can take a few days to work. No way to know an exact time, but, you'll probably take comfort in knowing it will be a miserable few days." She laughed. "Consider it my gift to you. A down payment on finding Karl, perhaps…?"

"Fine," he said. He let go of my arm and pocketed the device. Every muscle in my body screamed for me to take it. Pin him down, claw, scratch, pull his hair—anything to wrestle that thing from his grubby digits. It was bad enough my life was currently in his hands, but G's? I couldn't live with that. Unfortunately, my chances were slim with Cora here. I'd have to bide my time. Plan and pick my moment carefully. "I'll look for Karl, but if I find out you're lying—"

She waved him off and stood. "I'm not." Without another word, she swept up her coat and breezed through the door, leaving us alone.

Dylan patted his pocket absently. "Let's go."

I stared at him. "Just like that? Are you serious?"

He spun in a circle, arms extended, and laughed. "No one here to pay the bill."

"I wasn't talking about that." Though, I had a bad feeling in my gut as to the fate of the staff. "I mean Cora. You can't really buy what she was selling."

He narrowed his eyes and nudged me toward the door. "She wouldn't dare lie to me."

How could he possibly think that? Had he been paying attention at all? Cora Anderson thought herself to be above everything. Everything and *everyone*. But the thing I'd learned in my short—but agonizing—time with Dylan was that reason was impossible. Instead, I decided to ask him something equally impossible.

"If you care about me—any version of me—you'll hand over that device."

He did a double take, obviously thinking I was joking, then laughed and pushed through the front door.

I followed, doing my best to tamp down the anger boiling up inside. "G won't bother you. I'll make sure of it."

Dylan grinned—the kind of smile that would have made the Cheshire Cat proud. "S'okay." He waved the small device in the air before pocketing it. "I think I've got it covered."

Chapter Six

With a final, brutal yank, I managed to free Cade from the bars a half second before the vehicle plowed past us. For the longest time, we both lay there trying to catch our breath.

"You could have gotten yourself killed," Cade said after a few minutes. He sat up and crawled to the curb.

I followed. "Yeah. You, too."

He stretched out his leg and rotated his ankle. He hadn't broken it, but no doubt had incurred a bad sprain from me wrenching it free from the bars. Overall, he wasn't in great shape. The swelling in his eye had gotten slightly better, but the bruising on his face was darker. At least his nose had stopped bleeding. "Can I ask you something?" he said.

"If I say no, aren't you just going to ask me anyway?"

He laughed. "Why did you do it?"

"Assuming you mean save you?"

He nodded.

"I'd like to think you would have done the same thing for me if our positions had been reversed."

"Of course."

"'Sides, if I let anything happen to you, Noah would be a permanent pain in my ass—not to mention Kori. That chick is scrappy as fuck."

"Yeah, she is."

I stood and hitched a thumb over my shoulder. Sitting here, especially dressed the way we were, was going to attract too much attention eventually. "Sightseeing?"

"Sightseeing" was what Cade called getting a feel for the place. Saying or doing the wrong thing could be disastrous, he'd insisted on multiple occasions. Following his simple rules assured that we didn't commit some sort of disastrous faux pas.

Cade had a lot of rules.

I stuffed both hands into my pockets as we started walking. "Listen, about earlier…"

"It's not—"

"I'm sorry." I wasn't the type to apologize, but I hadn't really meant to lay into him like I had. This bomb inside my head was getting worse. I grew more and more unstable with each passing day. "You should have fought back. Your punches were weak, and I know damn well you're not a pushover."

He was quiet, and I just figured he'd let the conversation die. Cade wasn't a man of many words, and I was fine with that. I wasn't a damn chatterbox myself. But after a few minutes, he said, "I'm sorry, too. I know you're not my brother. You didn't commit all those violent crimes. You don't deserve what Cora did to you. I'm—"

"How do you know?"

"Know what?"

"How do you know that I don't deserve it?" I stopped walking and turned to him. There was definitely a resemblance between us. We had the same squared chin, the same dark hair and eyes. But when I looked into his, it was obvious that we were nothing alike on the inside. "For all you know, I could have been just as bad, if not worse, than your brother."

He snorted. "You saved me. Dylan wouldn't have done that."

"Ever? Even before things turned sour between you two, you're telling me he would have left you to die?"

"Probably not—but there's no way to know for sure. My brother has always been…off."

"Don't buy it. Sorry."

"You're rough around the edges because you've been through hell. I get it. But I believe you're a good person underneath it all. Someone who does the right thing."

He sounded convinced. Me? Nope. I knew better than that. I'd tried to tell Sera once. In the dark, during one of my weaker moments…

"What do you suppose landed us here?" Sera had been quiet tonight, and I was grateful for the sound of her voice now.

I snorted, then flinched when the action caused a spasm of pain. "Really, really bad luck?" Today had been one of the harder days in a while. Cora had kept me up in the lab hours longer than usual.

She snickered, a soft sound that had me desperately trying to picture what she might look like. "I'm being serious. You think it was random?"

Sera might have ended up here by way of random bad luck, but me? No damn way. I was here for one reason and one reason only. "What if it wasn't?" Involuntarily, my voice dropped. "What if there was a specific purpose?"

"What could it have been, though? Something to do with genetics? Blood type?"

My intent was to confess that I was there in that cell because the universe had deemed me worthy of such punishment. I'd been a monster in my old life. A heartless solider who'd spilled more blood than Cora ever would. But I couldn't push the words out—for a couple of reasons.

First, I didn't want Sera to start thinking she might be here because karma was kicking her ass for something she'd done. True or not, I knew the thought would fester and slowly eat away at her. And second, I didn't think I'd survive in here if she knew what kind of a bastard I'd been. This place was hell, but it was oddly comforting not to have all the hate in the room directed at me. For once.

"So, what now? Do we try to find them?"

He'd stopped walking to stare at something over my shoulder. "Um…"

I spun to see what was so damn interesting and froze. There across the street, exiting one of the buildings, was Cora Anderson. There were apparently endless versions of the bitch floating around out there, but I'd know the one that kept us captive anywhere.

I lunged forward, but Cade snatched my arm and hauled me around the side of the nearest building. I clamped down on the inside of my cheek to keep from snapping at him.

"Hang on!" He held tight, and we watched as she rounded the corner and disappeared. I was about to take a swing at him when the door to the building opened again. Dylan and Sera stepped out. They walked a few feet then stopped. It looked like they were arguing.

"Sera…" I started forward again, and again, Cade grabbed me.

"Whoa. We can't just charge in there."

I jerked away. "Why the hell not?"

"We have the advantage here."

"What advantage? He's there. She's there. This is what we've been waiting for. What's the fucking problem?" This was cut and dried from where I was standing. The best chance we'd had in a while—and he wanted to take it slow?

"We need to know what's going on before we charge in there. If Dylan is working with Cora—"

"Why the hell would she be working with him? He can't possibly have anything to offer her. Cora wants Sera. Unless Dylan has done a one-eighty, I doubt that's something he's willing to give."

"You're underestimating my brother. He's resourceful and will do anything if it means keeping Ava."

Anything to keep Ava...

"She's sick. Sera. Cora did something to her..."

Cade gave a small nod. "Maybe she offered a solution. Look—" He nodded across the street. "She's left—without Ava. There's more to this than we know."

"But in exchange for what?" Anything Cora Anderson put on the table would be for her benefit and her benefit alone.

Cade looked as skeptical as I felt. "Let's find out."

They started walking, and we followed far behind, careful to stay out of sight. It killed me, being so damn close yet unable to act. They took their time, waltzing down the street as though they had no place else to be. Dylan hadn't restrained Sera in any way, but I could tell by her walk, and the rigid set of her shoulders, that she wanted to be anywhere but there. He tried several times to engage her in conversation. She didn't seem interested in whatever it was he had to say.

A few blocks from where they'd started, the pair stopped in front of a large storefront. I couldn't hear what they were saying, but they appeared to be arguing again. I was about to step in when Dylan did the last thing I'd expect. He walked into the building—and left Sera outside. Alone. I was done being patient. This was my chance and I was taking it.

"G, wait." There was more to Cade's plea, but I blocked it out and darted across the street.

Chapter Seven

Sera

"Sera!"

My pulse quickened, and I held my breath as I turned toward the sound of footsteps stomping against the pavement. "G." A plea, a prayer, a cry of anguish against all the crap we'd been through.

I rushed to meet him, making it to the edge of the sidewalk as he got to my side of the street. He pulled up short, stopping a few feet away from me. I did the same, and for a moment, neither of us moved. Neither spoke. There was a nagging whisper in my head. A voice that kept pleading for me to… I had no idea. Nothing mattered in that moment. Nothing except the fact that he was here. He'd found me.

We were face to face…

He came a single step closer, gaze never leaving mine. His shoulders were taut, his entire body rigid. "Tell me that you're okay."

His voice was low and held the faintest off-pitch

note. I'd gotten so accustomed to his moods by simply listening to him speak. I matched his step with one of my own, forcing my hands to stay at my sides. All I wanted to do was touch him. His face. His arms. His hands… Any place we could connect physically, so I could prove to myself that he was really there and not some figment of my fragmented brain. "I'm okay," I whispered, hoping it was loud enough for him to hear.

He came another step closer, lifting his hand then hesitating and letting it fall slack at his side. "I've been looking. Since he took you, I've been—" He lifted his hand again, but instead of reaching out to me, his fingers curled into a fist. A shudder went through him, and he closed his eyes tight. When he opened them, my breath caught at the fierceness I saw there. "You know I wouldn't have stopped, right? I would have kept going until I found you."

I couldn't hold it back any longer. I took his fist between my hands and held it, coaxing his fingers to relax. His skin was warm and felt right against mine in a way I couldn't imagine anything else feeling. "I never doubted it. I knew you'd find me."

He deflated some, the tension lifting like a ten-ton rock from around his neck. His shoulders slumped, and he inhaled deeply. "He left you alone? Why didn't you run?"

I gave his hand one final squeeze, then sighed. "And go where? I have no chip, so…"

"So, without him, I could never find you."

Behind me, something squealed, and a door chime rang, bringing reality crashing back with jarring force.

Someone laughed, and when I turned, Dylan was

leaning casually against the building, grinning like a madman. He took a sip from the cup in his hand then waved it in my direction. "Oh. No. Don't let me interrupt. You were about to say…?"

"This is done." G moved to stand beside me. He was coiled and ready to strike. "She's coming with me."

Dylan didn't answer right away. He looked around then turned in a slow circle. "Where's the gang? I don't even rate the entourage anymore?"

G balled his fist and stepped between us. In all the times I'd tried to imagine his face, the movements of his body and subtle mannerisms that belonged just to him, I'd never pictured him so fierce. It was funny, since I knew, even back in that cell, he was a force to be reckoned with, but seeing it in action was so much more intense than hearing it. "It's just you and me."

"Sounds like a good time." Dylan held up his hands in surrender, but I knew better. He grinned at me, then focused on G. "Tell you what. How about we ask the lady here who she'd like to go with? *Sera*—who would you prefer?"

G faltered, looking from Dylan to me, then back again. His lips parted, and his brows lifted, then disappeared beneath his hair. "You can't be serious."

Dylan winked. "Go ahead, be honest. Who would you like to go with? Me or imposter me?"

G was confused. He kept alternating between Dylan and me, tense, as though waiting for some sneak attack. The possibility that I'd pick Dylan over him wasn't even in the top one hundred thoughts going through his mind right now.

I hated to do it…

"I'd *like* to go with G," I said. His expression relaxed into a smug grin.

G flipped Dylan off and threaded his fingers through mine. The contact was an even mixture of electrifying and comforting…

"We've never seen each other, but you're the most real thing in my life."

He snorted. The sound echoed through the cell. "That's not saying much. You know that, right? And really, are you sure? Because the smell in here is pretty damn real *sometimes."*

I smiled. It wasn't his words but his tone. I slipped my arm through the bars at the corner of his cell. Somehow, he knew. He did the same thing at the same moment. I saw the shadow on the floor in front of the cell. Just out of reach. I stretched, pushing my entire body against the bars until the pain made my eyes water, then let out a frustrated cry. I could almost feel the warmth coming off his skin.

A grunt, followed by a low curse. His shadow hand fell slack, clattering against the bars of his cell. "I know how you feel." Something slammed the wall. "Ever notice how they won't even let us see each other? They take me out the door on my end, and you out the other."

"Just another way for Cora to get into our heads."

He was quiet for a few minutes before clearing his throat. "My hands have calluses. They're rough. Scarred."

"No calluses for me, but I do have a scar. On my right thumb. Looks like it might be from a burn or something.

The skin is weird. A different pattern than the rest."

Material rustled, and in the hall in front of my cell, I caught sight of G's shadow again.

I slipped my arm through the bars and stretched toward him. Even though I knew I couldn't reach. Even though it was impossible. "I'd give anything just to touch you."

Now that I'd finally gotten what I wanted, I had to pull away—and I hated it.

"But I *have* to stay with Dylan," I finished, cringing as G's face went from triumphant to perplexed. Then, from perplexed to hurt.

"No, Sera." He took both my hands in his and shook his head. Just once. "Whatever it is you think he has on you, it's crap. It's a lie. A trick to make you think—"

"Cora gave—" Dylan caught my attention and gave the smallest shake of his head while patting his pocket. The same pocket he'd slipped Cora's kill device into. I couldn't go with G, and Dylan wouldn't let me tell him the truth, either. My making the choice to stay with Dylan, even though he'd have to know I had a good reason, hurt G—which is what Dylan wanted.

I stepped back, trying to block out the desperation I heard in G's voice. A step closer to Dylan. I refused to look at him, but I knew if I did, I'd see that same smug expression that I loathed. The one I'd been forced to endure for almost a month now. "You have to trust me."

I didn't know my family or where I'd come from. I didn't remember when my birthday was. The one thing

I did know was G. Better than anything—which is why, hurt or not, I should have known he'd never just walk away.

His expression turned stony, and he squared his shoulders. He stepped to Dylan, stopping inches away. It was strange seeing them face-to-face like that. Two sides of the same coin, one blackened and foul, the other cracked with bits of shine showing through.

"I don't give a shit what she says, she's not leaving with you. And on the off chance you do manage to somehow take her, then rest assured that it's only temporary. Because I won't give up." G's arms were stiff at his sides, fists balled so tight that his knuckles had gone white. "I will *never* stop."

Dylan wasn't threatened. In fact, he started laughing. He gave G a brutal shove. G stumbled back but held his ground. "You're me, so *I know*. There's no need to try and convince me. What do you think started this whole mess? I'm right where you are. I don't intend to let her go." He tapped the side of his head, his grin growing wider. "We're flawed, man. Fucked in the head, with lots of little loose pieces banging around inside. You don't remember yourself, so let me give you a little reminder—you're an asshole. A self-serving, sadistic jackass who only cares about himself—and Ava. She's the one thing—the *only* thing—on this miserable rock that means anything. I would do anything to get her back. Just like I know you'd do the same. I can't have you getting in my way. I won't."

Both boys looked at me, and a horrible knot formed in my stomach. Dylan had the device Cora had given him out of his pocket, finger hovering above the small button, before I could even blink.

"Dylan, don't…"

For half a second, he almost looked sorry. It didn't last, though. That tiny glimmer of humanity morphed into something hard and cruel, and without a single word, he pushed the button.

Chapter Eight

Sera's skin turned ashen, and Dylan looked smug. There was an object in his hand. Something I assumed was significant in some way, considering the shit-eating grin on the bastard's face. When nothing happened, though, he lost that grin. "Well, that's a goddamned letdown," he said. "She promised me—"

Whatever it was he said next was lost to an agonized sound. One coming from my own damn mouth. Everything grew hazy, and it felt like there was someone inside my head trying to rip their way out. I clawed at my skull, desperate to stop it. I was vaguely aware my knees had buckled, and that I was on my back, on the ground. There was a foul taste in my mouth, coppery with a tang of sweetness. I gagged and coughed, making the pressure in my head ten times worse.

Dylan laughed. "That's more like it." A pause. "Ava, let's go."

Sera had dropped to her knees and was beside me, my head in her lap and her clinging to my shoulders. Every few seconds, a small tremor pulsed through me, though she kept my body as steady as she could. Slowly, the pain started to ebb. With each second that passed, it lessened until it became a dull ache that made my eyes water just a bit.

I struggled into a sitting position, and when I was steady, Sera stood. She positioned herself in front of me, legs spread and fists at the ready. *Protecting* me. "One more step and I'll kill you."

"With what? That cute little glare of yours?"

"Go ahead and test me, Dylan." The fury in her voice, in her stance, was something to see. Fierce and brave.

Dylan laughed and made a swipe for her arm. When she violently smacked it away, his expression darkened. "Gonna be like that, then?"

"Damn right," Sera said with a growl. "I'm not leaving him like this. If you wanted me to come with you, you should have kept your word. We had a deal."

Dylan shrugged. I tensed, sure he'd make another grab for her. I wasn't confident that I could stop him right then. But instead of pulling a snatch and grab, he folded his arms and frowned. "You stay with him and you're as good as dead. Come with me and you have an opportunity to live."

"I'll take my chances with him," she said.

Another shrug. He lifted his arm and woke his chip.

No way. It was this easy? He was just going to walk away, after all that?

"Once I'm gone you're stuck. I'm guessing that

chip won't work when he's dead. You'll be stranded wherever he drops."

"Leave before I hurt you," she ground out. Even took a menacing step forward. God. She was even more perfect than I'd imagined.

Far too perfect for someone like me.

With one last look in my direction, Dylan smiled. "Enjoy her while you can, man." And then he was gone.

For a second, I stared at the spot where he'd been, then turned to Sera. She watched me with an odd mix of elation and fear. "Obviously I missed something. What's—"

She fell to her knees and collapsed against me, arms winding around my waist like a vise. I hesitated for a moment before locking my arms around her, as well. It was weird. I estimated that it'd been more than 372 days since I landed in Cora's cell. 372 days since Sera— the faceless girl who I'd come to depend on as much as I did my own limbs—came into my life. Her voice had become a source of comfort, her unshakable hope a light in the dark. But this…this was the first time I'd *really* gotten to touch her. Sure, she'd taken my hand earlier. But that was a hand. This…this was her. This was *Sera*.

My ghost. My dream.

I savored the feel of it, soft and warm and calming, while at the same time stirring my insides into a jumbled mess. My arms tightened, and I buried my face in the crook of her neck, reveling in the silkiness of her hair. But as many nights as I'd fantasized about touching her, about feeling her close and looking her in the eye—there were other things to deal with now.

Mainly, what Dylan had said.

It took every ounce of self-control I had, but I pulled away. "Why did that asshole think my eternal dirt nap was imminent?"

Lips pressed thin, she paled. "We should probably talk."

"How long?" I'd skipped us out—just in case Dylan changed his mind about leaving Sera behind. I felt bad about leaving Cade, but the guy could look after himself and could track me if he wanted. We'd been hunkered down in a public park just north of the center of town for over an hour now. It was cooler here than it'd been on the last world. There was a breeze that made it feel closer to the end of December than November. Still, despite the temperatures, the foliage was in full bloom. Brightly colored flowers, shades of blue and lavender, lined the walkway, while the trees overhead shaded us with golden leaves.

She shook her head and tucked both feet beneath her on the bench. She wore dark blue jeans that seemed a size too big, and a men's hoodie. Her hair, mostly free of the elastic it'd been pulled back with, whipped wildly in the wind. It looked darker than I remembered. Chocolaty brown. And her cheek bones, sharp and defined... They gave her an almost ethereal look. She was stunning, no doubt, but it was what I saw in her eyes, the hope and trust and emotion, that made her truly unique. No one had ever looked at me like that.

She kind of cringed a little. "When Cora gave him

the device, she said a few days. No way to know for sure."

The good news? I'd gotten Sera back. The bad news?

I was going to die.

"But there's a way to fix it? To neutralize the poison?" Dylan had flipped a switch that started the disintegration of a pod Cora had implanted in my body—one I hadn't even been aware of. It contained a toxin that would kill me if left unchecked. But there was an antidote. She'd given it to Dylan along with the device to release it. Of course, he—and it—were long gone. I might have called bullshit on the entire thing if I hadn't seen the look on Dylan's face when he pushed the button.

"Dylan has it," Sera confirmed with a nod. "We just need to get to him and take it."

Sounded simple. Sure. Except for one small problem. We were both on borrowed time. The pendulum was swinging over her head as much as it was mine. "And the way to fix the failing chip in your head is to find Karl Anderson?"

Again, she nodded. "The chips that Phil MaKaden stole, then implanted you and the others with weren't the standard kind. They were part of a special set she created and can do more than the others."

"More, meaning?"

She made a move to grab my arm but hesitated, the tips of her fingers grazing my bare skin. It took every ounce of self-control not to sigh like an idiot at the contact. "I... Sorry. Can I?"

I held out my arm and looked her in the eye. She

inhaled sharply, and my heartbeat sped up. After a particularly bad night, I'd once told Sera that if I ever managed to get out, I'd never let another living person touch me. Apparently she hadn't realized she was exempt from that statement. "You are the one person who never has to ask me that, Sera."

She flushed and cleared her throat, refocusing on my forearm. It took a minute of fumbling, but she finally managed to wake the chip. "See this?" she said, pointing to a small circle in the bottom corner. "There's a code—6256. It pulls up a hidden menu. Within that menu is a way to track Karl. She said it can do a lot more than that, but obviously she wasn't going to give up all its secrets."

"If these chips are that advanced, then why isn't she trying to take them back?" Knowing Cora the way I did—which was too damn well—she'd never let a piece of tech like this go. Especially if she had plans for it.

Sera frowned. "I thought about that. To be honest, though, it wasn't my main concern."

"One thing at a time," I agreed. I stood and glanced around. The sun was setting, and the park had all but emptied. It was just us and a tall man with a dog a few yards away. "We go after Karl, then we'll hit up Dylan."

She jumped from the bench. "Not a chance. We go after Dylan *then* we chase Karl."

"We find Karl first. We don't know how much time you have." The chip Cora implanted in her brain to help the serum work was malfunctioning. It could go at any moment. How the hell did she think I'd take the chance?

"But we know how much you have—and it's not long."

"I'm not debating this with you, Sera. I'm the one with the chip. I'm calling the destination." Was I being an asshole? Yeah. But I was looking out for her. First and foremost, it was always Sera first.

"Hey!" Cade crossed the park at a jog. He looked winded and pale. "I've been looking for you for hours!"

"Took you long enough to find us," I said.

He looked from me to Sera, and relief crossed his features. Huh. Maybe he wasn't just worried about payback. "You okay?"

"Debatable at this point," she said, shifting subtly closer to me. Someone else would have perceived it as weakness. Maybe think she was timid and afraid. After everything she'd been through, it would be understandable. But I knew that wasn't what it was about. It'd been just the two of us for so long. It didn't matter that Cade and his friends had freed us from a living hell, or that they'd tried to help get her back. We were so used to relying on each other, even if only for verbal support, that everyone else was the enemy.

"We have a problem. Two of them."

Cade groaned and rolled his eyes. "Why am I not surprised?"

I nodded to my forearm, where the chip had been implanted. "Grab on. I'll explain on the way."

Chapter Nine

Sera

I lifted the glass and drained the rest of the dark liquid. It was bubbly with the faintest taste of cherries and mint. Not great, but definitely not the most horrible thing I'd ever ingested. Cora's idea of keeping us hydrated had been tepid water that smelled strongly of sulfur. Anything was an improvement over that. Across from me, Cade and G were currently engaged in a stare down, both their drinks untouched.

Cade folded his arms and leaned back in the seat. His eyes narrowed, and he jerked his head from side to side. "I don't like it."

"Of course you don't," G responded with a snort. "Because you can't control it."

We'd skipped and found an out-of-the-way café that took a form of cash Cade was carrying; he'd been collecting money during their travels. We'd found a table and were trying to iron out the details of a plan that would allow both G and me to continue breathing.

The boys were having a hard time agreeing on logistics.

"I'm all for splitting up," Cade said through clenched teeth. He jabbed a finger against the tabletop. Something about the way he did it made me think he was picturing G's head. "But we've got a better chance—"

"No." I knew that tone. There was no arguing with G. He'd made up his mind, and nothing Cade—or I—could say would change it.

A part of me understood—and agreed. Sort of. We were going after Karl. We hadn't agreed on what we'd be doing with him when we found him—neither one of us believed Cora would fix my head just because she'd said so—but it was a step in the right direction. Cade would go after Dylan for the antidote. That's where the disagreement came in.

Cade wanted to skip home to his world, where Noah and the others had gone to keep Ash from Cora. Ash was under the protection of his military and, therefore, untouchable. Searching for Dylan would go quicker with Noah's help, Cade had insisted. G didn't agree.

"The two of you chased him together for a year," G said. "You couldn't take him down then. What the hell makes you think this time will be any different?" He narrowed his eyes. "If anything, you'd be less motivated than before."

Cade opened his mouth, but G cut him off.

"This is it, man. You want to help, then this is the way to do it."

I took his hand and squeezed. I recognized the

danger signs by just the tone of his voice. "Please don't take this the wrong way, Cade. You really have no idea how Cora played with our minds in that place—"

"And we don't trust you," G finished. It wasn't totally true, though. There was a part of him that trusted Cade—even if only a little bit—despite the fact that he kept insisting he didn't. He wouldn't have stayed with him otherwise. Maybe it was their blood. Different worlds or not, they were still brothers. That had to mean something, right? There had to be *some* kind of connection. Maybe there'd been a Cade where he'd come from. The memory might be fuzzy, but a fact like that had to leave some kind of imprint.

"We'll compromise." Cade leaned forward and planted both elbows on the table. "I'll go after Dylan alone—for now. But we don't have time on our side. You both understand that, right? If I don't have any luck, I'm *going* to get help." He pushed away from the table and stood. There was a resemblance to G. They had the same brown eyes and perfectly sculpted cheek bones. Their hair was the same shade of night. They even had the same frown, something they both wore too often.

For a minute I was sure G would argue. He was nothing if not stubborn. But after a tense moment, he nodded just once. "Fine."

Cade woke his chip and disappeared before our eyes.

"He'll find Dylan," I said, slipping my hand into G's. "I don't believe he'll let you die."

He glanced at me from the corner of his eye. "I'm not going to let *you* die." He woke his own chip and pulled up the secret menu. Finger hovering above Karl's PATH line, the thing that told us his unique frequency, he said, "Ready?"

"More than."

He jabbed the line, but nothing happened. "Crap."

"What's wrong?"

"I must have lost count. Guess we're on cooldown."

The sand in the hourglass was sliding, but the truth was, part of me was glad we were stuck. I'd been skipping, been dragged from one place to another, for almost a month now. I was both mentally and physically drained. Half a day or so to get my bearings and come to terms with everything that had happened? I'd take it. Of course, it was easier to swallow knowing Cade was out there, looking for a way to save G.

"Then we make the most of it. Food and rest. We both deserve at least that."

"Cade didn't leave any of this world's money. How are we supposed to pay for it?"

I smiled. It felt strange, yet wonderful. The first real grin I could remember. The muscles in my face were stiff, having not bent that way in God knew how long, but so help me, this would be the first of many. We could fix this, G and I. Together we could do anything. "I think I can take care of that."

G flopped onto his back, noisily chewing the last of his fries. The mattress on the other bed groaned, the sound tugging at the frayed edges of my memory in ways that threatened to drive me mad. We'd gotten a room and ordered more room service than we could both possibly eat, thanks to the cash I'd pickpocketed off a creepy guy on the street corner a few blocks from here. I'd mimicked what I'd seen Dylan do a hundred times while we were stuck together. I didn't think it'd work—but we'd gotten lucky.

I'd kicked off my shoes and lain back as well. This was nothing like the rooms Dylan and I had stayed in. The carpet was clean, and the sheets smelled fresh. The paint on the walls was pristine, and there were several vases full of fresh flowers.

"What do you think Cora really wants with Karl?" The silence between us was comfortable, but I wanted to hear his voice. I'd gone almost a month without it, and even though he and Dylan were *technically* the same person, clearly it wasn't even close to similar.

"Hard to say. He could have actually stolen something she wants back, like she said—or she could just want revenge because he left. Bitch is crazy."

"Do you think she'll keep her end of the deal?"

"No," came his response, instant and unwavering. There was anger in his tone, but also certainty. No one knew Cora's cruelty like G did. With me, she'd at least tried to present herself as human—most of the time. With him, though, she'd been a monster at every turn, heartlessly taunting and punishing him when he didn't do exactly as she wanted. "I'll make her. She's done hurting us. Don't worry."

I rolled onto my side so that I was facing his bed. He was still on his back, staring up at the ceiling. The slight rise and fall of his chest made the hard lines even more defined; I wondered what it would be like to run my fingers across. We'd lost so much time, locked away in those cells. There was a part of me that worried this newfound freedom wouldn't last. I wanted to do everything *right now*. All the things we'd talked about. All the things we swore we'd get to do together. "Do you remember our last night there? What you said to me?"

Cora came down this morning to claim him herself. She'd brought her entourage and dragged him from the cell. The whole thing had been eerily silent. G never kicked or screamed. He never thrashed or fought. He had, in the beginning. I'd heard the chaos and could only imagine the damage he'd done. It took six of Cora's men to subdue him. But she was a smart one. One threat to make me pay for his actions had rendered him as docile as a kitten.

Footsteps at the other end of the hall pulled me from my reverie. Soft voices, a creaking door, then the echoing snap as the cell was closed and locked. I waited until the footsteps faded again.

"G?" The question terrified me. One of these days, would he not be able to answer? Or worse, would he just not be there anymore at all?

A few moments passed. "I'm here. You okay?"

Was I okay? I was sitting on my ass in a cell. He was the one who'd been taken up. "Are you okay? What happened? You were gone so long. I thought…"

"Thought you could—" A violent string of coughs

filled the air, followed by a grunt of pain he tried to mask, and a moment later, the sound of something wet slopping against the floor. "Thought you could get rid of me?"

"Why were you gone so long? What did they do?"

"You know. The usual. We threw back a few beers. Played some pool. Nothing exciting." He coughed again, trying to cover up the sharp inhalation of breath with each new wheeze.

He was particularly bad off tonight. He only joked like this when it got really rough. "Why won't you tell me? If you think it'll scare me—"

"Scare you?" He laughed, a sound that seemed to rattle through the small space. "You're too tough to be scared, Sera."

"Then why not tell me? Why keep it to yourself? You're not alone here. You're—"

"I'll tell you." His voice dropped to a barely-there whisper. Not because he was afraid someone would hear, but likely because it was hard for him to breathe. The sound of his labored puffing was soft, yet the loudest thing in the room in that moment. "When we're free, I'll tell you everything."

He was quiet, and I figured he'd simply fallen into old routine. G had a habit of shutting down when this particular subject came up.

"Why is it so important for you to know?" The sun had gone down, and we hadn't bothered with the lights. I think we both liked the dark—it was a calming contrast to the harsh lights of Infinity. Sometimes Cora would go weeks without turning the lights off. Another person might not think that was a big deal, but when you craved some kind of schedule, any shred of normalcy you could latch on to, it was. G's voice was soft. Barely a whisper. "Why do you need me to paint you that picture when you know it'll be ugly?"

"Because I care." How could he even ask me that? After everything we'd been through together. "It's you and me. Us against the world. We survived that hell together, and I know we can survive this. I want to know what you went through. I want to help."

Another few minutes passed. The only sound was a faint buzzing coming from the clock on the nightstand between our two beds.

"Sera, what do you think will happen? After we wrap this up?" I saw his dark outline shift. "We're either going to find a way and live—or we won't, and we'll die. Say we live. What is it you think will happen after all that?"

I didn't quite understand what he was getting at, but the tone of his voice made me uneasy. "Like, where will we go?" I shrugged and smiled even though he probably couldn't see me. "I dunno. Someplace nice. Someplace warm."

"So your vision of the future is *us* skipping off someplace sunny and warm?"

"Well, I don't love the idea of going someplace bleak and cold." I tried to force the words out in a way that was light and airy but failed. Suddenly it felt like there was a pile of rocks sitting at the bottom of my stomach.

"You really wanna know what they did to me?" He

sighed. "They created something awful. They poked and prodded and did things to push me to the edge of sanity. They shredded my mind, then stitched it back together in the wrong order. They did things to my body that no human should ever experience, much less live through. It destroyed me, Sera. I'm unstable now. Hell, maybe I was *never* stable. But the things that go through my head at any given moment...the emotion..." He inhaled deeply. The sound brought goose bumps to the surface of my skin. "I will die trying to save you if that's what it takes. You're...important to me. But there's no *us*. The moment I know that you're safe, we're going our separate ways."

"Going our sep—"

"There is no us, Sera."

Chapter Ten

"That's not what you want." Her voice was so small, and she sounded so damn far away. Miles and miles. Possibly on another planet. Or, in our situation, another dimension. Even back in those damn cages, she hadn't felt as out of reach as she did right now. I'd get used to it. I had to. "I don't—won't—believe for a second that you want to just drop me someplace and move on."

Damn right I didn't, but that's exactly what was going to happen. If I lived that long.

You're important to me...

I rolled over so that my back was facing her bed. What a fucking joke. Sera wasn't important to me. She was everything to me. The reason I was still alive. The reason I wanted to *stay* alive. And that was exactly the reason I had to get this done and get away from her. Every mood, every feeling I had was ten times more intense than it should have been. Things that would induce a slightly angry response from a normal person triggered an increased adrenaline rush that had me jacked on strength and sent my pain tolerance through the roof. It wasn't just anger, either. Sometimes, when I looked at her, remembering all the nights I'd fantasized about kissing her, I had to physically distract myself because I was afraid of what I might do.

"What I want doesn't matter." What I wanted hadn't mattered long before Cora kidnapped me. I'd gotten my orders and carried them out, regardless of that little voice of reason, one that grew softer and softer with each mission, pleading for me to walk away. I was a soldier. Sometimes I couldn't remember *not* being a soldier. "What matters is getting you far away from Cora and the things she did—and that includes me."

The springs on the other bed creaked, and Sera's feet hit the floor with a thud. She didn't bother with the light, instead stomping around my bed in the dark and coming to stand over me. "Get up," she demanded.

And I did—just another reason I had to get away from this girl. Anything she asked for, anything she wanted, I would bend over backward to give her. I was afraid that might include the worst possible thing for her—me. It was funny when you thought about it. She didn't remember our early interactions—but I did. I'd been horrible to her.

"Please...why won't you talk to me?"

Her babbling was a constant echo in my ears. She'd been chattering nonstop since I'd arrived. It was close to driving me insane. I'd been here for a week now…at least that was my calculation. It was hard to tell. I hadn't left the cell they'd dumped me in, and there were no windows or doors to look through.

"Just a name. Tell me your name. Please?"

"Do you ever shut up?" I couldn't stand it anymore.

"Oh my God. Hi! Hello." God. She sounded so damn hopeful. What the hell did she think a conversation would do? "A guy. You're a guy."

"Give the lady a cracker. She knows I'm male by the sound of my voice."

"Do you know why we're here? Who took us?"

"What I know is that you're giving me a damn headache. Please. Shut. The. Fuck. Up."

"My name is—"

"I don't care what your name is," I roared. "I don't care where you're from, what your hobbies are, or why the hell you're here. If they're going to kill me, I'd just like a little bit of peace and quiet first. Okay?"

"Yes?" She was in front of me. I kept my head down.

"Look me in the eye and tell me you feel nothing for me other than concern."

I lifted my gaze to meet hers but said nothing. I had never lied to Sera. I'd chosen not to answer her questions on occasion, but I had never told her an outright lie. Now would have been a good time to start…but I just couldn't do it.

Her lip twitched, a small flinch of satisfaction, and I knew my silence had the opposite effect I'd hoped for.

"Kiss me."

I almost fell over. "What?"

"You heard me." She came a single step closer. There was almost no space between us now. "You asked me once if I remembered being kissed."

I remembered the conversation well. It'd been a few months ago…

It had to be close to dawn by now, and we were both hungry and exhausted. Cora would be back soon. She'd come with a small team to bring me upstairs. A new day of horrors. Sera had been up with me all night.

"What about cheeseburgers?" She laughed. It was a sound that used to grate against my nerves. Now? I lived for it. My estimation was that it'd been four months since I'd gotten here. Sera had worn me down, talking and talking until I couldn't ignore her anymore. Until I hadn't wanted to… "Do you remember what they taste like?"

"Cheeseburger…" I repeated. "Not sure we had that on my world. Or, if we did, I don't remember it."

She gasped. "No cheeseburgers? That itself is a crime. Can't remember what the inside of my bedroom looked like, but cheeseburgers? Those I remember."

"My turn." I shifted so that my back was against the wall of her cell. "Ever been bitten by a dog?"

"Instinct is to say no."

"Why?"

"I think I like dogs," she said. "Not sure if I had one, but I think I like 'em."

"I had one," I said before I could stop myself. "I, uh, it's weird. I remember this kind of black and white dog. Long hair. Odd-eyed."

"Name?"

Jax. "Wish I could remember."

"Funny how it works."

"It?" I knew exactly what she was talking about.

"The memory loss. It's like everything we were is washed away. Like, bleached from existence, but there are these stubborn stains, these moments, that just won't fade completely."

"What about your first kiss? You remember it?" I asked.

She was quiet for a few moments. "Nothing comes to mind. Maybe I haven't had it yet."

"Maybe," I agreed.

"Or maybe I did, and I just can't remember—which is kind of cool."

"How is that cool?"

She laughed. "Well, that first kiss is supposed to be something special, right? From where I'm standing, I'm lucky. I get to have my first kiss all over again once I get out of here."

My throat was dry, and the dank cell fell away. I found myself drowning in the fantasy of it. Her lips were probably soft as silk. I imagined them tasting like something exotic. Something I'd never tasted before. Something that once sampled, I'd never be able to live without. The thought was intoxicating, while at the same time, terrifying. "When we bust out of here, I'll gladly step up and do the honors."

...

"So?"

I snapped myself out of it. "So, what?" Obviously, she hadn't heard a damn thing I'd said. Maybe I should tell her the truth. Tell her that I'd been a monster before Cora pulled my nearly dead carcass off the battlefield. Maybe I should remind her how truly horrible I'd been to her when I'd first arrived. Point out all the cruel things I'd said during those long hours as her memory ebbed. "You think you feel something for me? You don't. If you could rem—"

"Kiss me."

The rest of the sentence stayed lodged in my throat, choking back the air and leaving me hollow. Her demand equally horrified and thrilled me. I'd thought about kissing this girl for a long time now. Here she was, finally standing in front of me and demanding it, and I was backtracking? What the fuck was wrong with me?

You're a monster, that's what's wrong *with you...*

I was trying to do the right thing. Sera had seen enough darkness—both in Cora's basement and before it. Morals weren't a strong suit in my old life, but because of her, I was determined to fix that.

I growled low in my throat and took a step away from her. "Not going there, Sera. I meant what I said. We're going to do what we need to in order to get Cora to fix that thing in your head, and then I'm going to take you someplace safe." I wouldn't bring her home. Like me, the place she'd come from hadn't been any better than the place she'd ended up. No. I'd see her off to someplace better. Maybe Kori's world. She'd spoken of it often. Green trees, mostly clean air. Sera could make a life for herself there. A life that didn't include me.

"Fine," she said. I think she folded her arms, too. I was trying not to look at her. "But before you do, kiss me." She closed the minute distance between us, her small body dangerously close to mine. To the hard lines and ugly scars I'd accumulated. Some had been there when I'd woken up in that cell. Souvenirs from the life I wished I could forget. Others, Cora had been kind enough to supply me with. "I've seen you, G. You're not afraid of anything. So what's the big deal? Just get it over with and kiss—"

The thundering of my pulse drowned out everything else. The buzz of the clock, her voice, my logic… I lost my shit. I grabbed her face and mashed my lips to hers, moving them furiously, greedily, like she was the meal I'd been deprived of from the moment I'd entered this world. Ravenous, I clutched her face, the tips of my fingers threading through satiny strands of hair. It was heaven—and it was hell.

It wasn't enough.

A soft noise of approval escaped her lips and almost sent me through the roof. I was moving before I even realized it, backing her across the room and up against the wall. When we'd gone as far as we could, I kissed her harder, drawing her bottom lip into my mouth and grazing it with my teeth.

She gasped, her fingers digging through my jeans and into the skin of my hips. In the back of my mind I hated the idea of her hands on me. Those fingers should never touch something so dark and ugly. The me that Cora had all but drowned knew I should pull away and stop this, but the me she created, the one born from endless torture and countless rounds of experimental drugs, chased the sensations. He reveled in the tightness down south and was almost salivating over the soft perfection nearly writhing beneath his touch.

She pulled away and sucked in a breath. I took the opportunity to drag my lips across her cheek and down the right side of her neck. She shivered, fingers curling into the thin material of my shirt. "That was"—another gasp as I tugged aside the collar of her shirt and grazed her skin—"some kiss."

"Yeah? I'm not finished."

The air rushed from my lungs as something ignited, the sudden searing pain in my chest quickly changing into an all-out explosion. I stumbled away from Sera and collapsed.

"G?" She fell forward and hit the carpet in front of me. I heard her, but my vision grew hazy. All I could make out was a vague, watery shape. "G, what's wrong?"

"I—" I struggled to pull the air in and push it out. Each inhalation burned hotter than the one before it. It was the pod, the one Dylan set off. Had to be. More of the poison must be leaking. "I'm okay. I just need to—"

There were several shouts outside, followed quickly by what I could only describe as pandemonium, a collection of panicked voices and terrified cries. Sera hesitated for a moment before hauling herself off the floor and making her way toward the door. As she opened it, I grabbed the edge of the comforter and stood. There was some swaying and a fair amount of nausea, but I managed not to fall on my ass again—which was a good thing. The situation outside our room had people in a panic.

"What the hell is going on?" She stepped aside so I could see into the hallway. It was utter fucking chaos. People were darting back and forth, screaming, crying, and calling for loved ones. Sera ventured out a few steps, and I turned toward the window. That's when I understood what the panic was about. There was a colossal wave of water heading straight for us.

"Shit!" With a clumsy lurch, I propelled myself forward, catching Sera's arm as I flew out the door.

"What—"

"Hurry!" I dragged her past the elevator and barreled through the door marked Stairs. My grip on her hand was like steel, and she stumbled several times, but I didn't slow down. There was no time.

"What am I missing?" She dug her heels in and grabbed the banister with her free hand. Not expecting the sudden resistance, her hand was pulled from mine. "Why are we—"

The entire building shuddered and shook, sending us both off balance. Sera caught herself before collapsing, while I latched on to the railing with both hands. The sound of breaking glass was just slightly fainter than the screams of those still on the lower floors. Screams that were cut morbidly short.

"Oh my God." Sera's face paled as the sound of rushing water filled the stairwell below us. She peered over the edge as I did the same. As far down as I could see, water was flowing in—and it was rising. Fast.

"Move!" I recaptured her hand and dragged her

upward. By the time we reached the top, we were both winded and the water was nipping at our heels. I jabbed a finger at the door a few feet away, the one marked Roof. "Through there. Hurry!"

We burst through and both stopped, frozen in our tracks. The colossal wave that hit the hotel moments ago wasn't alone. Another headed straight for us. It wasn't quite as high as the hotel, but that didn't make it any less intimidating. "What the hell is going on?"

"Tidal wave, tsunami—whatever it is, we're in the wrong dimension at the wrong time." I grabbed her hand and pulled her close, then braced myself against where the building jutted out. "Hold on tight."

The second wave hit harder than the first, shattering any remaining glass and surely wiping out anyone else still inside the hotel. The water leaked from beneath the door now, streams of it sliding across the rooftop and spilling over the edge.

"How long?" She clutched my waist tight and nodded to my arm. "How long until we can skip?"

"Not sure." I maneuvered so that I was still holding on to Sera yet was able to awkwardly jab at my forearm. I woke the chip and tried taking us to a random PATH line. Nothing happened. "I have no idea what time it is—but it should be soon."

The next wave reached us and collided with the building. The entire thing shuddered and groaned, but thankfully it held together. The wall of water exploded on impact, sending spouts like rockets in every direction. They cascaded outward and upward and overflowed across the edge of the roof.

It all happened in an instant. A mini wave crashed

over the side of the building, barreling along the rooftop. It wasn't big. Two or three feet at best. But it was enough because it struck at the same moment as another jolt of pain from the poison caused me to double over. Sera was ripped from my grasp and dragged along with it.

"No!" I let go of the building and made a swipe for her. It took three tries and a shitload of slipping as my feet tried to find traction on the slippery surface, but I managed to grab her hand—only to lose it again.

The force of the water took her feet right out from under her and carried her beyond my reach. Three ticks later and she'd reached the edge. "I can't—there's nothing to—"

Adrenaline surged. It overrode the still-there pain in my chest and cranked up my senses to eleven. My legs pumped faster, and my breathing quickened as water raged all around. I woke the chip as I ran, saying a silent prayer that the timer had hit zero. I reached Sera as another wave crashed into the building. The overflow from this one was more significant. When it made its way across the roof, the force of it took my legs out from under me and knocked the air from my lungs. I slid on the tarred surface, fingers scraping as I went for something—anything—to grab.

The last thing I heard as the current carried us both over the edge was Sera's scream.

Chapter Eleven

Sera

I was on the roof, and then I was weightless. From the corner of my eye, as I went over, I saw G being carried along as well. I saw his head smash against the brick as he slipped across the side, his body limp and falling like a stone. Toward me, at me—then past me.

He hit the water first, though, it wasn't like there was far to fall. The entire city of Wells was submerged, only a few of the tallest buildings now poking morbidly out from the surface of the raging flood.

The air rushed from my lungs on impact. Still, the only thing on my mind was G. I forced my eyes open, the water stinging, and flailed frantically to break the surface. I did. I sucked in a mouthful of air just before being pulled back beneath the swell. In my attempts to break the surface again, something knocked my leg.

G.

I broke through again and managed to keep myself up just long enough to fill my lungs and dive.

Everything was blurry, but I made out G's form, sinking farther down. I kicked hard, arm extended. My fingertips brushed his shoulder, but I couldn't get a hold. He slipped farther out of my reach.

I let out a frustrated howl and pumped my legs for the surface. Lungs filled once more, I dove again. Harder. More frantic. This time I was able to grab a handful of material. I tried kicking for the surface, but he was too heavy, and the current had increased.

My options were limited. Let go and kick for the surface and take the chance that he'd slip too far away, or try and activate his chip and hope like hell that our timer had run its course. There wasn't a choice. Option B was the only thing I could live with. If the timer wasn't ready, then we were both going to die. I refused to sacrifice him for myself.

I jabbed his wrist and woke the chip. Mimicking what I'd seen Dylan do a hundred times, I pressed the R button, which I hoped meant we'd skip to a random version of Wells—and out of here.

There was a rushing sound, and I was weightless once again. Not my favorite feeling in the world, but way better than drowning any day of the week. A blast of wind hit me just before my body slammed hard into the ground. Squealing tires and the scent of burned rubber assaulted my senses. Everything hurt, and I was pretty sure I was bleeding. The inside of my mouth was slick, and the tip of my tongue had a foul, coppery taste…

But I was alive and on dry land.

I pushed myself up onto my elbows, then sloshed the still-dripping hair from my eyes. We'd landed in the middle of the road—more specifically, in the middle of traffic. It was a miracle we hadn't been smooshed.

G was a few feet away, just inches from the front wheels of an SUV. I scrambled onto my knees and went to him as a crowd gathered on the sidewalk. My head fell to his chest, and I stilled, blowing out slowly when I heard the soft, rhythmic thumping and the sound of even breathing.

Brushing a clump of wet hair from his face, I leaned in closer. Just because there was air moving through his lungs didn't mean he was okay. "G? Please open your eyes."

He coughed and groaned, fingers going to the wide, bleeding gash on the left side of his head.

I lay my hand flush against his cheek, thumb gently stroking the hollow just beneath his eye. There was a faint scar there, and I wondered if he'd had it before coming to Infinity. "Please," I begged, only vaguely aware of the growing crowd. "Please just open your eyes."

He was kind enough to oblige.

His body went rigid, and his eyes popped open. The color visibly drained from his skin as he let out a horrible sound. One moment I was leaning over him, terrified that he wouldn't wake up, the next I was flat on my back, bits of concrete and gravel digging into my skin as I fought for air.

"I'll kill you," he said with a growl. His fingers tightened around my neck, and no matter how hard I tried to pry them off, they didn't budge. His grip was like iron.

"Stop," I managed to choke out. "Sera…it's… You're

safe. We—" Air was quickly becoming an issue, and the edges of my vision grew watery. His eyes glazed over, and his expression was haunted. He had no idea where he was—or who I was. I didn't think it was possible, but in that moment, I was terrified of him. "G—stop. You have to—"

There was a loud pop, and his eyes went wide. A second later, the pressure on my windpipe lessened, then disappeared altogether as G's body convulsed and slumped to the ground beside me.

I coughed and gagged, and when I finally managed to suck in a lungful of air, I saw three men in black standing a few feet away. The tallest of the group had an odd-looking gun trained on me. I held up my hand to surrender, but he fired anyway. I felt something imbed itself into my left shoulder, and a moment later, everything went dark.

The first thing I noticed when I came to was the smell. A disgusting mix of urine and mothballs with an underlying hint of rotten eggs. I forced my eyes open and shifted positions, stretching to relieve the kink in my back. Concrete. I was on the floor…

"Sera?"

I turned in the direction of G's voice—and instantly regretted it. Everything swam, and a series of sharp pangs shot down my neck and shoulders. "Can we agree to never do that again?" I stretched my hand and braced myself against the wall to stand. I was in a cell.

And so was G. There was an empty one between us.

A wave of panic, white-hot and paralyzing, rolled over me. It stole my breath and made my heart do double time. I backed away from the bars. "No… Oh my God, NO!"

"Easy," G said. His voice was soft and soothing as he pressed himself closer to the bars, closer to me. "Easy, Sera. It's not what you think. We're not back in that place. The locals picked us up. We're at a police department."

I blinked and took a closer look at my surroundings. Different cells. Much cleaner than the ones we'd come from. Ambient chatter in the distance. He was right. This wasn't Infinity. It was, however, still a cell. "Police. We got *arrested*?"

He frowned. "From what I've gathered, violence of any kind is a crime here."

Of course it was.

"Did you explain that it was just a misunderstanding? That I startled you?"

He lifted the hem of his shirt. Just below his ribs was an angry looking burn mark. "I tried. They wouldn't listen, and things escalated. I got angry, and we both know how that goes. They Tased me again and dropped us in here."

I fell back against the wall and slid to the floor. We really didn't have time for this. "That's not good."

"It's really not," a new voice said. "The punishment for violence of any kind here is generally death." Standing between our two cells, wearing a black suit and bright yellow tie, was Karl Anderson. He turned to the guard beside him and nodded once, and the officer went back the way he came. The newcomer chuckled.

"Ironic when you think about it."

"You…" I moved to the front of the cell. Karl Anderson stood on the other side, beaming like the sun. What were the chances that this was the Karl Anderson we were looking for and not this world's version of him? That would take coincidence to a whole new level. "Who are you?"

"Who am I?" The man winked. The grin on his face said it all. "At the moment? I'm your lawyer. After that? I suppose we'll see."

G let out a growl, and I actually took a step away from the bars. "You're—"

"Here at the moment to help you. As I said, we'll see what happens next." He leaned in a little closer. "I would suggest you play along…for your own sakes."

I glanced to G, who was checking the chip. He held up his forearm. Karl's PATH line was bright green.

I narrowed my eyes. "And why, exactly, would you be helping us? After what you put us through—" Cora had been the one in charge, but her husband, Karl, had taken part in his fair share of the atrocities.

He waggled a finger at me. "Technically I didn't put you through anything. Cora is the scientist. Any experimentation, as well as your removal from your home world, was all her."

"You did nothing to stop it." The venom in G's voice made me cringe. I was actually thankful for the bars.

Karl shrugged. "Nothing personal. It was simply business."

G rushed the bars and thrust a hand through, trying to grab hold of the older man. "I'll show you business."

Karl laughed, but he did take another step away

from G's cell. He gave up and refocused on me. "Now then. I can get you out."

"Why would you do that?"

"Because I believe we can help each other."

G slammed a hand against the wall and snorted. "Like we're gonna believe a word of what you say."

Karl frowned. "You should. They're preparing your funeral pyres now. So unless you plan on skipping alone—seeing as how you can't physically touch Miss Fielding from all the way over there—you have one way out of this. Trust me. Listen to what I have to say. If you don't like my proposal, then we'll go our separate ways." He smiled. "Before you make alternate plans, however, know that I'm well aware that you've been… shall we say, commissioned by my wife. But I believe I can offer you something better."

G mumbled something I didn't quite catch then pushed off the bars and began to pace. Me? I just stared at Karl. I hated him, but not nearly as much as I hated Cora. As far as I was concerned, he was just as trustworthy. But he obviously knew he was in danger. He'd been a man of limitless resources back on his world, but that had all come from his money. Money he no longer had.

Cora was relentless. No one knew that better than G and I did. She'd never give up trying to find him. He had to know that. He had to be desperate.

Desperate people were easier to manipulate. I knew that firsthand.

"Fine," I said, gripping the bars until my knuckles turned white. "Do it. Get us out of here, and then we'll talk."

Chapter Twelve

I was able to stay quiet as they unlocked our cells and led us through the building. I managed to keep my cool as Anderson bantered with the desk clerk, a pretty brunette with thick glasses who kept batting her overdone lashes at him. And as we exited the building, my fingers twitching to curl themselves around the bastard's neck, I focused on Sera and the apology I owed her for what I'd done.

But when he led us around to the side of the building, to a waiting car with tinted windows? That's when I lost my shit. I pushed him back against the vehicle and grabbed a fistful of his graying hair. Using the leverage, I pinned him to the hood. "What's your game, Anderson?"

Had to give the old dog credit. He kept his cool, twisting to find Sera. "If you'll kindly instruct him to let me up..."

She laughed. "*Instruct him?* You've met him.

Multiple times. No one instructs him to do anything."

God was she wrong. One word from her and I'd crawl naked over broken glass.

"But if we wanna know what he's selling, you have to let him up, G."

Against my better judgment, I released him and took a step back. He made a show of adjusting his jacket and dusting off some speck of imaginary dirt from his shoulder before clearing his throat. "So, I suppose my wife offered you something in return for finding me, yes?"

"I guess that's technically correct," Sera said. She kept her expression neutral. "Though she made the offer while I was still with Dylan."

"Might I ask what she offered you?"

"A chance to survive." She tapped the side of her head. "Apparently the chip you crammed in here is going to kill me if she doesn't fix it."

"Interesting…" He turned to me. "And you? What did Cora offer you?"

"Nothing," I ground out. From one point of view, we were offering Anderson too much information. But in the back of my mind, a part of me hoped that maybe he could fix Sera. That maybe we didn't need to rely on Cora's word. "She was kind enough to give Dylan my kill switch, though." Maybe he knew where there was an extra vial of the cure hanging around.

"Which he's activated," Sera added.

"Ah. So you don't have a lot of time left, do you?"

"Before you write us off, we're not the only ones you have to worry about. Dylan is looking for you, too— and he's perfectly healthy."

"Who could forget about Mr. Granger? What did she offer him?"

"She told him there was a way to get Ava back. *His* Ava."

"Again, interesting… And in return, I assume she wants the flash drive I stole. Correct?"

"Which I have to wonder," I said, glancing over at Sera, "why are we not just taking it?"

She folded her arms. "Ya know, I'm really not clear on that."

"You could try, but obviously I don't have it on me. How stupid would that be? Besides, this is much bigger than you realize."

Sera sighed. "What is it you want?"

"I simply want to be left alone. You find a way to keep them from tracking me, and I will gladly fix the chip myself."

"Fix the chip yourself," she repeated. "You?"

"I'm no scientist, but I do know a little about my wife's work. I imagine that the chip in your head simply needs to be neutralized. Is that what Cora told you?"

I looked from Sera to Karl. "Even if we believed you—how the fuck are we supposed to find a way to hide you from them?"

Anderson shrugged. "I'm sure the technology exists in one of these worlds. You simply have to find it."

"Oh. Is that all?" We had to wrap this up or there was a good chance I'd go for his throat again. I felt my control ebbing.

His grin widened. "I'll even give you a little something up front. A retainer of sorts." His gaze found me. "If you think Cora is going to let her go, you need to think again. She made that deal while Sera was still with Dylan, correct? Still in what she considered a somewhat controlled environment. Now that the two of you are together, it will become another matter entirely."

"You're saying they'll still come after me?" There was a twinge of defeat in her voice, and I hated it.

"I'm saying that you're far too important to her to be allowed to walk away. She won't want you alone with this version of Dylan."

"Don't call me that." I made a move to grab him again, but Sera took my hand.

"Wait—why?" She glanced from me to Anderson. "What is she afraid of?"

"He can be a bit...unstable." Anderson's grin morphed into a mock frown. "You're too important to her to lose to one of his random violent outbursts. And should the serum she administered him kick in..."

"I would never hurt Sera."

Karl laughed and spread his arms wide. With a nod toward the building, he said, "Except, you did, didn't you?"

My fists tightened, fingers twitching, but I didn't correct him because he was right. He was right, and I fucking hated him—and myself—for it.

"Cora's personal security are all early members of a project called Alpha—an earlier trial. You are the newest version."

"What is Alpha?" Sera nearly pushed me aside to get to Anderson. She grabbed him by the lapels and gave an impressive shake for someone so small. The last thing I wanted was for her to hear any of this, but short of dragging her away—which would look suspicious—I was stuck. "What is it that they did to him?"

"Alpha was Cora's attempt to score Infinity a government contract by creating better soldiers. The first batch weren't impressive enough for the muckety-mucks, so my wife went back to the drawing board." He flicked a finger at me. "That's where you came in. You were part of the *improved* project. It went better than the first, results-wise, but had some, um, undesirable side effects."

"The mood swings and amped emotion," Sera said.

"That, and Cora insisted she would be able to control the subjects. Your boy here proved her very wrong—which is impressive, considering the serum didn't technically work." He dislodged himself from Sera and straightened his coat.

"What do you mean, it didn't work?" She glanced at me, then quickly back to Anderson.

"In order to activate the serum, the test subject needs to reach a certain level of stress. This triggers an enzyme that then attacks part of the brain—namely the hippocampus. There are synapse issues and neural connection problems—it's all very boring, I assure you. My point is, G here fought it. He has yet to allow himself to slip over that edge." Anderson leaned in close and winked at me. "Quite impressive considering the physical stress they put you through in that lab."

I lifted my arm to strike him, but he rushed on.

"Bonus tidbit—every test subject, as well as each member of my wife's personal guard, has a termination pod." He tapped his chest dead center. "Right here. Get hit there, and it's all over in a matter of minutes. A hard enough blow would shatter the pod and release the poison instantly—unlike the slow disintegration of yours."

At least now we knew how to deal with Yancy if he came sniffing around.

"So, that's my pitch. Do we have a deal or not?"

Sera didn't hesitate. "Deal—on one condition—you tell me where we can find another antidote for the Alpha poison."

He shook his head. "I'm sorry. As far as I know, there was only one vial of it left—and you said Dylan has it."

"Then how do we make more?"

"You don't. The ingredients are a bit hard to track down at the moment, not to mention the recipe is unattainable. You're going to have to settle for what I offered you. Nothing more. Nothing less. Deal?"

"Deal," I said before he changed his mind. I had no idea how we were going to do it, but it was another shot at saving Sera. I wasn't ruling any option out. Either we took down Anderson, and Cora made good—or we got the bastard what he wanted, and he fixed her chip. No matter what, Sera was *not* going to die.

"You've been unusually quiet," she said. We'd run our timer to cooldown and were currently tucked away in the back corner of an all-night diner. The first world, the one where we'd encountered Anderson, was a no-go. We both agreed that staying to sniff around was a bad idea after what had happened with the police. The second place we landed was a bust. That version of Wells was stuck in an era where they still used horses for travel. Their technological advances had topped out at the invention of the light bulb. We called it and moved on to our current stop.

"Trying to figure out what the fuck we're supposed to do." I slammed my empty cup down. "I mean, where do we even start? I doubt we'll be able to walk into a store and ask for a cloaking device for realm-traveling assholes."

"That's not what's bothering you."

Her tone was even, and her posture relaxed, but she was upset. I saw it in her eyes. And why the hell wouldn't she be? I'd tried to kill her. "There's nothing I can say, Sera. Not a damn thing."

"Why do you feel like you need to say something?"

I lifted my empty cup and stared at her over the rim. The reddish mark across the front of her throat had started turning bluish purple. Every time I looked at her, it was all I saw. "Why would I need to say something after trying to kill you? Is that *really* what you're asking me?"

She rolled her eyes. "You didn't try to kill me."

"Were you there? Because I'm pretty sure—"

"Don't you think I heard you?" She leaned across the table and grabbed my hands. I was tempted to pull them away, but her touch was so warm. So soft. "The nights you'd wake from a dead sleep screaming. How you'd throw yourself around the cell, fighting an enemy only you could see?" She straightened. "You won't tell me what they did. Fine. But I can imagine. That kind of thing takes time to get over. And with what Karl said—"

"You don't get it." That time I did pull my hands from hers. "Time isn't going to change anything. I'm not going to *get over* it." I slammed my fist into the side of my head. "They broke me. Went in and messed up all the wires. I'm barely human now. I opened my eyes on that street, and I saw her. I saw Cora—and in that moment, I would have stopped at nothing to kill her. In case you've forgotten, that her was *you*."

"You act like I'm clueless." Her lips twisted into a scowl. Even glaring at me like she was, pissed off and putting up with none of my shit, she was the most beautiful thing I'd ever seen. She shook her head. "I know exactly who you are, G. We're both screwed up. Maybe not in the same ways, but I have no illusions that you're perfect. I have no delusions that we'll ever live peaceful, boring lives—and I'm fine with that. Infinity will always be a dark cloud over our heads. The difference is, if we stick together, it won't matter."

"It will *always* matter. My mood is too unpredictable. I could turn on you in a heartbeat." I snorted. Cora always referred to me as a dog, and in that moment, I realized how true the comparison was. I was feral—borderline rabid—and I wouldn't put Sera in danger just because I wanted her in my life.

"I don't believe you'd ever hurt me on purpose." She folded her arms. "And that's it. We're done talking about it. Time to focus on Karl. Rattle off an idea. Anything."

I felt myself getting worked up. She could probably see it, too. This was her way of distracting me. "We shoot them both."

"That's a nice thought." Her lip hitched, and my heart sped up as she aimed her smile at me. "But probably not realistic. Next?"

"Infinity? If anyone would have the tech Anderson wants, it'd be them."

"Better," she said with a nod. "More specifically, Cora herself. Or that other guy. Phil? Rabbit? Whatever he's called." There was a note of uncertainty in her voice.

"I know Cade said the other versions of Cora were nothing like the one we dealt with, but…" I didn't want to go to Phil for help. She didn't know it, but neither did she… "Maybe we could approach another version of Cora. Best to go right to the source."

"No." She shook her head slowly, and I could see the fight in her eyes. There was a memory on the verge of breaking free. "He's the better choice."

I pushed the chair away from the table and stood. There would be no dissuading her. I suppose we'd see just how badly Cora had tampered with her memories. "Let's go Rabbit hunting."

Chapter Thirteen

Sera

*F*inding Rabbit was harder than we'd anticipated. It made me wonder how Cade and Noah did this for so long without going crazy. They'd been searching for not one person but technically five.

We checked the phone directory and when the library opened the next morning, we hopped online. There was no trace of Phil MaKaden or Infinity in this version of Wells. There was—unfortunately—a listing for Cora Anderson.

"Have I mentioned that I don't love this idea?" We were standing on the sidewalk in front of the address we'd found for this world's Cora Anderson. The place was a dump. A shack covered in spray-painted graffiti and a roof that looked ready to cave at any second. The lawn was overgrown, the tree branches all but lying across the front porch, and in several places, even growing through it.

"I vote we bail." G glared at the house like it might

eat him. "There's no way that any Cora Anderson living in this shit hole knows anything about multiverse travel."

I sighed. While I mostly agreed with him, we were already here. It would be stupid not to at least check. We had time to kill, anyway. We still had a little time left on the cooldown, and we'd spent the entire night at the table in the diner. Any longer and I was worried we might arouse suspicion. We didn't know anything about this place, and the last thing we needed right now was to break some weird law and get tossed into jail again.

Without another word, I forced my feet to move me forward and climb the rickety porch steps. Three knocks on the wooden door—there was no doorbell—and after a pause, the thing creaked open with a horrible wail. "Yeah?"

"I—uh, hi." It was Kori…only not. This version had onyx-colored hair and dark makeup. I couldn't make out the specifics, but there was a tattoo on her right hand.

She looked past me to G and smiled. "What can I do for *you*?" Her gaze raked over him, with her mouth open slightly and chest puffed out. She licked her lips, purposefully slow, and leaned a little closer as I fought the urge to knock her back.

"Cora," I snapped, irrationally irritated by the way she was leering at G. "We're looking for Cora."

Kori shrugged and pushed open the door. "She's coming off a three-day bender but, eh. You can try talking to her. Wouldn't get too close, though, if I were you. Don't think she's seen the inside of a bathroom in a couple of days." She led us down the hall to the living room, where this world's Cora Anderson was splayed out on the couch, surrounded by empty liquor bottles. Standing unnecessarily close to G, Kori said, "I'll be upstairs if you need *anything*."

G grabbed one of the bottles closest to us and lifted it to his nose. Cringing, he tossed the thing across the room. Next, he slammed his foot into the bottom of the couch. The whole thing shuddered, and Cora groaned. "Wake the hell up."

"This is just…weird," I said.

She wore a red polka-dot robe and, from the way it was hanging open in the front, nothing underneath. Her hair was matted down, and her face was streaked with old makeup. I couldn't imagine the other Cora looking like this. With her pristine hair and expensive clothing, the most disheveled I'd ever seen her was when she'd once slapped me and a hair had slipped free from one of her bobby pins.

G kicked the couch again, and this time her eyes flickered open. "Wha's rong?"

We both covered our noses as a blast of fetid breath wafted our way. "Jesus," G snapped. "This is a waste of time."

I hated to give up, but he was right. This Cora couldn't have found her way through an empty room, much less designed any kind of complicated tech. I scanned the small space, finding a clock above the door on the far wall. "Timer should be up by now."

G nodded and hitched a thumb back the way we came. "Let's head outside. Skipping in a building makes me antsy."

I felt the same way. Dylan used to do it, and more

times than not, we ended up inside another building. It was hard to explain to the inhabitants, not to mention dangerous. You could end up in someone's living room or, say, in the jail cell of a murderer. There was a chance no matter where you were. Every version of Wells was different. Just because there wasn't a building in the exact spot you were standing in on one Earth didn't mean it wasn't there on another. But why tempt fate? Chances were just better outside.

We closed the door behind us and walked to the middle of the front lawn. G lifted his arm, but hesitated. "Is this really what we're gonna do? Bounce from place to place on the off chance we can hunt down this goddamned tech?"

"What other choice do we have?"

"We find Anderson and *make* him give us the flash drive."

"You said so yourself—the chances of Cora holding up her end of the deal are slim. What happens when we hand over the flash drive and she doesn't keep her word?" Of course, the same could easily be said about Karl. Neither one of them was what I'd consider trustworthy. We needed some kind of insurance policy.

"This whole thing—" G gasped and clutched his chest. "Fuck."

He dropped to the ground, and I went with him, grabbing his face in my hands and forcing his head up so that we were eye to eye. "Breathe," I said, trying to keep the terror out of my voice. "Please just breathe. In. Out. In. Out."

He covered his mouth as a series of coughs racked his body. When he moved it away, his palm was covered in blood. "Probably not a good sign," he said with a wheeze. He swiped the back of his hand across his lips, then ran it down the side of his jeans

"Cade will find Dylan." If he didn't, I'd go after the bastard myself. "He'll get the antidote."

With my help, he got back on his feet and woke the chip. But instead of pulling up the PATH menu, he looked at me. For what felt like an eternity, he just stared, gaze unflinching and attention intense. He was standing absolutely still.

"G?"

The movement of his chest as he breathed seemed to slow, then stop, and a flash of panic rolled through me. Just when I was sure he'd stopped breathing, he jerked forward, grabbing the back of my head and dragging me to him.

His lips were like fire. They moved with fury and intent and sent a wave of warmth crashing through me. It only vaguely registered that we were still standing on Cora Anderson's front lawn and that we should be moving, skipping off to our next destination to get Karl what he'd asked for. But I couldn't bear to move away. This kiss was different than the first. It was desperation and passion, but also tasted of acceptance.

Of goodbye.

He didn't believe he'd make it out of this alive.

G was the one who broke away first, moving back just far enough so that I could see the golden flecks in his chocolate-colored eyes. He said nothing as he lifted his arm, eyes still locked on mine, and woke the chip.

A moment later, we were someplace else.

Chapter Fourteen

Two skips after we met drunken Cora Anderson, we finally caught a break. Phil MaKaden, or Rabbit, was alive and well on this world, as was Infinity. We'd landed in front of their building, a glass-covered skyscraper extending far into the clouds like some metal beanstalk. Above ground instead of below—I wanted to take it as a sign that they'd be different. That this *skip* would be different.

Sera had looked Rabbit up and found him right away. One quick phone call and we were on our way to meet him. He all too enthusiastically agreed, leading us to believe he knew her on this world—which worried me.

"So, what's the story?" She kept trying to talk to me. I'd been giving her simple, short-and-sweet answers.

"We go with the truth."

"And that is?"

"That we need tech help." We were on foot since we

had no idea what kind of money public transportation used here. Thankfully Rabbit's place wasn't far. I picked up the pace, pulling ahead of her.

She wasn't having it. She caught up and grabbed my arm, yanking me to a stop. "Tell me what is going through your head right now."

"We don't have time for this." I pulled free and started forward again.

She jumped in front of me. "Yeah. We do." I tried to sidestep her, but she blocked me, bringing her hand to my cheek. It was warm and soft. "Since when do you not tell me what's on your mind?"

She had a point. I'd refused to tell her all the fucked-up things Cora and her team did to me, as well as the truth about my old life—including the fully intact memories I had of it—but I'd never held back what was going through my head. Even the stupidest things.

"Cheese," I said out loud. Sera had been quiet for the last hour. I wanted to hear her voice.

Needed to hear her voice.

"Cheese?" Something rustled, and the cot in her cell scraped against the floor.

"Yeah. Cheese. I miss cheese."

Sera snickered. "You don't remember your name, but you remember cheese?"

"Don't you?"

She thought about it for a minute, then said, "I think so. I want to say I loved cheddar."

"Brie is my favorite, I think. With tomato and garlic."

She laughed again. God. I'd sing show tunes in a chipmunk voice for hours if she'd just keep laughing like that. "That's oddly specific."

"What about you? Is there anything you remember? Something that you miss?"

"I know it's weird, but I want to say peas."

"Peas?"

"Yeah. I think I kind of loved peas." I recognized the sound of her sliding down the wall to the floor. "I have this watery memory of this huge bowl of peas. There's tiny slivers of carrot and caramelized onion…"

"God. You're making me hungry."

"Do you like peas?"

"Honestly? I have no damn clue."

And despite the situation, and our rumbling bellies, we both broke out into hysterical laughter.

I sighed. Not telling her was stupid. I couldn't hide it anymore. "It's getting worse."

"It'll be okay. Cade will—"

"I'm not talking about the poison," I said quietly. I closed my eyes and sucked in a breath, holding it to the slow count of five. When I blew out, I opened my eyes. Sera was still standing there, watching me. There wasn't even the smallest hint of anger or fear in her expression. Just understanding and acceptance, and for some reason, that only made my anger worse. "I'm swinging in all directions every few seconds, and it's giving me whiplash. Remember how Anderson said I had to basically lose my shit to activate the serum?

It's getting harder not to give in…"

"That kiss on the other world—"

I laughed. The sound was grating and cold. "If you knew what I'd really wanted to do to you…" I inhaled and held it again, this time to the count of seven. There was a small voice inside my head that kept fighting for my attention, but I tamped it further down, mesmerized by the expression on her face. "I wanted to tear you up—in the most painfully exciting ways."

"G—"

I moved in closer, bringing my lips just shy of touching hers. "I know you've wondered what it would be like." My pulse spiked as she inhaled sharply, the sound sending a thousand mind-numbing volts through my body. Pain wasn't the only tool Cora had used to try pushing me over the edge. "I could show you. I could make you beg me to—"

"Enough." The sound her hand made as it connected with the side of my face echoed in my ears. The faint, lingering sting, along with her expression—a gut-turning mix of fury and understanding—had me backing away. "Snap the hell out of it."

"Sera, I—"

Her expression softened. She took my hands and pulled me a bit closer. "This is the serum talking, not you."

God, I wanted that to be true. More than anything, I wanted it to be true. "How? How do you know that for sure?"

She smiled, and it wasn't tentative or forced. There was nothing fake about the grin currently aimed at me. A weapon. It was the only word I could muster to describe it. That smile was a nuclear weapon with the capability to obliterate all my doubts. All my self-hatred. "Because I know you. Now, come on. We need to keep moving."

And that was that. Argument, discussion—total clusterfuck—over.

"I don't think going to Rabbit is a good idea."

She frowned and let go of my hands. "I'll admit the version we're used to dealing with has always creeped me out—"

"It's more than that." Fuck. Could I tell her? *Should I?* Was there even a chance I could do this and not attack the guy—especially in the frame of mind that I was?

"It's our best option right now." She started forward and, when I didn't follow, turned back and took my hand. With a squeeze, she was tugging me forward. Pulling me from the dark once again.

Rabbit's place hadn't been far, but it still took us almost twenty minutes to get there on foot. By the time we'd made it to his front door, the pressure was back in my chest and the inside of my cheek was raw and bloody from my teeth clenching down.

I lifted my hand to knock, but the door swung open and a familiar face came into view. "Ava! I was so glad you called..." His gaze hit me, and his expression soured. "What's he doing here?"

"We need your help," she said. Without waiting for an invitation, she shouldered past him and dragged me with her. "What do you know about Infinity?"

He blinked. "Infinity? You mean the computer place in town?" Rabbit's eyes narrowed, and his nose scrunched up. Like he'd smelled something offensive. "Or are we talking about what I offered you?"

"Huh?" Sera glanced at me, then back to Rabbit. Something flashed in her eyes, and she took the smallest step back.

"Are you—" Another round of chest spasms had me on my knees, coughing up what felt like both lungs. When I managed to get it under control, I swiped a hand across my mouth, quickly bringing it to my side to hide the red smear.

Rabbit snorted. "He's not looking good, Ava."

"He's *not* good. That's why we need your help."

"You're asking me to help *him*? Seriously?"

I used the wall to haul myself upward. "Did I piss in your damn Cheerios here? What the hell is your problem?"

"You stole my girl, asshole." He glared at Sera. "Something I'm *still* not over, by the way."

"You're—" Sera's face paled. She even backed away another step. "We weren't together."

Rabbit's face contorted. His eyes narrowed, and his lips pulled back into a vicious sneer. "Is that what you need to tell yourself? That the whole thing was a dream?"

"More like a nightmare," she said, voice cracking.

There was fear in her eyes. "It's okay, Sera."

But she didn't hear me. From the way she stared ahead, unmoving and dazed, she didn't see me, either. She was lost in something. A memory, a feeling, something linking back to her past. Those shadows were the worst. There, but not. They lingered just beyond reach, no matter how hard she chased.

I could help her. I could turn the light on and illuminate the feeling of dread she couldn't quite put her finger on when she looked at Phil MaKaden—any version of him—but refused. Early on, when she'd still had her memories, she'd admitted to wanting to forget. She'd been so desperate to leave her past behind. It was the one good thing—the *only* good thing—I could give her. Blissful ignorance.

"I might not know you, but part of me does *remember* you." She was shaking her head. "I felt it needling me when you unlocked my cell. It's bugged me since back at Infinity, in the lab just after we escaped. But now…just now when you looked at me like that—I remember you looking at me that way a hundred times. That anger and…and entitlement."

"Unlocked your cell? You've lost your mind," Rabbit snapped.

Sera laughed, nodding her head a little too enthusiastically. "Actually, I have. And even if I never get it back, I will still remember you."

I stepped up beside her. She was shaking, anger rolling off her like I'd never seen before. "We're leaving," I said. "Rabbit is off the table."

"Off the table," she whispered. There were tears in her eyes, but her expression was anything but stricken. It was fierce. Deadly. "But—"

I nodded and carefully took her hand. She tensed for a moment before catching my eye and allowing me to lead her out the front door. It still took all my willpower to leave him standing.

Chapter Fifteen

Sera

G walked us to the front of Rabbit's yard and gathered me close. I didn't argue as he pulled me to him, gentle as though I was made of glass. I didn't make a sound as he kissed the top of my head and lingered for a moment before skipping us to another Wells. I didn't question him when he led me down the foliage-lined street and tucked us away below the shade of a large oak, or when he gently nudged me to sit on the wrought iron bench beneath it.

For a while we just stayed like that. Just sitting under that tree, out of the sunshine in an odd sort of silence. The quiet with G had never been an issue. Now, though, it felt heavy. Maybe he was afraid I'd snap again. Lose my cool and start screaming, or worse, crying. I didn't remember the details of my old life, but I recalled a cloudy memory of someone slapping me, someone of the male persuasion, and telling me he didn't need to see the *waterworks*.

"Whatever it is you remembered, it's in the past," he said softly.

"I know that." The words came out low, almost weak, and I hated myself for it. I'd cried in those early days at Infinity. I couldn't remember my name, or what foods I liked, but I remembered that. I'd cried a lot. G never made me feel weak, though, and each day I cried a little bit less. Each day some of his strength seemed to seep into me. Strength was the only way to survive.

"And even if it weren't, I would have never let him hurt you."

"I know that, too." I thought about his face when he'd taken me from the house. How his eyes had sparked with fury and his muscles wound tight. His final glance at Rabbit, a threat of something worse than death, both terrified and elated me. He was capable of bad things, dark things. Far darker than I'd imagined.

"I just need to stop and breathe, okay? I need to think. Then we can get back to it."

It took a minute, but when he understood what I meant, he jumped from the bench and glared at me. "This isn't up for debate. We're not going to him for help. On any world."

It wasn't like I wanted to. In fact, the thought of seeing Rabbit again—any version of him—actually made the acid in my stomach roil, and I had no idea why. Worse than that, though? G's insistence. There was something off about it. "What are you not telling me?"

"Nothing."

So it was back to the one-word answers? No. "Liar. Tell me."

He closed his eyes tight. "Don't ask me this, Sera."

It was more his tone—guttural and raw—than the fact that I knew he was hiding something that made me twitch. "G—"

He opened them and pinned me with a furious glare. "Don't ask me again."

More than anything, I wanted to push it. He knew something, there was no doubt in my mind. But he was also dangerously close to the edge. The rapid rise and fall of his chest, the slightly shuttering vein in his neck, and the rigid set of his shoulders… He'd confessed to worrying about activating the serum. I didn't want to chance being the cause of it.

I sighed and sank back to the bench. "Fine. Okay. That leaves only one option."

"Cora."

"Not a choice I love. Also, one we're not very equipped to deal with." I reached across and tapped his chipped arm. "Let's see if we can find someone who can give us a little insight."

"Insight? Like who?"

I held up his arm so that he could see the translucent blue screen—Cade's frequency. His PATH line was green. He was in the same Wells as we were.

It took almost three hours to find Cade, and by the time we did, G had deteriorated further.

He looked like crap, and Cade must have noticed, too, because he was staring. "You okay?"

"Sure."

He frowned, then rolled his eyes. "My brother used to do the same thing. We had an ATV accident when I was fourteen. On the outside everything was coming up rockets, on the inside, he walked home with four broken ribs, a broken toe, and a dislocated shoulder all without saying a damn thing."

"Your brother is a goddamned psychopath."

"Technically *you're* my brother."

G leaned back and kicked his feet onto the empty chair beside me. "Rest my case."

"Anyway," I said. I glared between the two of them then tapped the table. I hadn't forgotten about G's refusal to go after Rabbit again, and had no intention of letting it slide, but I knew better than to fight him outright. Especially with the poison still working its way through his system. I'd have to play the cards right. We'd filled Cade in on our little jailhouse visit from Karl and had spent the last half hour trying to decide whose deal held more weight. "Do we have a consensus?"

"No," G said as Cade nodded and remarked, "Yes."

I groaned and let my head fall to the tabletop. "This is getting us nowhere."

"Maybe we should switch. You guys try catching up with Dylan, and I'll chase the tech."

"No." G's face left no room for argument. "I'm not leaving her fate up to—" He gasped and stumbled from the seat, coughing and wheezing like he couldn't catch his breath. Doubling over, he fell to the floor.

Cade and I both jumped up, but he was around the table and to him first. "Hey," he said, hauling G up. "Hey, look at me. Take it easy. Deep breath. Slow."

G struggled several times but got the coughing under control—but not before he tried to hide the blood. "G…"

There was so much more of it now. Small pools instead of simply a smear.

He flashed a painful grin when he noticed me staring. "Sera, please. I'm okay. This isn't—" The coughing started again, but it was different now. More violent with a rattling wheeze. This time he couldn't get a handle on it.

"Is he…" The waitress lingered a few feet from our table. "Is he all right?"

"Doctor," Cade said as he braced G's body to keep him from flailing around. "Ambulance. He's been poisoned. Hurry!"

The girl paled and bolted off.

"Is that a good idea?" We needed to get him help, but we knew nothing about this world or their medicine. "What if they do something to make it worse?"

Cade's brows knitted together, and his lips twisted into a grim frown. "I'm not sure anyone can make it worse at this point. We have to do something. Now. This is the only option."

A few minutes later, sirens blared, getting louder and louder. G had given up trying to stand and was struggling just to breathe when the EMTs came. From there, everything moved at warp speed.

They loaded him into the back of the ambulance, ushering Cade and me inside as they slammed the doors closed. The ride to the hospital was surreal, watching them work on G as he lay there, still coughing up blood, so much blood, and hearing them talk—

yet not really understanding the words. I was numb, terrified in a way that I'd never been before. All the horrible things Cora did to us, all the threats she made, none of them had shaken my very core like this. Seeing him like this stripped me down to bone.

When we arrived at the hospital, they whisked him away and demanded that we wait in the designated area as they worked. The place was busy. Nurses and doctors hustled back and forth, breezing here and there, none stopping to talk to us. I curled up in a large chair while Cade paced the room. Back and forth. Back and forth. Every once in a while, he'd stop and look around like he'd forgotten where he was before resuming his trek. He seemed genuinely concerned.

"You look worried," I said when I couldn't stand it anymore. Normally the pacing wouldn't bother me. God knew I'd listened to G do it for as far back as I could remember. But now it was grating, making me jumpy and raw.

Cade frowned. "I am."

"Me, too."

"He'll be okay," he said, finally claiming the seat across from me. "My brother is as stubborn as they come."

"But he's not your brother."

Cade sighed. He leaned back in the chair and tilted his head toward the ceiling for a moment before sighing. "Isn't he?" He lowered his head and pinned me with what I could only describe as an apologetic gaze. "He's Dylan. Doesn't matter what he calls himself or what's been done to him. Those things don't change who he is underneath it all. Whether he's shattered like my Dylan or just badly bruised, he's still Dylan."

"Destroyed," I said, my voice barely a whisper. Thinking about the way he'd said it broke my heart. "He feels like he's been destroyed. By Cora. By what she did to him…"

"I think he's stronger than that."

"Your Dylan wasn't," I pointed out.

"My Dylan lost the one thing that kept him tethered. G hasn't. He has you."

"He can't wait to leave me behind." The words, and the thought, were like acid in my belly. "He feels like he's dangerous—and he's right. He is. But I don't believe he's dangerous to *me*."

"I don't, either."

"Have you come across him many times? Alternate versions, I mean?"

"You'd think my answer would be yes, considering how long we've been doing this, but no. G is the first alternate version of my brother that I've had any real interaction with."

"Mr. Granger?" A tall man in a white coat poked his head out from behind the closed doors. His expression was grim.

Cade jumped up and was across the room in three long steps. I followed close behind. "How is he?"

The doctor frowned. He hesitated for a minute, and a sick feeling bubbled up in the pit of my stomach. He glanced between us and sighed. "Sit down. We need to talk…"

Chapter Sixteen

"Now," the doctor, whose name was Mitching, had returned with Cade and Sera, and had settled on the chair by the window. I'd passed out for a while, and since waking up, no one would tell me shit. "The EMTs informed me that you thought you'd been poisoned. Is that correct?"

"Yeah." They'd made me put on a hospital gown, and I had no clue where my clothes had gone. The smock was itchy and smelled like bleach, and I couldn't wait for him to spill it so I could take the damn thing off.

"We did extensive testing and discovered no trace of any type of poison in your system. We did, however, find a virus."

"A virus?" Sera's lips turned downward, and she paled just a little.

Cade, on the other hand, looked hopeful. "So you can treat it? Medication to kill it?"

The doctor's expression grew bleaker. I knew the answer before he even opened his mouth. "We've been able to stave off the symptoms with a fair amount of success by using moderate doses of adrenaline, but I'm afraid that's just a bandage, and we'll begin to see diminished effects sooner rather than later. We can't treat it because we have no idea what it is."

"You've never seen it before?"

"We've never encountered anything like it. It's multiplying at an exponential rate. The virus quickly overtakes anything we give him."

"So, what's the prognosis?" Though, I knew. Poison or virus, without the antidote I might as well just dig my own damn grave—which would have been fine if Sera's life weren't on the line as well. I needed to live long enough to make sure she was okay.

"I'm not sure what to say." His gaze darted to the door, and he stood. I got the feeling he couldn't wait to get out of that room. Fingers lingering at the handle, he said, "We'll keep you here for tests, and we'll do our best. It doesn't seem contagious. I have a virus specialist coming in from the city in the morning. He might know more than we do here."

As soon as the door closed behind him, Cade was by my side. "We have to find Dylan. Now."

"Yeah," I said, throwing the covers off and swinging my legs around. The room spun for a moment before coming to a grinding halt. "That's a great plan. Why the hell didn't I think of it before?"

Cade rolled his eyes then grabbed my arm. At first, I thought it was to restrain me, but I realized he'd seen me sway. It was a subtle touch to keep me from falling.

Probably casual in hopes that Sera hadn't noticed. "What we need is a trap."

Sera snorted. "Haven't you guys tried that, like, a million times already?"

"She has a point. If it were me—which, it kind of is—I'm pretty sure I wouldn't keep falling for the same crap over and over."

"Exactly," Cade said. He nodded in my direction. "Which is why this time I think we can pull it off."

"Why? Because of me? Not sure where you're looking, but I'm half dead." Right now, I wouldn't be able to go two rounds with a two-legged cat. What good would I be?

"What would you do? If you were in Dylan's shoes, chasing Karl with no luck?"

I thought about it for a minute, then sighed. "Hard to say. If it were *me* and Karl was proving to be impossible, I'd go full throttle at Cora." I turned to Sera. "She said she had a way to get him back to his Ava, right? That's what he's after."

She nodded.

"Then I'd go at her. Yeah. If it were me, I'd get tired real fast of trying to shake down someone else's problems, and just deal with my own."

Cade smiled. "My thoughts exactly. So let's work with *that*."

Maybe I was doped with the good stuff because I still didn't understand what he was getting at. "How exactly can we *work with that*?"

"Dylan is going to be hunting Cora. Everyone is hunting Karl. I say we bring everyone together. Lead them all to one place and make our stand."

"But where?" Sera asked. She frowned, gaze lingering on me for a moment before focusing on him. "We still need Cora to fix the chip in my head and for Dylan to hand over the antidote. Where could we convincingly lure them both that would give us the upper hand to do all that?"

Cade's grin widened. "The one place they couldn't go. Home."

Cade's plan was an outline at best. It lacked meat, but even I had to admit it started with a solid foundation. We agreed that since time was an issue, we'd have to build on it as we went. Step one? Getting me the hell out of this hospital bed. To do that? I needed drugs. Specifically, adrenaline.

As the doctor said, it was a bandage, but it was one that worked. For now, at least. Whatever the virus was, the adrenaline kept it at bay. We didn't know how long it would last, so acting fast was in our best interest.

"Okay," Cade said. We were outside a park after having skipped from the hospital. He fished into his inside pocket and pulled out a small plastic bag. He'd managed to liberate me a handful of syringes and several vials of adrenaline. I went to grab it, but Sera beat me to it. "Don't overdo it. Remember—diminishing effects."

She wrapped the handles of the bag around her wrist and gave a short nod. "He won't."

"We're clear on the plan?" He'd only asked us fifteen times since we'd landed here.

I sighed. "We find Karl and tell him we've tracked down a way to cloak him from Cora."

"We convince him that, in order for us to give him the tech," Sera said, "he needs to come with us."

Cade nodded. "Bring him to my home world." He pointed to my arm. "The frequency is programmed in."

"In the meantime, you're going after Cora." Sera tried—and failed—to hide her shudder. "You're going to tell her you have Karl and are willing to exchange him and the flash drive for the information on how to fix my chip."

"This whole convoluted plan still has a lot of holes," I said. Granted, it was all we had, but still. There were too many variables. Too many chances to fuck it all up. "This hinges on a lot of probabilities. Us tracking Karl down and convincing him to come, all in a reasonable amount of time. You being able to do the same with Cora, without her just wiping you from the face of the Earth…"

"And Dylan," Sera said. "You're assuming he'll end up following Karl or Cora. If he's wanted for murder on your world, do you really believe he'll skip back there?"

"I know he will. Dylan is smart, but he's also obsessed with getting Ava back. There's nothing he wouldn't do now that it looks like he's got her almost in reach."

"What about G? Won't he be arrested—or worse—as soon as we get there? If Dylan is as big a criminal there as you say, won't they shoot first and ask questions later?"

"I'm going home ahead of you. I'll give the general—Kori's dad—a rundown of our plan and get Noah." His gaze rested pointedly on me. I didn't argue. We were out of time. "We *will* find Cora, and we *will* get her to my world. Dylan *will* follow."

I nodded. "All right."

Cade woke his chip, then hesitated, lifting his head so we were eye to eye. Another moment, and he held out his hand.

I took it and squeezed just once. "Be safe."

A flicker of something flashed in his eyes, and his lip twitched, so slightly that it was barely noticeable. "You, too."

With a few flicks of his finger, he was gone, and Sera and I were alone once more.

Chapter Seventeen

Sera

I wasn't saying much, but I could tell the adrenaline they'd given him back at the hospital was wearing off. Every once in a while, when he thought I wasn't looking, he'd cringe. His skin was pale, and his movements were stiff.

We'd traveled to Karl's current PATH line, but after two hours of searching, the line went red, meaning he'd skipped to another version of Wells, and we moved on, hoping to have better luck in the next place. "How do you feel?"

"I'm fine, Sera."

"We could do a dose of adrenaline if you want. It's been—"

"I'm good."

We'd walked the street for a little over an hour. It was like searching for a needle in a haystack. I didn't know enough about Karl to make an educated guess as to where he'd go when arriving someplace new. We searched two of the town's hotels and happened to get super lucky when we arrived at the third. Karl was registered—under his *real* name, which seemed careless. We'd gotten his room number and took the *liberty* of letting ourselves in to wait for his return. Apparently in this Wells, everyone was honest and trusting. None of the doors had locks.

Now we waited, and every once in a while, G glanced at me like there was something he wanted to say. After ten minutes, he cleared his throat. He flipped off the light by the bed and sank into the chair beside the dresser. "I'm not thrilled where this is all headed, but I want you to know I wouldn't change what happened… Getting thrown in that cell, I mean." He inhaled. "Cora put me through hell, but it was worth it. For me, at least."

After having been through what we both had, would I change it if I had the chance? I got the impression that G knew more about my past than I did, but the glimpses I had been able to recall weren't pretty.

There was a shadow over my memories, the few I retained. The nameless places and faces, the muddy situations and bits of conversation… The shadow was so dark, so crushing, that sometimes I was sure I didn't want my memories back. Still, to have never lived through Cora's torment and abuse? Was my old life worse than that?

The truth was, it didn't matter.

"For me, too," I said softly. I sank onto the edge of the bed a few feet from where he sat. Despite the horrible things that had happened to me since being torn from my home, I didn't want to go back—for several reasons. I held up my arms, staring down at the twin scars on each wrist. "I don't know what happened there, but home wasn't a happy place for me. I think you know why that is. Why you won't tell me—"

He stood and moved to step in front of me, taking both my hands in his. "Sera, I'm sorry. I—"

"Just answer one question." He wouldn't like it, but I had to know. "Tell me one thing, and I won't ever ask you again."

He didn't answer, but he hadn't moved, either. I traced over one of the scars. "These—I did these? I tried to hurt myself?"

"You did."

"How do you know?"

He thought about it for a while, and just when I was sure he'd avoid it altogether, same as he always did, he said, "I remember more from my first days at Infinity than you do. I remember you telling me what you'd done."

"Why?" My throat was thick, and the corners of my eyes stung. "Did I tell you why I did it?"

He shook his head. No words. Just a simple side-to-side motion that I was sure wasn't a no, but a refusal to tell me.

"I wouldn't have survived in there without you." Heat rushed to my cheeks. "My time at Infinity was horrible, but you were there. If I skipped that, then, well, there'd be no you."

"You might have had a Dylan back home."

I shook my head again. "No. I couldn't have." I lifted my upturned wrists higher. "If I had a you where I came from, then I wouldn't have done this."

He pulled away and dropped his gaze to the floor. "Maybe I'm the reason you did that." There was such heaviness in his tone. Such remorse. It was like he'd already been charged, put on trial, and declared guilty.

I laughed. "You're the reason I didn't do it back in Cora's cell." We'd talked about it. There'd been so many nights we'd debated the act. Broken and defeated, we'd come up with ways to do it. It'd been talk. A way to ease some of the misery and make it seem like we had a choice. Like there was some small fraction of our existence we could still control. But in the predawn hours, we'd each beg the other not to go through with it. *"Stay and fight,"* I would say to G, while he would tell me, *"I can't do it without you."*

"I believe we're stronger together, G. I know you know that."

"I'm stronger with you. You're stronger without me."

I stared at him. "How can you say that? How can you—"

He lifted his head and took a wide step away. "We've been over this. Nothing has changed."

I wanted to hit him. "You stupid, stubborn ass!"

"Sounds about right." His expression softened, and for a moment I was sure he'd reach out to me. But he didn't. Actually, he took another step away. "If you could see the things inside my head, you would run the other way. No version of Wells would be far enough away from me, Sera."

I glared at him. "I thought you knew me better than that."

"I remember more than I told you," he said. The guilt in his eyes was surpassed only by the pained expression on his face. "About before."

"So?" I wasn't angry at him. I wasn't even hurt. If he remembered more and hadn't told me, there must have been a reason. If he wasn't telling me the truth about my scars, then I had to trust him. No. It wasn't anger I felt, but concern. We'd been each other's only lifeline in that hell. There'd been no reason to lie, because we never expected to get out alive. "Were you a serial killer? Did you slaughter hundreds of innocent people?"

"You're not far off," he said, grim.

I rolled my eyes. "G, there's nothing you can say that will make me believe you were a serial killer."

"Why not? Look at Dylan. Look at the blood on his hands. Look at all the things he's done without thinking twice." He rushed me, stopping a fraction of an inch from my face. "I am him. Never forget that."

I pushed him hard and folded my arms. The chair beside the dresser wobbled, then tipped and fell to the floor with a clatter. "You are *not* Dylan. And you weren't a serial killer."

"I wasn't," he confessed. "But I was a soldier in an unnecessary war. I've got blood on my own hands— probably more than Dylan."

This was what he'd been afraid to tell me? That'd he'd been a soldier? "War is bloody," I said. "It's violent and people get hurt. You can't possibly—"

"I liked it, Sera." He closed his eyes for a second, and when he opened them, I saw the most intense self-loathing. It was crushing, the hatred I saw there. Deeper than the oceans and wider than the entire sky. "I was in my element. I loved the violence of it. The rush it gave me… I was a *good* soldier. Obedient. I never disobeyed an order—even when I knew it was blatantly wrong. Immoral and cruel."

I opened my mouth, but when no words came, I closed it and backed away another step. Not because I was afraid of him. I wasn't. This changed nothing about my feelings…though maybe it should have. If he was right, and the memories weren't distorted in some way—which I believed they were—that would make him more like Dylan than I cared to admit.

Correction: it would have made the old G more like Dylan.

When I found my voice, I said, "You've told me a hundred times. That was another life. One that's come and gone. One neither of us will be able to go back to. Maybe you *did* like the war. Maybe the violence of it all gave you a rush. Maybe it didn't… But either way, the person on that battlefield is gone. He's still locked away in Cora's basement, and he's not ever getting out."

"How can you look at me the same way after hearing what I just said?" His lips twisted, a disgusted scowl on his face.

"You're flawed," I said, giving in to the inevitable pull I felt for him. I stepped to him and pressed a single finger to his temple. "Things are a little jumbled in there." I let the finger trail down the side of his face, moving slowly across his cheek and stopping at the corner of his lip. I felt him shudder beneath my touch, then I ran the tip of my finger ever so lightly along his bottom lip.

"Sera," he warned, but didn't move away.

"I don't remember the day you arrived at Infinity."

The serum they used to try and wipe my memories hadn't worked at first, and then when it started, almost everything from G's first few weeks there faded. "I can't recall the early days—but even without those memories, I always knew you were there for me. I might not be able to tell you what we talked about, but I know we talked."

"We did." His voice was unsteady, like he was trying to catch his breath.

They'd stopped giving me the serum about a month after G arrived. At least, that's what his estimate was. "Even before we each stepped out of those cells, before I laid eyes on you, I knew you were special to me. Most people don't go through what we did. But we survived it, and I don't care what you say, we only got through it because we were together. I got through it because you gave me strength. *You* made me a survivor."

"I can't do this anymore." I pulled my legs in close and wrapped my arms around them, making myself as small as I possibly could. Maybe they would overlook me next time they came down. Maybe they would forget I was here. It'd been a month now. I kept the wrapping paper from the straw they brought each morning. Sometimes, when I didn't get a new one, I ripped an existing one in half. I needed it, to keep track of the time. It was the small bit of stability I had left to cling to. It only felt like a few weeks, but the boy in the cell next to mine, G, said I'd lost time. I lost memories.

"So your plan is to, what? Give up? Great idea." G's

voice echoed down the hall. His cell was next to mine, but sometimes seemed like it was on the other end of the Earth.

"They're going to kill us."

He sighed. "Maybe. Maybe they are. But I have no intention of making it easy on them."

"We don't even know what they want from us." So far, they hadn't done anything horrible. At least not that I remembered. Blood tests and medical exams. It was the waiting that killed me. The uncertainty of what was to come.

"We don't," he confirmed. "But whatever it is, I'm not giving it to them—and neither are you."

"How can you expect me to fight them?"

"How can you expect not *to?" There was a rustling sound. "You are a survivor, Sera. You won't roll over and die."*

"How can you say that?" I grabbed the bars and yanked violently. Of course, nothing happened, but it made me feel a little better. A little warmer. "You don't know me. You don't even know you.*"*

"Maybe I don't know who we were—but I know who we are now. And who we are is two people who can deal with this. Together we can get through this. Together we will be strong enough. I will not let you give up. You're made of steel, Sera. You might not see it yet, but you're a fighter."

I leaned my head closer to him, stopping just short of brushing my lips to his. He was so much stronger than he gave himself credit for. So much more…everything. I loved his flaws, but the depths of my admiration for his strengths, for the things he couldn't—*wouldn't*—see about himself? Those were boundless. "And if you think I'm going to let you get away from me, you're crazy. After all we've both been through, we deserve each other. *I will not let you give up.*"

I was too close to him to see his reaction, but I felt it. His entire body stiffened, and both arms twitched at his sides. But he didn't move. He wouldn't. Not if he could help it. The thing about G—whether it was because of all the things Cora had done to him or because of his past as a soldier—was that he hated the feeling of being out of control.

A small part of me felt a pang of guilt as I pushed in and brushed my lips to his. Even smaller than that speck of guilt was the desire to stop. I could kill two birds with one stone.

I knew it was a bad idea. The desk clerk had said we'd just missed Karl, but that didn't mean he'd be gone for long.

But I couldn't stop myself.

"Sera," he said again. He kept insisting he didn't want this, but his eyes said otherwise. There was hunger there. A fierce need that, despite the situation and all the things that led to it, made me weak in the knees. "What are you doing?"

"Is your heart racing?" I placed my hand on his chest.

He swallowed and nodded once without speaking.

I rose onto my toes and leaned close, brushing my lips against his ear. "Do you feel the blood zipping through your veins?"

I felt him nod again.

My lips lingered for a moment, my warm breath tickling the side of his neck. "How do you feel?"

He stiffened and sighed. "That's what this is about?"

I should have let him think that. If he thought that I was doing this to get him all worked up to save one of the precious doses of adrenaline we had, then I should have been more than fine with it. But I wasn't.

"This is about proving something to you," I said as I moved my lips down his neck. I barely grazed the skin. "If it offers a double reward, then I'll mark that in the win column."

"I'm not going to kiss you again." The statement was crystal clear; it was the delivery that lacked conviction. "I'm poison. Inside and out."

"Then poison me," I said. I brushed my lips to his again, this time slightly harder. He stayed absolutely still. I pulled away. "Do it so that I can show you I won't break. I'm not fragile, G. I'm made of steel. You told me that, remember? I'm a fighter, so let me fight for you."

He stared for a moment before letting go of a growl. "You deserve... They made me a monster. There's nothing gentle or kind left in me anymore."

"First, I don't believe that." I gripped the hem of his T-shirt, hesitating for only a fraction of a second before lifting it up. Despite his protests, he moved his arms and allowed me to pull the material over his head. "Second, maybe I'm not interested in gentle..."

Chapter Eighteen

She let the shirt fall to the floor beside us. The sound it made was, in reality, barely there. A muted *thud* and nothing more. To my ears, though? It signaled the gates of hell being unlocked and pushed open wide in an earsplitting invitation for the demons to come out and play.

An involuntary growl escaped my lips as she pressed herself against me. I felt her breath on my chest, a scorching alarm that my control was in danger of slipping. My mind clouded, and my breathing quickened. She was right about one thing. The pain had ebbed, the newly released adrenaline chasing it to the far reaches of my mind, even if for only a short period of time.

She ran her hands over my bare skin, fingers curling to let her nails graze the planes of my chest. The sensation was unlike anything I'd ever felt. No one had ever touched me like that. There was so much need, but also an unparalleled sense of connection. Sera's fingers moved with not only lust, but something far deeper and more complex. Something I never expected anyone to feel for me. "Tell me you want me to stop…"

Yes.

"No," I responded, my voice hoarse. If she stopped, I would break. I would crumble into a million pieces with no way to put myself back together again. "I don't."

"Tell me you don't like how this feels."

I don't.

"I can't." The words came out harsh, the monster Cora created rabid and fighting to get his hands on her. But that thing would have to battle me. It was closer than it ever had been to overtaking me, but for the first time, I felt confident that I could beat it back. I was sure because I refused to taint her in that way.

"All I'm going to do is touch you, G. We're not taking it any further than that. Not now." Her hands continued to move, up and down my chest, caressing, playing with the lines and ridges that came from Cora's mandatory gym sessions. Small circles and feather light skims, each touch bringing me closer to madness and peace all in the same instant. "You need to see that you're not poison. Not to me."

She was wrong. So very wrong.

"You can kiss me." Hands still moving, slow and frustratingly high, she lifted her head to stare at me. "If you want…"

Perfectly pink lips parted, her body all but pleading for me to do it. I closed my eyes, remembering what she'd tasted like. No words came to mind, only a feeling of peace. Kissing Sera had been like coming up for air after suffocating. It'd been like uncurling my body and using all my muscles after being knotted up and chained in one position for what felt like decades. While I hadn't told her the whole truth, I'd surely told her enough to send her running—and she was still here.

Maybe...

My fingers twitched, and before I realized what she was doing, her hands were at her shirt, lifting it over her head. Slowly, carefully, like one wrong move would have me disappearing.

She wore a simple tank underneath it. The neckline, while not overly low, gave the smallest preview of what lay beneath. The way the material shifted as she breathed in and out, creating a frustratingly perfect tease, was what tore at the remains of my protest. It broke me in the most amazing way.

"You told me once that we were fighters. That together, we could deal. Whatever your life was— whatever Cora did to change you—is irrelevant."

"Irrelevant? Are you cr—"

She covered my mouth with her hand. "Because even if some small fraction of what you think of yourself is true, I negate it. I'm your light, and you're my darkness."

I moved her hand away. "You don't need any more darkness in your life."

"Don't I?" She took my hand and held it to her chest, over her heart. "I believe everyone needs an even balance. You can't have one without the other."

My arms encircled her waist and hefted her off the ground, across the room, and to the bed, where I set her down on the edge. "Are you sure that's what you want?" My voice sounded wrong. Deep and desperate. The protests I'd had moments ago, the ones I would have sworn life and limb on, were forgotten. I stood in front of her. Inches separated us, but we didn't touch.

"I think I've had more than enough time to think about it." She lifted her head to look up at me, voice trembling just a little.

I dropped to my knees beside the bed and leaned forward but stopped before brushing my lips to hers. I wanted to. In fact, I'd never wanted anything more. But that inner voice kept stopping me. Whispering all the ways that I was bad for her. With great restraint, I ran a single finger across her cheek, skimming it lightly over her bottom lip.

I ran my finger down her arm, tracing random patterns against her skin just like she had on mine. The soft whimper that escaped her lips and her quickened breath were the only response I got.

My pulse pounded in my ears, so damn loud that I could barely think. The world fell away until all that was left was Sera. Really, she was always what it came down to. Every one of my actions since stepping across that cell threshold had been motivated by her existence. She was the sun in my world, and I was simply a planet caught in her gravitational pull, helpless. Without her light, I would wither and die.

I leaned forward, lips lingering at her ear. "You're right." I didn't dare move an inch closer. "The last thing I want to do is leave you behind." I knew I had to—that I should—but the actual act of walking away? It was inconceivable. "Hell, I don't even know if I *could*."

"Then the solution is simple." She wrapped her arms

around my neck and pulled me to her so that there was nothing separating us. Without hesitation, she kissed me.

Or, she tried. I pulled away.

"Please don't do this, Sera." It was two parts begging her to listen, and two parts praying that she wouldn't.

"You can't get rid of me. Not that easily."

My resolve broke. The action terrified me, but I couldn't deny the hold she had over me. I pressed my lips to hers, hesitant. She pressed back, moving her lips ever so slightly. I responded, unable to resist.

I brought my hands to her face, skimming both cheeks then up to thread my fingers through her long hair. A soft noise escaped her, and she wrapped her arms around my waist, pulling me closer. Nothing. There was nothing on any version of Earth that could compare to this. Nothing would come close to the euphoric feeling.

"While I'm sure this would be entertaining to watch for Cora, I'm not the voyeuristic type…" The door creaked open.

The room came crashing back, the remnants of the adrenaline rush making me twitch. Karl stood in the doorway. He came into the room and closed the door behind him, as Sera stood and pinned him with a glare. Me? I didn't know whether to kill him—or thank him for the interruption.

"Adrenaline helps with the symptoms of the poison." She smacked the side of her head. "Oh. Wait. I don't mean poison. I mean *virus*."

Karl snickered. "Oh, yes. Giving in to those teenage hormones was *all* for the sake of quelling the symptoms, I'm sure."

Sera said nothing, and I had to remind myself to stay where I was.

"Cora always wondered what you two would do if given the chance. She wanted to conduct an experiment. Stick you both in the same cell for a few days and watch what happened."

Sera's face paled. "You're a sick bastard."

He lifted his hands and shook his head. "I said Cora, not me. I'm the voice of reason who talked her out of it. She is the one with the weird obsession with the lot of you." He shrugged out of his jacket and laid it carefully on the bed before bending down to retrieve my shirt. "Moving on—since you're here, I can assume you've found me what I requested?"

"Sort of," I said.

"It's more complicated than handing over a piece of tech." Sera looked from him to me, then back again. "But yes. We found a way to keep you off Cora's radar."

He clapped his hands and grinned. "Wonderful." He waggled greedy fingers. "Let me have it, then."

"Yeah. Like she said, it's more complicated than that." I yanked my shirt from his hands and shrugged it over my shoulders then tugged it into place. I had nothing to be shy about, but a small part of me was too conscious of the assortment of scars that covered my body. I hadn't given it a second thought when it was Sera's gaze, but someone else? It made me itch in ways I wasn't comfortable with.

Sera nodded. She was totally at ease, and I was in awe of her calm. One wrong flinch and we could blow this. "It's not something that can be given to you. It's something that has to be done to you."

"Done to me? Like Cora's chip?"

"I don't think it's a chip," I said. "I didn't get the specifics from MaKaden."

Sera cringed, and I regretted not running it by her first, given their history, but it was the most convincing sell. Karl knew Phil—Rabbit to Cade and Noah. He knew the guy was a genius, and if anyone could perfect the tech he wanted, it would be him.

"So I have to go to him?" Karl's eyes narrowed. I couldn't blame the guy for being suspicious. Not with a woman like Cora.

We'd agreed to keep things as close to the truth as possible. Less chance of a mix-up that way, considering all the moving parts in this plan, as well as the fact that we were improvising a large portion of it. "The Phil from Cade's world has what you need. He can make you virtually invisible to Cora."

"This is the Cade who freed you, yes?"

"Yeah."

"And I assume I'm not supposed to be suspicious?"

I shrugged. "You can be whatever the hell you want. You asked for a way to free yourself from Cora, and that's what I got. Take it or leave it—but hold up your end of the deal and tell me how to fix Sera's chip."

Karl thought about it for a minute. His gaze darted between Sera and me. "Cora followed Ashlyn to Cade's home world. She couldn't get to her."

"Their military is protecting her." Cade had been right about that, at least. Cora couldn't get to any of them there. "They've given me permission to bring you there for the procedure. You'll be given twenty-four hours to leave. Then if you don't skip out, you'll be fair game."

"Fine," he said. He grabbed his jacket and shrugged it back on, then gestured toward the door. "Let's go visit another world."

Sera let out a breath and pushed past him to open the door. Without waiting, she stepped into the hall—and gasped.

Dylan was standing at the other end.

Chapter Nineteen

Sera

Maybe if I hadn't frozen the moment I saw him... If I'd just ducked back into the room and quietly closed the door... Of course, that hadn't happened. I'd stopped dead in my tracks, giving Dylan ample time to take in the sights, turn around, and spot me standing there with my mouth hanging open like an idiot.

G was right behind me, Karl pulling up the rear. For the longest moment none of us moved. No one spoke or breathed. Of course, I'd spent enough time with Dylan to know the silence never lasted as long as I wanted it to. Eventually he reacted—and everyone paid the price.

He came closer, stopping five or so feet from where we stood. A cruel laugh, followed by two quick pats of his jacket pocket, and he grinned. "Miss me, baby?"

"Not even a little bit, asshole."

G came up beside me. "So what's the plan, Dylan? Gonna rush all three of us? Pretty sure that might go badly for you."

"Gotta say, man, I'm really disappointed to see you're still alive and kicking." Dylan's grin got even bigger. He patted his jacket pocket again. "I don't think it's gonna be an issue too much longer, though."

G laughed. "That right?"

"Feel like handing Karl over? I promise to make the rest of this quick. You know… Kill you, steal the girl. Yada, yada."

"Think we'll pass. You understand. But, if you feel like making things easier on yourself, you can hand over the antidote."

Dylan fished into his pocket and pulled out an odd-looking weapon. "I don't think you'll need it."

The next few seconds were a complete blur. G grabbed my hand, and from the corner of my eye, I saw Karl's fingers knot into the material of his shirt. He jerked up his wrist, waking the chip and skipped us to a random frequency—but not before Dylan launched himself at me. The contact wasn't much. His fingers brushed the toe of my shoe—but it was enough. We all skipped together.

The second we landed, they were at it. Dylan lifted the weapon, and G let out a horrible roar. Karl backed away, lingering on the edge of the fray. We were still in a hallway—it looked like the hotel we'd just left, except the walls were painted deep blue instead of the hideous floral wallpaper. The carpet, which had been bright yellow, was now a neutral beige.

"I'm done waiting for that shit to kill you slowly." Dylan took aim at G. "Time to be done with it."

I rushed him, taking us both to the ground. We hit

hard, and he immediately swung out. The blow caught me in the gut, and I coughed, rolling off him and gasping to catch my breath. I wasn't a fighter like G was. I was fairly sure I never had been. In fact, I had watery memories of being weak. That me, whoever she'd been, was dead, though. This girl, Sera, she was strong. She was able to stand on her own and do what needed to be done.

G roared and charged again. He bent seconds before impact, jamming his shoulder into Dylan's stomach and lifting him off the ground as he barreled past me like a freight train.

As they fought, Karl dragged me away from the fray. "Probably best to steer clear. A man battling himself is a dangerous thing."

I watched them, riveted by the scene, the ferocity of it. It was something out of a nightmare. Two versions—one dark, the other, well, darker—squaring off against each other. Dylan swung with a roar. His attacks were ruthless and bold with a clear statement: death and destruction. G pivoted, ducking with ease and retaliating with an expertly placed jab of his own. His moves, while just as brutal, screamed not of devastation but of defense. Of survival. Dylan fought to harm. G fought to survive. They were both in so much pain, but for as many ways as they were the same, they were vastly different. And in that moment, I realized what the biggest difference was.

Dylan had been hiding behind his anger, lashing out ever since he'd lost his Ava. He'd hurt anyone he could just to feel something. G had embraced his anger so that he didn't have to dwell on the pain Cora had inflicted. Despite the fact that he kept denying it, the only one he continuously hurt was himself. But, it'd always been that way.

They'd brought him back a while ago. I'd managed to mark the passing days, but we had no way to measure the hours and minutes as they ticked away. Maybe it'd been an hour. Or maybe it'd been ten minutes. Who knew?

I was about to call to him, to ask if he was okay, but he let out an enraged howl. For a second, I thought they had come back. That they were trying to drag him away again. It took a moment to realize that we were alone.

He thrashed. Incoherent screams and random sounds of chaos. I heard the ping *of the metal bowl they sometimes gave us water in. It clattered and clanged as it whipped around the cell, at the mercy of G's rage. The metal springs on the cot groaned and creaked, followed by something—presumably the metal frame—crashing against the wall. It wasn't until I heard a rhythmic dull* thump *that I tried to stop him.*

"G," I said carefully. When he got like this, it was so hard to talk him down. "G, please. Listen to me. Hear me…"

He let out one last roar. There was a thud *as something hit the floor, then…nothing.*

I went to the far end of my cell, the one closest to his, and slid down the wall. "When they bring me upstairs, when they're…" I swallowed and tried to keep my tone even. "When they're doing their work… *I picture myself fighting back. I imagine getting free and attacking them.*

I punch, and I kick, and I use whatever I can get my hands on with the sole intention of watching them bleed." I expelled a shaky breath. "Sometimes I feel guilty about it. Like I'm a bad person or something. For getting angry. But I'm not. It's okay to be angry, G."

"It's so easy, isn't it?" Material rustled softly. "When there's nothing but pain and you can't feel anything but helpless. Anger is easier. It's more comfortable than pain."

"I think it's okay to be angry to block out the pain, but only if it's a temporary thing, ya know? Like, we're using it now. To survive."

A red light flashed in the hall. It was followed by a shrieking sound. The chaos caught the attention of the boys, who had just climbed from the ground and were faced off and catching their breath.

"What do you suppose the law is like here?" I heard G say. His grin was wicked, almost inviting Dylan to make a move. "Come at me again so we can find out."

Dylan hesitated. There was fury in his eyes. His gaze flickered to Karl. "We're not done." His attention swiveled to G for a second before ultimately landing on me. "None of us."

Without another word he disappeared around the corner. G nodded in the other direction. "Right now, that seems like a good plan. Go!"

We managed to wind our way through the chaos of the main lobby—people had come pouring from their rooms when the alarm sounded—and out the front door without anyone stopping us. After the scene the fight caused, we decided it was a good idea to keep a low profile. The timer was up, so we were stuck here for the next twenty-three hours or so. I didn't have any desire to spend them in a jail cell.

After wandering around a bit, we finally settled on a low-budget motel on the far side of town. Neither G nor I questioned it when Karl whipped out his wallet and slapped the currency of the land down on the clerk's desk. There was more to Karl than outward appearances—and I wanted no part of any of it.

"So," Karl said, flopping onto the first bed. "How are you two enjoying your freedom? Shall we trade war stories?"

G braced his boot against Karl's hip and gave a violent shove. The older man slid from the bed and landed on the floor in an overly satisfying *thud*. G grabbed one of the pillows and yanked off the comforter, throwing them down beside him. "First, you'll be sleeping on the damn floor. Second, this isn't a friendly vacation. The only reason I haven't killed you is because we need you. Otherwise, you'd be dead. I haven't forgotten the time we spent in your basement."

Karl grabbed the edge of the other bed and hauled himself off the floor, making a great show of his struggle. "As I said, Infinity was Cora's baby. I had a hand in it now and again, but all the sub-level projects were her ball of wax. I handled mostly the public face of the company."

"That doesn't make you any less responsible," I said. I understood G's anger because I felt it, too. "You knew what she was doing to us. You didn't do a damn thing to stop it. That makes you just as guilty."

His expression soured. "I can tell you with one hundred percent honesty that I regret not stepping in. Things got out of control, and by the time I made the decision to do something, it was already too late."

"So instead you decided to steal from her and run away when you could have acted?" I sank onto the edge of my bed. "Classy."

"You haven't said yet..." G narrowed his eyes. "Why *did* you run? Weren't you and your batshit wife blissfully happy?"

Karl frowned, and even though I hated to humanize him in any way, there was sadness in his eyes. Regret. "I loved my wife. I still do. But she is out of control."

"So what was the actual plan? I mean, you had to know she'd follow you, right?"

"Honestly? I'd hoped she'd be arrested and I could leave without her realizing. At least not right away." He sighed. "Like I said, I love my wife. My plan was to simply leave and find her again. To start over."

I stared at him, sure I must have heard wrong. "Find her again? As in, you were going to, what, hunt down another version of Cora?" Just like Dylan... What the hell was wrong with these people?

"That's the gist of it, yes." He lowered his head, almost like he was ashamed. "I want to be with Cora, but my Cora had taken her interest in science way too far. It overshadowed everything in our lives."

"Too far?" I got the feeling we were talking about something other than stashing teens away in a jail cell and wiping their memories. Suddenly I was very curious about the thing Cora was desperate to get back.

"What was on the flash drive you stole?"

He hesitated for a moment, then sighed. "I guess you could call it a recipe."

"A recipe," G repeated. "We're not talking about chicken noodle soup, are we…"

Pulling out the chair beside the small desk in the corner, he settled heavily. In that moment he looked so much older. Tired and world worn. It made me wonder what the other versions of him were like. The ones Cade insisted were so different. "The recipe on the flash drive I stole is for the virus."

"The virus—" I couldn't help it. I gasped. "The one she put in G's pod?"

"A slightly different version, but yes. She plans on releasing a contagious strain of it, then selling the antidote only to upper-class families and making it impossible for those lower on the food chain, so to speak, to afford the medicine. Cora was desperate to destroy the second and third tier citizens on our world." He let out a noise that sounded vaguely like a snicker. "My Cora is a bit of an elitist…"

My mouth fell open, and when I looked over at G, he had the same reaction. "What the fuck is wrong with you?" he roared.

Karl cleared his throat. "Now her desire is to find it and go home to release the virus, then offer the antidote as a way to get back into the president's good graces—as well as make a fortune and be rid of society's rubbish. As I said, this is Cora's plan. One I couldn't condone—which is why I left and took the recipe with me."

"Because that made so much more sense than

handing her over to the cops?" G bolted off the bed and stalked the few feet to where Karl stood. He loomed over the older man, and even though a part of me knew I should stop him from doing whatever it was he might do in a fit of rage, another part wanted to let things play out. Karl deserved whatever he got. That, and then some.

Karl shrugged, though it was obvious he was uncomfortable with G's proximity. "There was no reason for me to turn her in. Ashlyn had given the authorities all the ammunition they needed to know about Cora's illegal activities. I simply hedged my bets on the off chance she managed to talk her way out of things." He snickered, a faraway look in his eyes. "My Cora could talk herself out of almost anything…"

Thankfully, G kept his cool. His shoulders rose and fell before his fists curled tight for a minute. He backed away slowly, then settled on the bed beside me.

"This is a problem," I said, refusing to look at him. "Now that we know what's on that flash drive…"

"We weren't handing it over to Cora, anyway," came his clipped response. "But when Anderson gets what he wants, he's handing it over to us." G's gaze swiveled toward Karl. "That clear?"

We had a plan that involved us getting what we wanted and the bad guys getting, well, nothing. But things could go wrong. The plan, or at least parts of it, could fail.

Karl nodded and smiled. It was the kind of smile that screamed *I have a secret*. "Absolutely. Trust me when I tell you, I will do whatever it takes to keep Cora from producing that virus. *Anything*."

I swallowed back the growing unease, extremely uncomfortable with the way he was looking at me. At the way he said, *Trust me*.

He folded his hands in his lap and relaxed his shoulders. "Anything…"

Chapter Twenty

Sera slept fitfully while Karl knocked off like a fucking log. Must be nice. The guy obviously had no trouble sleeping with his demons. Me? I lay awake in the bed all night, a million sins bouncing around inside my head. I decided to tell Sera the whole truth then changed my mind at least thirty times over the course of the night. Arguments ranged from how it would hurt her, to how it would destroy me when she turned away—which she would, there was no doubt in my mind. She'd accepted me when I told her I still retained watery memories of my previously violent life, but what would she say when she knew the whole truth? That I knew exactly what she'd come from? When she heard all the things I'd been hiding from her about the past? In the end, though, I knew that I had to come clean—just not yet.

First, I had to make sure she survived today so she could hate me tomorrow.

"How many hours do we have left to kill?" Sera pulled a hoodie over her head and shrugged into the sleeves. Karl had supplied us with fresh—though ill-fitted—clothes. I didn't ask where he'd gotten them, but they were all brand new. "Because I'm getting munchy."

"The young lady brings up an excellent point." Karl rubbed his belly. "I'm quite hungry myself. Maybe we should go out and find a bite? Or, perhaps we could stay here while you fetch something?"

I ignored him and focused on Sera. Something was bothering her. Her eyes moved nonstop, gaze continually flickering to Karl and away again. Did she think he'd double-cross us? Was she worried this was all some elaborate plot to drag us back? I would die before letting that happen—to either of us.

The clock on the nightstand between the two beds flashed a neon green three o'clock. "A little over an hour now." We'd spent the day holed up in the room, not wanting to tempt fate after all the bad luck we'd had. Dylan was still here, his frequency line was green, and we didn't know anything about this world.

But we were all getting antsy, and I found that when that happened, I had a shorter fuse. I had less control over my emotions and tended to lose myself to Cora's serum. The poison had progressed as well. When I'd woken, the first thing I'd done was steal off to the bathroom with the bag and dose myself with adrenaline—but it wasn't working nearly as long, or as well, as it had been. Four hours later and the effects were already beginning to ebb.

"So, we're clear on things, right?" Karl sat in the chair by the door. Other than complaining about his growling stomach, he hadn't said much. I had noticed him watching Sera, and it bothered me. "We leave here and get you to MaKaden. You give us the flash drive."

"That was the agreement," he said with a forced smile. "I'll gladly hand it over as soon as you get me the tech that will shield me from Cora."

There was something about the way he said it that made me think he was lying. Or maybe it was the fact that everything that came out of his mouth was a lie. Either way, I stood and took a step toward him. "How about you hand it over now. You know that I'll keep my word. I'll get you to MaKaden."

He stood as well, a wholly fake smile smeared across his face. "I will make you a deal. You go out and get us something to eat, and I'll hand over the flash drive. I believe that you'll keep your word."

Sera snorted. "That's awfully trusting—"

"What the fuck?" No. There was definitely something wrong here. He'd never just hand over all his cards. "Something's up with you."

"Up?" Karl stepped back, nearly tripping over the chair. "What do you mean?"

"That's the second time now that you've tried to get me to leave. Why?"

His eyes darted to Sera, then back to me. "I merely suggested going out for some sustenance. If you'd like, I can—"

"G… I think you're overreacting. Maybe—"

"No way." I lunged forward to drag her across to my side of the room, but Karl was closer.

He latched on and yanked her to him, locking her in place by wrapping his arm around her neck. "Don't," he said, breathing fast. His smarmy expression was gone, replaced by wild eyes and scrunched up lips. "You don't understand."

Sera struggled, but Karl only tightened his grip. "We had a deal," she cried, fingers still trying to pry his hold loose. "You said—"

"I *said* that I would do anything to keep Cora from releasing the virus."

"What the hell does that have to do with us? We promised we weren't going to give her the drive."

He shook his head and readjusted his hold on Sera. I could easily dislodge it, but I didn't want to chance her getting hurt in the process. There was nothing but desperation in his eyes. Desperation made men careless—and dangerous. "To do with *her*, you mean."

"With Sera?" I took a small step toward them. "What does the virus have to do with Sera?"

"Sera *is* the virus." In his grip, her face went pale, the blood draining to leave horror. "Her blood is the key component for the recipe used to create it. Without her, Cora has no leg to stand on."

"She could just nab someone else from Sera's home world," I challenged.

"No," Karl said. "No, it's not like that. The serum we gave her to wipe certain parts of her memories changed the structure of her blood. It changed her very physiology. Sera is one of a kind. A true rarity. Irreplaceable. It was an accident, the virus. Something Cora stumbled on while testing the irregularities in Sera's blood created by the serum."

Sera pulled against his grip but Karl held tight. "So, you're, what? Going to kill me to keep your crazy wife from making the virus?"

At least this explained why Cora was so desperate to hang on to her. Another step closer. "Killing her isn't the answer."

The guy looked almost sorry. "I'm afraid it's the *only* answer. Even if she manages to get her hands on the flash drive, without the girl's blood, her plans cannot proceed. Think about it." He shook his head from side to side. "One death to prevent billions."

"You know I'm not going to let it happen, right? There's no way you can think I'll stand here while you hurt her. You have to know that if it comes down to Sera and a billion nameless, faceless people, I'm *still* going to choose her."

Karl struggled for a moment but managed to slide his free hand into his pocket. When he pulled it out, he had a tiny syringe. "Take another step, and I'll inject her with the virus. I don't want to do it that way, but I will."

I cursed and threw up my hands, taking a step back instead of forward. "Easy. Just think about this. Cora isn't going to get that flash drive. You have my word."

Karl started dragging Sera toward the door. "I can't take that chance. You must understand that there are far too many lives at risk."

A familiar feeling bubbled in my gut. "Anderson," I warned.

He got her to the door, opening it. Before stepping into the hallway, he slowly changed his grip to her forearm. The needle was poised inconspicuously behind his fist. "Struggle just once and I will depress the plunger. Are we clear?"

Sera nodded.

Without a word, he stepped into the hall, eyes still on mine. I followed, trailing just enough so that he wouldn't perceive me as a threat, but close enough so that he understood I wasn't going to stand there and let this happen.

Down to the lobby and right out the front door—no one said a word as he smiled and nodded his way through the small crowd. Sera had stopped struggling. Her movements were stiff and forced, and every once in a while, she'd turn and I'd catch a glimpse of her face, still horrified by what Anderson had told us, while at the same time, terrified.

When he reached the edge of the building, he rounded the corner and tucked himself away in the alley between the hotel and another large building. The scent of food wafted from around the front, and my stomach gave an involuntary gurgle.

"Just trust us," I heard Sera say as I entered the alleyway. "We don't want to see her hurt anyone, same as you."

To the bastard's credit, he did look apologetic—not that it would save him. I was going to rip his damned heart out for this. "I am truly sorry, Sera."

"Then don't do it," Sera said and nodded toward me. "We're about to skip to Cade's world. She can't get to us there. The drive—and my blood—will be safe. You might be a bastard, but you're not a killer like your wife."

She must have sounded convincing to Anderson, because he withdrew the syringe a few inches. But I heard the bullshit in her tone; she didn't believe a word she was saying. Now that Sera knew the truth, she'd be worried about Cora using her to end the lives of countless people, same as Karl was.

On some level, I understood where he was coming from and what must be going through her mind. Sacrifice one to save the many. Blah, blah, blah. But unfortunately, that *one* was Sera. If it were anyone else, I probably wouldn't have hesitated even a moment. But her? There was no way in hell. I'd let the world wither and die in favor of her every single time.

"How can you be certain? How can you possibly—" The rest of the sentence was lost to a grunt as Karl flew sideways into the wall, knocked there by the black and gray blur that zoomed into the alley from the other end.

Dylan let out a horrible wail as he positioned himself over Anderson. The old man struggled and thrashed, and at first, I thought he was trying to free himself. But when his hand wriggled free, just after Dylan delivered the first blow, I caught him digging into his side pocket.

As Dylan hefted him off the ground, a triumphant grin on his face, Karl tossed something in Sera's direction. It bounced several times before coming to a stop right at her feet.

The flash drive.

Chapter Twenty-One

Sera

Dylan struggled with Karl a few feet away, unaware that the future of countless lives now lay at my feet. I wondered how something so small could determine the fate of so many. How the blood inside my own veins could potentially put an end to innocent lives.

"Where's the flash drive, old man?" Dylan dragged Karl into a choke hold, causing him to grunt and gasp. Our eyes met, and he gave the smallest of nods.

I lifted my foot and slammed it down. The plastic burst and cracked beneath my shoe as I ground my heel around nice and hard, making sure to smash it into as many bits as possible.

Karl coughed and laughed. In fact, he was laughing so hard that Dylan let him go and took a step back. "What the hell is so funny?"

I smiled and lifted my foot.

Dylan stepped closer and bent low to examine

the remnants of silver and blue. He nudged it with his toe, dragging some of the broken bits away from the pile. I saw the exact moment he understood what had happened. His face drained of color, turning white then flooding with scarlet. His shoulders shook. The rage on his face and in his features, in every breath, seeped from his pores like poison.

He whirled on Karl, who was wearing a grin similar to mine. "Tell me there's a copy. That you have a duplicate."

"Afraid not. That was the one. The files on that drive are now gone for good."

"What was on it?" he demanded. He grabbed Karl's shirt and hauled him away from the side of the building. "What the hell did she want with it?"

Karl's grin grew wider. "Something she will never have."

His reaction was instant—and fierce. Dylan grabbed both sides of Karl's head and twisted hard. Just once. The man's expression never changed; his eyes didn't get a chance to widen. There was no gasp of surprise or scream of terror. One second he was alive and enjoying Dylan's anger, the next he was gone. Nothing but a heap of flesh and bone piled on the concrete in a dirty alley.

My breath caught, choking back the air like someone had lodged a rock in my throat. I tried to swallow, to shove the rock down, but my body just didn't listen. It was too preoccupied with the sight of Karl, previously alive and smarmy, now lifeless. He wasn't a good man. He didn't deserve my sadness or pity, but he was human, and no human deserved to die like that. *For* that…

G came up beside me. He took my hand and squeezed. It was stupid, but that single action, that one reassuring touch, was the fuel I needed to pull my shit together.

I breathed in deep, then blew out slowly. I had an idea and hoped he went with it. I pointed to the mess of plastic and metal on the ground. "Before you decide to turn your anger on us, you need to know something. That was a decoy. I stole the real one from him last night."

I didn't expect Dylan to believe me so quickly, but the color returned to his face almost instantly, and his posture relaxed a little. I supposed it made more sense that I stole the flash drive rather than destroying it, since it had technically been the key to my salvation. That was, before I found out what was on it and my role in the whole mess. "Where is it?"

"Someplace safe," G chimed in.

"Cora offered you the deal to return you to Ava while we were together."

"We were never together," Dylan snapped. "Or did you forget how many times you reminded me of that?"

I didn't owe Karl Anderson anything, but he'd technically been trying to save lives by stealing that flash drive from Cora. It was the right thing to do. Maybe I could still see it through. Still make this work. For all those innocent people, for Karl, for me…

We'd told Cade we were bringing Karl back to his world, but maybe we could bring someone else instead. "You know what I mean. She made that offer to both of us. We get her the flash, and she gives each of us the thing we wanted."

"Your point?"

"My point," I said, "is that we can still do that. I'm willing to let you in on the deal—I get the chip fixed and you get your Ava back, just as planned—if you give me the antidote for G."

He seemed to consider it for a moment before bursting into a fit of hysterical laughter. "Do I look that stupid to you?"

"She's not joking," G said between clenched teeth. "Considering the position you're in, I'd take the offer and run with it, man."

"The position—" More laughter. "Dude, *you're* the one dying."

"Dylan," I tried. I could see I'd lost him, though. In reality, I probably never had him.

He held up a hand and collected himself, making a show of straightening and taking a nice deep breath. "Here's my counteroffer. You take me to the flash drive. Hand it over, and then I'll give you the antidote."

"What about Sera's end of the deal?"

Dylan shrugged. "I'll let her tag along. If Cora wants to fix her head, then so be it."

"No deal," G said, while at the same time, I nodded and said, "Fine."

G growled and grabbed my arm. His expression was the perfect mix of anger and fear. "We can't trust him. What's to say he doesn't steal the drive and leave without giving me the antidote?"

I frowned, trying hard to play my part as well as G had. He was positively perfect. "We're not arguing about this, G. I'm not taking any chances. You're too far along now. You've got hours—maybe a day."

"Seems to me like the lady has spoken." Dylan grinned. "Well?"

I took my time, looking from G to Dylan while I bit down on the corner of my lip. "The antidote first." I held out my hand. I doubted he'd give it to me, but it looked more convincing to try again rather than to agree to his terms so easily. "We're far more trustworthy than you."

"Nope." He shook his head, smile still in place. "I've been burned one too many times. You have my word, though. I'll hand over the antidote just as soon as I have the drive in my hot little hands."

I hesitated, and he sighed.

"You're not my Ava, but you're still her. A version of her. I don't want to see you hurt or in pain. If this tool makes you happy, then I'll do what I can to give him back to you."

I didn't believe a single word of it, but I forced a smile and nodded. "I guess we don't have much of a choice."

"I guess not."

"I don't like this," G said as he woke his chip. I took his hand while Dylan slipped his into my free one. His grip was a little tighter than necessary, but I didn't complain. We were almost at the end of the tunnel. This whole horrible ride might just have an end in sight.

Everything shimmered, and when it cleared, we were still standing in the alley, but the buildings were different. The dumpster was empty and the garbage that had littered the ground a moment ago was gone.

"So it's on this world?" Dylan let go of me and poked his head around the corner. "Anything I should know? Specifics about the culture, et cetera?" He winked. "Wouldn't want to get arrested before your boy finds his meds."

"Normal world. We didn't notice anything off-key when we were here to hide the drive." G motioned toward the head of the alley. "Let's get moving. The faster we're done with this the better."

We rounded the corner and started down the street. I kept glancing at Dylan to see if he recognized the area. So far so good, but I didn't know how long that would hold up. I mean, this was his home. How long could we walk the streets before he realized where we were?

"So, I've never really gotten a chance to chat myself up," Dylan said as we walked. He grinned at G like he was in on some secret. "What kind of world do you come from?"

G's jaw clenched. I knew he wanted to snap, but I hoped he'd see the benefit of keeping Dylan distracted. "Don't know," he said after a few moments. "Cora stole my memories—or did you forget?"

"Yeah, but you must remember something? Were you up the Andersons' ass like my brother? Did you have a brother?" He stopped walking for a moment to laugh. "Are you cheating on an Ava of your own with this one?"

I thought G would lose it then. His face drained of color, and he held his breath—probably counting. "No."

Dylan seemed disappointed. "I met Ava when I was in first grade. We hated each other."

"There was a version of me who hated you?" I offered a mock gasp. "How surprising."

"I won her over by fifth grade." He winked at me.

"And hey…if something happens and I can't get back to my Ava, you'll learn to love me, baby."

"I'm sorry," G said. He stopped walking and was deathly still. After a few seconds, he turned to face Dylan. "That you lost your girl. It sucks, and given how things turned out for me, I have a pretty good idea where your head's at. I understand why you're so monumentally fucked up. It doesn't give you a pass on the shit you've done, but I *get it*." Like a snake, G lashed out and grabbed hold of his shirt front, dragging him close. With a violent shake, he added, "But talk about Sera like that one more time, and I will shred you. We clear?"

For a moment, all Dylan did was stare. There was the smallest hint of a grin on his face. "We are *exactly* the same, you and me. The sooner you get right with that, the better off you'll be."

G snorted and shoved him away. "We are *nothing* alike."

Dylan shrugged and started walking again. "Guess we'll see, eh?"

And that was it. From there we went along in blissful silence. I kept my eyes peeled for our backup, and G kept watch on Dylan, who strolled along like he didn't have a care in the multiverse. After about fifteen minutes, I saw what I'd been looking for. Thankfully, G saw it, too.

He stopped walking and grabbed Dylan by the arm, twisting him around so they were face to face. "Know what? This is shit. Just give me the damn antidote."

From there, everything turned upside down.

Dylan laughed, and G punched him hard enough

to knock him off his feet. I screamed—catching the attention of the three men in black fatigues a few yards away. The same ones Cade promised, when we'd concocted the plan, he'd have patrolling the city for our arrival.

They barreled across the lawn and separated the boys. Dylan raged, realizing exactly what we'd done and where he was. He screamed and cursed and fought like a wild dog. G simply dropped to his knees and placed both hands behind his head as I did the same, all the while wearing an extremely satisfied grin.

On to phase two.

Chapter Twenty-Two

The officers cuffed me and loaded me into the back of their van without an ounce of objection. This world's version of me wasn't so subdued. He'd kicked and shouted and cursed until finally one of the soldiers had to come back and sedate him. The rest of the ride was blissfully quiet.

They'd cuffed Sera, too, but I wasn't worried. Not when they separated us, leading her in one direction while they nudged me down a different hall, or when they deposited me in a small jail cell and locked me in nice and tight.

I estimated that it'd been a little over an hour when I heard footsteps in the hallway. Heavy footfalls, giving way to softer, faster ones. I hopped off the cot and pressed myself closer to the bars. "Sera?"

A few seconds later, she came into view. "G? You okay?" She skidded to a stop in front of the bars, hands reaching through to grab mine immediately.

"He's fine," someone said from behind her. Cade was there. Noah, too. But the speaker was Karl Anderson. "My men knew right away who our Dylan was. This young man complied without causing a scene."

"So, you're the good version of Anderson, huh?"

The old man laughed. He was more battle-worn than the Karl Anderson I'd become familiar with, rugged where the other Karl was smooth. But there was a light in his eyes not present when you looked at evil Cora's husband. Something that made me want to trust him. "One of many, I hope." He stepped back and motioned for the soldier behind him to unlock the cell.

The moment he did, Sera threw herself into my arms. When she pulled back, her expression was grim. "They searched him, G. There's no antidote."

I didn't tell her, but I hadn't expected there to be. Dylan was too smart. If it were me, there's no way I'd be carrying the stuff with me. I'd have it tucked away, someplace nice and safe. "We'll deal."

"We've got people working on it," Anderson said. He wore a black suit adorned with a bright red sash that was decorated in medals.

The soldier in me recognized the superiority of his rank and respected him for it, but the prisoner in me, the one who'd been kept stashed away in the Infinity basement, had to breathe deep and remember his control. "Appreciated, sir."

Sera nodded her thanks to him as well, then turned to Cade. "Everyone is okay? Kori? Ash?"

"They're fine," he said with a smile. "Cora is actually out of the country right now, so Kori is kind of sitting on pins and needles." He glanced over his shoulder at the General's retreating form. "But she met him. I've never seen the old dog tear up before…"

"So, what now?" I interjected. As nice as the mushy shit was, it wouldn't solve our current problems—which were many. "You have him in custody?"

Noah nodded. "Fucker is locked up tight, and that's where he's going to stay."

"Not gonna work," I said, folding my arms.

Noah glared at me while Cade raised a brow. "Why?"

"Because Cora is going to be expecting him when she gets here. She made a deal with him—not you."

"So?" Noah waved his hand down the hallway. "Get a haircut and act like an even bigger dick than you already do. Problem solved. Instant Dylan."

"Problem not solved," Sera said. "There's too great a risk that Cora will know he's G and not Dylan. She's got trackers in the both of us. She's too smart not to check all her bases before wandering into enemy territory."

Cade frowned. He knew she was right. "Let me talk to Rabbit. He's—"

"Phil MaKaden?" Sera's face turned ashen.

"Yeah." Cade smiled. "He's a friend. You met a version of him when we freed you, remember?"

I took Sera's hand and squeezed. "MaKaden is kind of a—"

"It's fine," she said. There was the slightest pitch in her tone. No one who didn't know her would ever hear it. "Sorry. You were saying?"

"Yeah. Rabbit? He's apparently working on base full-time now."

"A lot's changed in a year, man," Noah said with a smile.

"It has," Cade agreed. He turned back to me, then nodded to the other end of the hall. "There are bunks down there if you guys want to rest a while. I'll check with Rabbit and see what we can do to keep Dylan in line. The general won't even consider letting him out unless he's sure he can be controlled."

"Not to worry, though." Noah let out a hoot. "Our Rabbit is a genius. I'm sure he's got something we can use."

I turned in the direction of the bunks, but Sera hesitated. "Actually, is there any way I could see him? Dylan?"

Noah's mouth fell open, but Cade nodded slowly. He knew what she wanted, and although I could tell he felt it was a waste of time, he pointed to the entryway at one end of the hall and said, "Through that door. Tell the guard you have level nine clearance, and when he asks for the password, give him Jenga."

"Jenga?" Sera quirked her brow.

Cade waved as he turned and followed Noah down to the other end of the hall. "Don't ask…"

We'd stood in front of Dylan's cell for twenty minutes. When he'd finally acknowledged our presence, it was only to flip us off and roll onto his other side.

"He's not going to tell us where it is," Sera said as

we made our way to the bunkers. We'd been told to go there after we were done here. Rest up—because that was likely, right? With all the crap going down, a nice little nap was just what the doctor ordered…

"Probably not." We got to the bunk room, but instead of sinking onto one of the ten beds, I slid down the wall. The pain was back, and it was getting harder and harder to breathe. The more I moved, the more obvious it would become, and I didn't want her to know. Not just yet.

"Then I'll go to Rabbit. He's like some super genius here, right?" She sank to the ground and balanced on her heels in front of me. "If my blood is the main ingredient, then maybe he can use it to create a cure. A vaccine."

I shook my head. I didn't have the energy to move right now, and she couldn't go by herself. If she was alone with him… "You can't."

"Like you could stop me." She thrust her chin out defiantly and stood.

"I'm *asking* you not to go."

Her brows rose, and her eyes narrowed. "Why?" She took a step away from me. "Tell me what you're hiding."

I tried. I really did. On one hand, she deserved to know. But on the other, that missing knowledge amounted to a certain level of freedom. Freedom she'd never get back if she knew.

When I didn't respond, she sighed. "I know you believe whatever it is you're not telling me is for my own good, but I'm a big girl. A fighter—your words, not mine. But you've believed in me, in my strength, for more than a year now. What changed?"

Silence.

"I'm sorry, G. I'm going. He—"

"Sera!" I managed to grab her arm and tug her back to the ground. "You're right, okay? There's something I haven't told you."

"About?"

"About when I first got to Infinity."

She settled down, tucking her legs beneath her. "Okay…"

Deep breath. I nodded to her wrists, trying not to cringe when she lifted them to glance at the scars there. "I lied. About not knowing the specifics."

"You… Why would you lie?" Her tone wasn't angry, really. It was more confused. Hurt.

"Honestly? Several reasons—one being you asked me to."

"*I* asked you to lie to me?" Now she was angry.

"Not really in those words, but you told me you wanted to forget. You felt the serum starting to work. Your memories were fading, and you confessed that you were glad about it."

"Why would I possibly be—"

"You and Rabbit, on your world, you were engaged."

"Engaged?" Her face was pale.

"No. I mean, yes. But engaged is the wrong word."

"There's another word for engaged?"

"It wasn't your choice, okay?" Anger bubbled in my gut. I remembered her words perfectly. The night she'd told me, it'd been a turning point for us. For me…

...

She'd been quiet, the girl in the cell next to mine. Ava. Usually she chattered away until the early morning hours, but tonight she was oddly silent. It shouldn't have bothered me. I couldn't count the number of times I'd begged her to shut up. But for some reason, the silence felt wrong.

"Hey," I called out. "You alive over there?"

Silence.

"Hey? Av—"

"I tried to kill myself." It was barely a whisper, but I heard it as clearly as if she'd been standing right next to me.

I jumped to my feet and flung myself at the bars. Part of my brain registered the response as ludicrous. Why the hell did I care what she did? Another part, though… Another part was frantic. I tried to convince myself that it was because if she was gone, then I'd be here alone. For all my bitching, the idea terrified me. "What—what did you do? Hey! Someone help us!"

She laughed, a soft sound that was almost airy. Almost, if you could ignore the bleak undertones as it bounced off the dank walls around us. "Not today. Not here. Back home. Right before I woke up in this place, actually."

"I—" What the hell was I supposed to say? "Sorry"? "Bet you wish you hadn't failed"?

"Uh, why?" I didn't know if it was the right thing to ask, but I had nothing else.

"My father made some very bad investments. Our

family was in heavy debt to a man named Phil MaKaden. He agreed to cancel their debt in exchange for me."

I'd seen some twisted things in my time, but this was a new level of fucked up. "They sold you to him?"

She chuckled. "Yeah. I guess that's a really good way to put it. He treated me like property, after all. I wasn't a person; I was a possession. He kept me under house arrest. Treated me like some trophy he'd take out when he got bored."

I wanted to say something comforting, but I had zero experience with this kind of thing. Instead, I simply sat there and let her keep going. Maybe if she purged this poison, she'd be at peace for however much time we had left.

"I couldn't take it. Being someone's possession... I killed myself—at least, I thought I had. When I woke up, I was in a cell at Infinity."

"Ava, I'm—"

"Don't!" Something crashed against the wall. "I hate that name. Sera..." Her voice shook a little. "My middle name is Sera. After my grandmother. I always planned to run away. Use it and start a new life. Now it looks like I'll never get the chance."

"We could still get out of here." I didn't believe it for a second, but I felt compelled to comfort her. "Who knows? Maybe they'll even let us go."

She laughed, a sharp sound that made me cringe. "I doubt it, but even so, it wouldn't matter."

"Why not?"

"Because I'm losing it all. Everything. My life is starting to fade, G. I'm forgetting things. You know what, though? I'm not sorry. I'm not sad. Maybe this is the

best thing that's ever happened to me. Maybe for a short time, before they do whatever it is they plan on doing with us, I'll have peace…"

When I was finished spilling my guts, her mouth fell open, eyes going wide.

I felt a spark. A small flicker of life inside me. I climbed to my feet and chased it, the weight that had been crushing me for so long starting to lift.

If I wanted her gone, truly safe and out of my life, the truth—the whole truth—might do it.

"How do you remember all this?" Her eyes narrowed. "Every tiny detail?"

"Because I lied about that, too." I banged my fist against the side of my head. "I remember *everything*. Every moment of my miserable, garbage life before, and every single second of my life after. Every word you ever said to me—and every single one I ever said to you."

She stood and turned away from me.

"I was horrible to you. I shouted at you and cursed at you and told you I'd rather die than hear your constant yapping." I started pacing. I stalked the room from end to end, muscles tight and fingers twitching like an addict. "You just kept talking. Over and over. You kept repeating your name, *Ava Fielding*, and how you *hated* it. How you would do anything to shed it. Sera. Your middle name is Sera. You loved it. Something about your grandmother…." She'd turned and watched me. I didn't stop, and I didn't look at her, but I saw from the corner of my eye each time I passed.

I stopped pacing, winded, and slumped back against the wall on the other side of the room, as far from her as I could possibly get.

"I didn't know if my memories would fade, so I carved my name into the wall of my cell. Dylan Granger. I didn't want to forget. I wanted to remember. To never let go of who I was—because who I was *deserved* to be in that hell. Ending up one of Cora's lab rats? It was *more* than I deserved."

"G—"

"Then the next morning they took you. You were gone so long, I was sure I'd never see you again, and that was when I realized I missed hearing your voice. I *needed* to hear it. I was crazed that day. Each hour that passed and your cell remained empty, I grew angrier and angrier. I shouted for them to bring you back." I couldn't help it. I laughed. "Cora had taken me, but she wasn't sure what to do with me until that day. That was the day she decided how perfect I'd be for her Alpha project." I pushed aside the jarring memory of my first session and focused on Sera. "When they brought you back… You were dizzy. Sick. You knew someone was there—that *I* was there—but you couldn't remember my name. You couldn't remember yours."

"You told me my name was Sera."

"And I said that I was G. When you fell asleep that night, I kept the G but gouged the rest of my name off the wall, wanting to erase the person I'd been. I wanted to start over as G. You couldn't remember the horrible person I was, and I was glad because I wanted to be better. I wanted to be better for you. A few days after my sessions started, I told them that the drugs they gave me had taken my memories as well. Cora hadn't expected it, but she was thrilled."

"I—" She reached for me, but hesitated, letting her arm fall to her side.

I pushed off the wall, drawn to her despite feeling— *despite knowing*—with every fiber of my being that someone like me did not deserve someone like her. She might not remember herself, but I did. She'd been kind to me—even when I'd been cruel. She'd whispered words of comfort and encouragement in those first days—even when I'd threatened her. She'd remembered me—even when she didn't remember herself. "I hated you in those early days, and I think it was because you made me *feel*. I came from a place of violence and death. I was numb, and you took that away, and it terrified me."

I crossed the room to where she stood, pale and trembling. I cupped the side of her face and tilted her head so that we were eye to eye. "I love you, Sera. I have never loved anyone or anything in my entire life. It doesn't matter if you hate me for the lies I've told, or if you don't feel the same now that you know the truth, but that won't change anything for me." I laughed. "And maybe this is easier for me to do now. I was hollow back then, back in my old life before you. I did what I was told, went where I was told, and felt what I was told. Maybe coming clean now is easier knowing I won't have to deal with the fallout. If you hate me, I won't have to live with it because I'm a goner anyway."

I sucked in a deep breath, then kissed her.

I poured everything I had into that kiss. My heart,

my soul, and every ounce of life she'd made me feel since waking up in the godforsaken cell. I gave it all back, hoping to hell she could find a way to see past it all, yet knowing in the deepest parts of my heart that she shouldn't.

When I pulled away, all she did was stare.

"Sera? Say something. Please…"

Her complexion had gone pale, and her eyes were wide and unblinking. She just stared like she'd never seen me before. Her response was to back slowly to the door and slip out, all without taking her eyes from mine. All without saying a word.

I had my answer.

Chapter Twenty-Three

Sera

After being asked not to wander the halls of the base, I was directed outside, where I settled beneath a large pine tree. I was on overload. I just needed a minute—or a lifetime—to think.

I knew I had to have been Ava. But to hear G call me that, to listen as he admitted to knowing about my life, that had been devastating. I wrapped my arms around myself and fought back the urge to vomit. Deep down, a part of me thought the scars were self-inflicted. But thinking and *knowing* were so incredibly different. To consider that my life had been so unbearable that I'd tried to opt out made me queasy. It churned the acid in my belly and made my head spin with even more questions than I'd had before.

Despite all of that, a part of me understood why G had kept it from me. Understood and sympathized. I didn't remember how he'd treated me when he first got to Infinity. I didn't recall the harsh words. But it all made sense. Sick, twisted sense. He'd gotten to know me. To care about me. And when the time came, and he had the ability to wipe the horrors of my life away, he'd taken it. Could I honestly say that I wouldn't have done the same thing for him? If I had the opportunity to wipe his slate clean, I would take it in a heartbeat.

I knew I should be mad that he'd lied. That I should fear the person he'd been—because he'd never lost it. That person, unlike the person I was, wasn't gone. He'd tried to bury him, but that heartless soldier would always be there, would always haunt him. But just because that person was still with him didn't mean he hadn't changed. A heartless man wouldn't have cared about someone else. He wouldn't have tried to keep me from learning the truth. His motives weren't selfish. They were pure. Misguided and foolish, but pure.

I was up and moving before I really even understood what I was doing. My feet carried me forward, and I asked for directions as I went, eventually ending up at the science building, in front of the lab next door to Cora Anderson's.

I knocked twice, then pushed it open. "Hello?"

He was inside, standing across the room and bent over a long work table. His hair was shaggy, long in the back and on the sides, and was dyed a dark blue. When he turned and our eyes met, my gray to his dark brown, a wave of panic washed over me, and I had to force my feet to move me into the room.

"Hi. I, uh, sorry to bother you, but I'm—"

His eyes were wide, and his lips parted just slightly. Poor guy looked like he'd seen a ghost. "Ava..."

"Sera, actually." Another step forward. I could do

this. For G… "I'm—"

"Right! Right, sorry. Sorry. You just look so much like her." He tugged at the longer strands of hair on his head. "Ya know, with longer hair and stuff. And the still breathing part…"

"I'm really sorry to bother you." One more step. My heart was racing, and goose bumps had popped up all over my skin. "I was hoping to ask you a favor."

He cocked his head to the side, then squinted. "Sure. What did you—are you okay?" I must have been doing a shit job of hiding it because he stood there, obviously confused by my reaction. "You look ready to pass out."

When he made a move to grab me—more than likely to help me to the chair beside his desk—I jerked away violently. I didn't remember him. Not really. It was more like a hazy feeling. His voice was the ghost that had haunted my nightmares, his watery face one of the many devils that danced in my head. Now that I knew, now that I understood why the sight of Phil MaKaden turned my blood cold, it was hard not to see him as he'd been in my old life. "Don't. I'm okay."

He looked stricken, and in that moment, I believed what Cade had said about him. This Rabbit was kind. He wasn't like mine.

"Have they told you? About what's going on?"

He nodded, still watching me. His moves were slower now, though. Softer and more controlled. As he walked across to pull over a chair, he kept his eyes on me. "They gave me the rundown. What did you need?"

"The poison killing G—virus, actually—it's made from my blood. We thought your Dylan had the antidote, but apparently he's hidden it."

"And he won't tell you where."

"No." I held out my arm. "Do you think you can…"

"I know they'd planned on trying to cook up an antidote."

I nodded. Good. That was good. But planned wasn't good enough. Waiting wouldn't work. We didn't have time. "Can you—"

He frowned. "Not sure what other mes you've seen, but here I'm a tech guy." His smile brightened. "Pretty rockin' one, too. But medic stuff? Not my bag."

My arm fell slack at my side.

"I can draw the blood, though. Get it to someone in the lab and put a jump on it. That work?"

A spark of hope ignited in my chest. "I can't tell you how happy that would make me."

He nodded and slid off his stool, rummaging around in a cabinet before approaching slowly. When he reached me, he said, "May I?"

I nodded, and he went to work. "You knew me, huh?"

I swallowed as he tied off the rubber strip and ran the sterilizing wipe across the inside of my arm. "That's not an easy answer."

"Right. They messed with your head, yeah?"

"Yeah." The needle was uncapped.

"But you remember something about me. Not something good, I take it?"

"Not something good," I confirmed.

He slid the needle in, and I cringed—but there was no pain. Unlike the millions of times Cora had jabbed me, quick and heartless, Rabbit was careful and tender. Nothing like my fuzzy memories of the cruel man who'd viewed me as property.

"That kinda sucks, ya know? I'm not a bad guy. Have a few bad habits…" He lifted his free hand to his lips and made an inhaling motion with a boyish grin. "But I'm really not a monster. Not here, anyway. Drag to know there's a dick version of me running around out there."

He withdrew the needle and taped a piece of cotton to my arm. I forced a smile. "I'm sure there's more good than bad."

He smiled. "I'd bet my hands on it." He fidgeted with the needle a moment before setting it down. "I, uh, can take a peek into your head if you want. Ya know, since you're here?"

"Peek into my—"

He tapped the side of his head. "You're the one with the chip, right? Or is that your friend as well?"

Oh my God. It hadn't even occurred to me to ask him about the chip. I'd been so worried about G…

"They were planning to give me a crack at it, anyway," he rushed on when I hadn't answered. "Long as you're okay with it, that is."

"Yes!" I realized I sounded like an overenthusiastic child. "I mean, that would be great. Thank you."

His entire face lit up. "Killer! This is the shit I live for." He clapped his hands and kind of jumped. "I've been tinkering with chips lately, with Cora's help, and I think we're moving in the direction of the ones the guys have now."

He patted a large chair on the other side of the room. He had an odd-looking tube in his hand, with red lights and a small keypad.

"Is this going to hurt?"

He waved the tube-thing. "Nah. This bad boy will just give me a general reading. Chip power, where exactly they have it embedded. Just some basics. You won't feel a thing. Promise."

I nodded and settled into the chair…and waited. Rabbit moved the device back and forth, over the top of my head, down the sides, and around in a circle. He had an odd look on his face, which worried me, but I didn't ask. Knowing Cora, I didn't want to know. Maybe she had the thing booby-trapped.

For ten minutes, he skimmed his device back and forth, up and down, all without saying a word. There were a lot of *hmms* and *huhs*—even an *ahh*…but no words.

Finally, when I couldn't stand it anymore, I said, "Are those sounds of joy or anger?"

He set the device down and straddled the chair across from me. "Well, I guess that depends on your point of view. From mine, it sucks salty balls. From yours, it's probably more of a cute kitten playing with those balls."

"So, that means…?"

"There's no chip in there, Sera. Your head is empty. I mean, not empty. Your brain is in there. Fluid and goop, too, but nothing manmade is floating around inside."

"That's impossible. Couldn't your machine have just missed it? The last of Cora's tech was a little more advanced, right?" I didn't want to insult him, but he had to be wrong. There was no way the whole chip story was…a lie.

Oh my God…

Rabbit shook his head and grabbed the tube thing, flinging it up into the air, then catching it again and giving it a good wiggle. "Designed this baby myself. Trust me, your head is clean."

I jumped from the chair and whirled around, almost knocking Rabbit backward. "I have to go!"

He fumbled and called out an apology for whatever slight he thought I was fleeing from, but I ignored it and burst from the building.

Chapter Twenty-Four

It'd been almost an hour since Sera walked out. I tried looking for Cade or, God help me, Noah—any kind of semi-friendly face. What I encountered was actually the opposite. Everywhere I went on the base, people stared. There were whispers and pointed fingers and angry glares. It was understandable, I guessed. Understandable—and all too familiar.

Before Cora yanked me from the reaper's grasp, I'd been a monster. Coldhearted and emotionless, I'd obeyed my orders without question. Our world was at war. Not with another country or alien enemy, but with each other. Our own people were the targets of the government's wrath. Obey the rules and conform to the regime or pay the piper—and I was one of the pipers.

It was fitting, me going out like this. It's how fate had intended me to shuffle off anyway. The day Cora Anderson had found me was the first—the only—time

I'd hesitated on an order. I'd been called to a house to relocate the child of a couple who hadn't paid their taxes. I was almost across the field with the kid when I hesitated. I set her down, not 100 percent sure why at the time, and told her to run home—just seconds before a crowd of angry villagers came at me.

"G?" I turned and saw Sera rounding the corner. She was pale and winded, but the expression on her face wasn't one of fear.

"You okay?"

She threw herself at me, arms wrapping around my neck as she let out a strangled cry. "She lied. There's no chip."

I didn't return the embrace, instead pulling away, sure I'd heard wrong. "How... Are you sure? One hundred percent—"

"There's no doubt. Rabbit checked."

"Rabbit? You went to see Rabbit?"

"Since we couldn't get Dylan to spill, I thought maybe he could help with an antidote..."

"You went to see Rabbit for *me*?"

"How can you sound so surprised?"

I blinked at her. Once. Twice. Three times... "What I told you before—"

"Was what one Phil MaKaden did. Obviously, it wasn't easy. But he's not the Phil from my world. This one is different."

"And the other stuff I said? The things about me? About my life before? About the fact that I lied to you?"

She hesitated. "I—"

"Guys?" Cade poked his head around the corner.

"We need you in the briefing room."

Sera shuffled from foot to foot before letting out a soft sigh. "We should probably get down there."

"Yeah."

"Cade filled me in, and I want to be sure I have this whole thing straight," Karl Anderson said. He stood at the front of the room—it kind of looked like a classroom—and was bent over a thick notebook. When he lifted his head, our eyes met, and he gave me the smallest nod. "An alternate version of Cora Anderson abducted Miss Fielding and yourself and kept you locked in a non-government version of the Infinity Division for scientific experiments. Is that right?"

"Correct, sir." I hadn't had much interaction with the other Karl Anderson. A passing visit as he and Cora popped in on daily tests, then when he was with Sera and me for that short time. But the difference was instantly obvious to me. This version had a presence. It was commanding, but also trustworthy and loyal. This was not the kind of man who would hurt people for money.

"She's poisoned you. Is that right, son?"

Again, I nodded. "They created something from Sera's—Ava's—altered blood and put it in a pod they implanted. The pod has been damaged, and the poison is leaking out. Well, not really a poison, sir. It's more like a virus."

Karl frowned. He turned to Cade. "And we're sure your brother doesn't have the antidote?"

Cade's expression twisted into an angry scowl. "He

won't tell me where he hid it. Nothing is going to make him come clean, Karl. He's back where he started. We'd have a better chance of the virus just evaporating away on its own than convincing him to help us."

"And you're okay?" Karl turned his attention to Sera, who was sitting next to me. "This malfunctioning chip they said was in your head is working fine?"

"Actually, it's not there," Rabbit said from the far corner of the room. "My guess is Cora lied to keep her in line. Make her think she had to come back."

Sera nodded. "Without me, she can't make more of the virus."

"And she doesn't have the flash drive." Karl folded his arms. "It was destroyed?"

"It was," Sera said. "But what if she found her way back home and somehow recreated it?"

Karl glanced around. Cade and Noah, Rabbit in the corner, Sera and I sitting in the chairs at the front, and two people I didn't know, who'd been very quiet on the far end of the room. "Then this is still a threat? She could possibly recreate this virus and let it loose anywhere. Even here."

"We know she tried to follow when I brought Ash here," Noah said. "She couldn't get to us, though. This version of my mother is the worst of the worst—and she's smart. More than that, she's motivated. If she wants Ash dead and has that virus, she won't need to get to her. She can just let it go."

"Then we need to consider this an active threat."

"Agreed," Cade and Noah said at the same time, while the two nameless people in the corner nodded silently.

"And you have a plan?"

"We had a plan, sir," I said. "It involved drawing her here and forcing her to help Sera."

"But that's not needed anymore, correct?"

"Correct," I confirmed. I was still thanking the higher powers that she was going to be all right.

Anderson narrowed his eyes. The intensity of his gaze was heavy, but there was no animosity there. I wasn't sure what I saw. Compassion? Concern? Was he just as creeped out as everyone else that a guy with the face of a killer was walking the base, free and clear? "But you still need an antidote."

The virus was getting worse. I was losing the feeling in my legs—my hands all but gone—and every once in a while, my eyesight would grow watery. Everything would spin, then snap back to normal. With each inhalation, I felt an increasing twinge. Not a stabbing really, but almost an itch. At first it was localized to the center of my breastbone. In the last few hours, it had spread. Now I felt it reaching out all the way past my shoulders and halfway down both arms. There wasn't much time left. I needed the antidote, or I was going to die.

I would finally get what I deserved…

I thought about all the blood on my hands. All the innocent lives I'd delivered to oblivion simply because I'd been following orders. All the families I'd fractured and all the pain I'd caused. I thought about Sera and how when this was over, she deserved peace. She had earned a good life far from the violence of the old one, and as long as I was with her, as long as I still breathed, that would never happen. I'd proven time and time again how weak I was. I'd never be able to walk away and leave her behind. I would attach myself to her like a parasite, sucking the goodness from her life and ultimately dragging her back to hell.

Dylan was right. I was *exactly* like him.

Standing, I looked Karl Anderson directly in the eye and said, "Your focus right now is stopping that other version of Cora. While she still lives, she's a threat to you, to Sera—to everyone everywhere. The antidote is out of reach, and I've made peace with that." He was confused, but before he—or anyone else—could argue, I left the room.

I knew she'd follow.

"Are you insane?"

I didn't slow. If anything, I picked up the pace, rounding the corner and making my way back to the barracks. "Is that supposed to be a trick question?"

"Without the antidote, you're going to die."

That time I stopped. "What's your point?"

Her mouth fell open, her eyes narrowing to thin slits. "You… Are… Have you lost your damn mind?"

"You heard what I said to you earlier. Hell, you walked out, so I know you get it."

"I—"

I clamped my hand across her mouth. "No. There's no way to talk your way out of it, because in the end, it's true. I deserve to die, Sera. For everything that I did. We can't afford to have resources split between the antidote and Cora. She *needs* to be the focus."

She pried my hand loose and glared. "What you did is in the past. It doesn't matter if you can remember it or not, it was another lifetime ago. You're not that same person. Not anymore."

"Why? Because *you* say so?"

"Yes!" she screamed.

For the longest time neither of us said a word. We both stood there, in the hall right outside the barracks, breathing heavily and staring at each other.

"Do you really think you're the only one who feels this way?" she said softly. "Like they don't deserve to be here?"

"You cannot possibly be referring to yourself!"

"I absolutely am." Her voice rose a bit. "Yes, you have blood on your hands. Don't I?" Before I could argue, she rushed on. "How many people do you think Cora has already killed with that virus—the virus she made using *my* blood? How many people will die if she manages to make more?"

"How can you consider that your fault?"

"It's *not* my fault," she fired back. "Just like the things you did weren't your fault. You were brainwashed, G. Raised in a harsh society that made you believe their way was the only way. How the hell could you have known better?"

Part of me knew she was right. The war had waged since before I was born. We were raised to believe the only way to maintain order was to follow our commands to the letter, never questioning, never straying. But another part of me, the part she'd woken in that cell in Infinity, raged against the facts. It told me I should have been able to see the truth. I should have stood up to them sooner. I should have protected innocent lives instead of taking them. What I did, how I changed… It was too little too late.

"I'm not saying it'll be an easy road." She took my hands. "Neither one of us has had it easy. But I stand by what I said before—if we stick together, we can get through anything."

"Stick… What are you saying?" I wanted to leave her behind for her own good, but I'd still been crushed when she'd walked out the door earlier. When I thought she didn't accept me. Now she was saying… "You can live with it?"

She brought her hands up to cup the sides of my face. The warmth her touch gave me, calming and exciting in the same instant, stirred every ounce of tamped-down emotion within me. "I told you I wanted to be with you. Did you really think that had changed? I knew there was something in your past, G. Cora chose each of us for a reason. My living with it isn't the question. The question is whether or not you'll let *yourself* live with it."

Chapter Twenty-Five

Sera

After Cade came to talk to G, I wandered around for a while on my own. The base—Fort Hannity—was much different than I imagined. First and foremost, there was no actual Infinity. There was, but it wasn't a place or an entity on its own. It was a project conceived and overseen by this world's version of Cora Anderson, Noah and Kori's mother, in cooperation with the military.

They didn't harm anyone with the science, instead using it to learn and explore, but the idea behind it still scared me. The evil Cora—what G had started calling her—had used that same technology to steal me away from my home. I had no idea if there'd been an Infinity Division where I'd come from, but I'd had firsthand dealings with evil Cora, and it was terrifying. When I thought about the damage she could do if she were to let the poison out into the world—any world—my blood ran cold. That same technology, the one the

Infinity of this world used for good, she could use to destroy millions. Those fears were probably why I found myself back outside the door to Dylan's cell.

"What do you want?" He was lying on his back, staring at the ceiling with his ankles crossed over each other. His jeans and T-shirt were gone, replaced with a dark blue jumpsuit.

I sank to the floor just on the other side of the bars. "Honestly? I'm not sure."

"Come to poke the lion?"

"No."

This time he sat up and faced me. There was venom in his expression, but also pain. He'd been so close to getting the girl he loved back. "Gloat?"

"That would be petty."

He slid off the cot and stalked to the bars, wrapping his fingers around until they were white as snow. Placing his face against them, pushing so hard that it made him look almost alien, he said, "Then, What. Do. You. Want?"

"To talk."

His gaze lingered, hard as stone and cold as ice, before he let go and took a step back. Slowly he sank to the ground in the center of the cell, facing me, and folded his hands in his lap. The turnaround was crazy. One minute he'd been rabid, the next it was like he was ready to chat about the weather. "So, talk."

"I'm not going to pretend to understand what you've been going through since losing Ava. But I do have to wonder what you think she would have thought about the way you handled it."

For a minute his expression turned stormy, eyes

narrow and brows drawn, his lips mashed into a tight, thin line. His posture was rigid, and the set of his shoulders taut, arms so wound that you could see every vein. He held it for a long time before breathing out audibly. His face didn't change, but his body relaxed some.

"Contrary to popular opinion, I didn't wake up one day and decide to go on a murder spree."

"So why do it?"

"I was angry. On top of keeping me from her, they were going to put me to death." He let out a horrible sound. Somewhere between a snort and a strangled cry. "All because I couldn't live without her."

"You killed Noah's sister. The girl your own brother loved. Your friend. How can you possibly justify that? How could anything that happened have been her fault?"

"It wasn't," he said softly. For the first time since I'd met him, Dylan looked young. Almost innocent. He looked tired and beaten down and utterly lost. "None of it was Kori's fault, and not like it's any excuse or consolation, but I felt horrible. Each and every time, I hated myself a little bit more."

"Bullshit," I said, folding my arms. "If that were the case, if you felt any kind of remorse, you wouldn't have done it over and over again." I grabbed the bars and leaned into them. "You don't continue to murder people if you *feel bad about it*!"

"I went to the house that day to see her—our Kori. My only intention was to talk to her. To tell her what my brother had done. Ava was her cousin! She missed her, too. She was family—and I was trying to get her back. I thought if anyone could talk sense into Cade, it'd be her. I was—"

"You couldn't get her back, Dylan. That's what everyone kept trying to tell you. You wanted to skip out and find a different Ava. The key word is *different*. She would never have been *your* Ava."

He glared at me but kept going. "I got there, and we started talking. I told her right off the bat that Cade had freed me. That I was going on the run…"

"Did she threaten to call the police?" I swallowed. I hated hearing the pain in his voice because it humanized him—and that wasn't something I wanted to happen. Not after everything that he'd done. Everything that he continued to do by not giving us the antidote.

Dylan laughed, a grating sound that tore right through my flesh and gutted my insides. "Kori? God no. She offered me money. Supplies. She even tried to give me the keys to her car…"

"I don't understand," I said, sickened. "How could you… Why…"

"I just lost it," he shouted, jumping up and launching himself at the bars. With a pointless shake, he sank to the ground again, shuddering. "I snapped. I saw her standing there, still alive, still breathing, and I thought about Ava. I thought about my brother and the council that had so callously sentenced me to die when all I wanted was the girl I loved back."

"That's not an excuse."

"I know it's not. And every single second I live—no matter how much longer that will be—I will hear her pleas. I'll hear all of them, begging me to stop. Crying and screaming for me to think about what I was doing."

If I was going to do it, now was the time. I'd come here for a reason, and that reason wasn't to hear his confessions. "Dylan, I'm not your Ava, but you said before that you don't want to see me hurt."

"I don't," he confirmed. He folded his arms and frowned, and I knew he understood exactly what my reason for coming was.

"Then please, please, tell me where you hid the antidote for G. Don't make me go through what you did. Don't be the reason I lose him…"

"The antidote isn't hidden, Sera." It was the first time he hadn't called me Ava. "I don't have it anymore."

The entire world came to a screeching halt, and the air in my lungs turned to cement. I would have accused him of lying if not for the utter torment in his expression. "You—"

"After I left you, Cora found me. I told her I'd used the poison. Gave her the antidote back."

"Why would you do that?" I wasn't sure if I wanted to curl into a ball and cry for days or rip open the door and shred him limb from limb.

"Because I wanted G to suffer like I was."

I jumped to my feet and punched the bars. Pain bloomed in my knuckles, radiating to each finger and up my wrist. I ignored it. "I'm the one suffering, Dylan. *Me!*"

"I know and I'm sorry. Let me help you. That's why you came here, right? To get my help with Cora?"

I didn't respond, not trusting myself to open my mouth.

"I can get the antidote," he rushed on. "I saw her snap it into the back of the locket she wears around her neck."

He was playing on the one thing I wanted more than anything. Did I dare believe him? "How do I know I can trust you not to screw us over?"

Instead of the trademark grin I'd grown so accustomed to, Dylan frowned. There was so much pain in his eyes. So much suffering. Still, that didn't ensure his loyalty. Dylan was faithful to himself—and to Ava.

"I've done enough damage in the name of her memory. Let me do just one good thing. Something she could be proud of me for."

I hoped to God that Ava—that I—was enough motivation for him to stay on the straight and narrow. At least for a few hours.

Now came the hard part. Selling the idea to Karl Anderson...

Chapter Twenty-Six

"I can't believe any of you are even considering this."
I'd been stalking the room from end to end for the
last hour while they went over the plan.

The *plan*… Ha.

"What other choice do we have?" Sera begged me
to walk into this with an open mind. To see it not as
giving in to Dylan but as taking down a monster. One
even bigger than him.

I opened my mouth but closed it when I had nothing
constructive to offer. They were right, in a sense. We
had no other choice. And if it weren't for the fact that
Cora Anderson was still out there and still a threat to
the entire multiverse, then I would have quietly slunk
away to die in peace.

"She's not going to come alone. You all know that,
right?" In the corner, Dylan sat in a metal folding chair
with shackles around both his wrists and ankles. "She's
going to bring every bit of muscle she can scrounge."

"So?" Noah snapped. If anyone in the room was unhappier than I was about Dylan not rotting away behind bars, it was him. They'd been exchanging death-glares since the moment the guards marched him in, and if it wasn't for Cade, I had a feeling Noah would have gone for the guy's throat. "Planning on switching sides?"

"I said I'd help take her down." All eyes in the room swiveled toward him, and he frowned. With a nod in Sera's direction, he added, "I'm doing this for her. Screw the rest of you."

At the front of the room, Karl Anderson looked to be holding together just barely better than his son. I couldn't imagine how he felt. This was the person who killed his daughter then fled into the multiverse with his tech. He probably never expected to get his hands on him again, and now that he had, instead of hanging from a noose—or whatever the hell else this world used to put people to death—he was sitting nice and cozy in the same room.

"Moving on," Anderson said between clenched teeth. "I will feign unconsciousness, acting as the version of me who stole her information." He fished into his pocket and pulled out several flash drives. Setting them down on the table in front of him, he said, "Do any of these look like the one she had?"

"This one." Sera reached across and grabbed a bright blue one with a silver stripe. She rolled it around in her fingers before setting it back down again. "Perfect match."

Karl nodded to Rabbit, who stood and took his place at the front of the room. He held up a small red cube. "I've created a trap of sorts. Cora can skip in, but she shouldn't be able to skip out. This bad boy should fry her chip so she's stranded here."

"What about the rest of us?" Kori, who'd been quiet until now, sat in the corner next to Cade. She glanced at him, then down to her own arm.

Cade frowned. He took her hand and squeezed, then pulled her closer and wrapped an arm around her shoulder. "Rabbit knows the chips are important. He'd never risk them all." He pinned his friend with a pointed stare. "Right?"

"Course not. Anyone with a chip will have to steer clear at first. Thirty yards to be safe. Fifty to be certain. It's a one-time use, so after the initial blast, you'll be okay." He snickered. "Do you really think I'd risk losing those chips? Those babies are going to jump us years ahead!"

"Focus, Phil," Karl said.

He fought a grin. "Right. Right… Anyway, after… whoever…sets off the device—"

"Dylan," Sera said. She glanced over at him. "It has to be Dylan. He's the one she's coming to meet. I'll be with him, but Cora knows how…motivated he is."

I expected him to protest, but instead he sat there, sullen and silent.

"Okay," Rabbit said with a nod. "After *Dylan* sets off the device, the cavalry should be clear to swoop in and clean up the mess. Deal with her guard, et cetera."

"Not gonna be that easy," I said. These people had no idea what the hell they were dealing with. "Cora's guard has been enhanced. Yancy alone could probably take out everyone in this room with his hands tied behind his back. The only one who has a shot at him is me."

"You?" Rabbit quirked a brow. "Why you?"

"Because I was part of Cora's Alpha project."

The others in the room had no idea what I was talking about, but Rabbit and Karl? Yeah. They knew something. Rabbit's mouth fell open, and Karl visibly paled.

"She went ahead with Alpha on that world?" Rabbit looked from me to Karl.

"What's Alpha?" Kori asked from the corner. She glanced at Cade, who shrugged.

"It was a theory here. Cora refused to continue with it due to the side effects." Karl came around the table and stopped a few feet from me. There was a hint of respect in his eyes, but also the unmistakable taint of fear. "Are you telling me you're an Alpha, son?"

I stood. "I am, sir."

The older man suddenly didn't seem as thrilled to have me there as he was before.

"Still think I should get that antidote?" I leveled my gaze at him and snickered, deep, dark, and wrong on so many levels. "Because I'd caution you against it."

"G!" Sera cried. "Stop it."

Karl faltered then took a step back, shaking his head as if to clear away cobwebs—or more likely, thoughts of murder. If he had even the slightest inkling of what I was capable of, he'd put a knife through my chest right now. "And you're all right? Stable?"

"I have my moments, sir." Why lie? These people didn't deserve to be locked away with a loaded gun. They'd seen enough trouble; I had no intention of adding to it. Maybe at one point in my life I wouldn't have given it a second thought. But things were different now. *I* was different now. My stay at Infinity, meeting Sera, meeting Cade… These things changed me dramatically, and it was only in the last few days that I'd come to realize just how drastic that change was. "The truth is, the serum never fully activated in my system. I never got… I guess you could say, worked up enough."

"To trigger the full effects," Rabbit said with a nod. Sounded to me like he knew a bit more about the thing than simple theory, but who the hell was I to judge?

"Basically," I said. "But make no mistake, I'm still dangerous. I don't *want* to hurt anyone, but that doesn't mean it won't happen." When he didn't say anything else, I decided to throw in my pitch. They were either going to see me as an asset or stick me in a box and bury it. One way or the other, I had to know where I stood. I flexed my fingers and rolled my neck. "You seem to have a pretty good idea of what Cora did to me. You've got a pretty good idea of what I can do…"

Rabbit squinted, staring at me like he was trying to see through my damn skull. "I don't understand how you're so calm. So docile."

"I'm not. It's a constant battle to stay in control. Cora's theory was that because I never gave in to the madness, not really letting go, I've managed to maintain my humanity." I glanced at Sera, then quickly looked away. "Because of her."

Anderson frowned. "And to defeat her guard? To take down this Yancy? Are you prepared to lose yourself?"

"Lose yourself?" Sera was beside me in an instant. "What does that mean?"

I ignored her, focusing first on Anderson, and then settling on Dylan. He gave me a knowing nod then let his gaze fall to the ground. "Yeah," I said finally. "Yeah I am."

Dylan had contacted Cora an hour ago. Her line had turned green almost immediately, and she'd phoned. He'd given her instructions on where to meet—the back end of a park—and we'd come to wait.

Dylan pulled his jacket tighter and glared at me. "Shouldn't you go skulk off into the bushes with the others?"

"Aren't you going to try and escape?" I countered, knowing full well that any attempt on his part to cut and run would result in a near-fatal electrical shock to his system, thanks to the cuff Rabbit had shackled around his ankle. Still, a guy could hope.

The others were waiting, scattered around the surrounding area. Anderson had his best men—his words, not mine—ready and waiting to pounce. I'd tried to get Sera to stay behind, but she, as well as Dylan, argued that it would look more convincing to Cora if she was with Dylan, considering what was at stake. As far as the bitch knew, Sera still thought there was a life-threatening chip in her head, so it made sense. If Cora believed we'd learned otherwise, it might jeopardize things.

Still, I didn't like it.

"He's right, G," she said, taking my hand and squeezing hard. "You should hide. She could be here any minute."

I hesitated, hating the idea of leaving her here with him. Leaving her as a sitting duck for Cora...

"Like I'd let anything happen to her?"

I glared at him, mentally counting to five in order to keep from smashing his face in. "I think you'll do whatever it takes to get what you want."

"Which is her safety," he replied. Our eyes met, and his lip twitched with a grin. One I'd seen in the mirror a thousand times before. "After everything I've been through, do you really think I'd let her die?"

"You were willing to walk away from her before. When you thought the chip would kill her, you left her with me. So, yeah. I do."

"I think we both know I would have never let her die. What would you do to keep her alive?"

I grabbed the front of his shirt, and Sera gasped. "I'd rip the world apart for her."

Dylan smirked then dislodged my grip. "Then we're on the same damn page." He gently pushed me back and straightened his shirt. "Like it or not, you and me...? We're the same damn person. Different circumstances, but the same. We're the monster, G. Not the devil. Remember that because it's pretty damn important."

He was right—but he was also wrong. We weren't the same. I could see that now. I was a monster. That much was true. But my days of hurting people, innocent people, were over. Dylan? He was the monster *and* the devil.

Chapter Twenty-Seven

Sera

I'd held my breath as G walked back to the tree line. His gait was stiff, tension evident in every step he took. He'd refused to tell me what Karl had meant when he said *lose yourself.* I still didn't know much about the mysterious Alpha project G had been a part of, other than the fact that they'd essentially tortured him. Unfortunately, that wasn't going to change right now.

"You ready for this?"

Dylan had changed from his jumpsuit back into the blue jeans and black button down I'd become accustomed to. His eyes moved constantly, surveying the area over and over, and I wondered what was going through his head. He'd agreed to help us in exchange for jail time instead of execution, should Cora not keep her end of the deal and return him to Ava. He'd serve a life sentence—that wasn't up for discussion—but he'd be allowed to live. Maybe he thought Cade would help him escape again. Maybe he didn't believe they'd actually go through with it. Who knew? It was possible he truly thought Cora would keep her word. If it'd been me? I would have chosen execution. Sixty-five years or so confined to a cell? Been there. Done that. Never, ever going back.

There'd been a lot of debate on the subject. On one hand, no one thought he deserved to get what he wanted. If Cora kept her promise to him, and nothing went wrong, he would get Ava back. But, on the other hand, if that happened, it would be like none of the carnage occurred. They still weren't 100 percent sure what would happen with other worlds—and people from them, like Ash, Kori and me—but if Dylan went back and saved Ava, then this world's Kori would still be alive. Rabbit's theory was that it would only affect those with this world's frequency, so nothing should change for the rest of us.

I hoped he was right.

I sighed. "I'll never be *ready* for it. Seeing that woman makes my skin crawl." There was something I needed to say, and since Karl was on his way over, it was now or never. "You were right."

He quirked a brow.

"What you said about me—about her. How she was able to see past your flaws to the person underneath. I understand now."

His gaze flickered to the tree line. "Other me isn't a saint, eh? I could have told you that. I bet he's just as bad—if not worse—than I am."

"Not even close."

He lost his grin. "The right person, the perfect person, will see through all of life's bullshit," he said. "They're the ones who forgive you when you can't forgive yourself."

"I know." And it was dead-on. G wasn't able to forgive himself right now. He would, though. It might take a long time, but I knew he'd get there. I could forgive him for the both of us, for the time being, because I could see the parts of him that he couldn't. The bits of brightest light peeking out from beneath the dark.

"She was that for me," Dylan said. He grinned, and for the first time since I'd met him, it was a genuine smile. "She was the only one who saw *me*. If you're really that for him, don't let go, because without you… Without you, he'll just become me."

I still believed there was something wrong with Dylan on a fundamental level. Heartbreak and tragedy were part of human life. How you chose to deal with them defined you. Dylan had chosen the bloody path. Still, Ava must have *seen* him. She had to have understood what he was on a basic level—and she'd loved him regardless. When you stripped all the carnage away, all the pain, it was beautiful. That kind of love was pure.

"Clear on what to do?" Karl stopped a few feet from us and sank to the ground.

I rolled my eyes. He'd only asked us a thousand times already. "Yeah. Nothing. Act like the chip is in my head, and that I'm still worried it's going to kill me."

He was wearing the closest thing to a pinstripe suit we could scrounge up, but I didn't think it would matter much. The other version would have had to change clothes, right? To fit in on different worlds? As long as

it looked pricey—which Karl assured us that it was—
we should be okay.

He handed Dylan the flash drive and said, "No
funny business."

"We're past that now," Dylan replied, sullen.

Karl nodded and laid his head down, closing his
eyes. I was impressed by how his breathing evened
out, and with the stillness he maintained. Though, I
supposed that was why he was a solider and I wasn't.

We didn't have to wait long before Cora and her
crew appeared. They walked through the back gates
like they owned the world, her men all in deep purple
and led by Yancy, and Cora wearing her signature white.
Instead of being dressed to the nines, though, she wore
simple pants and a knit sweater with flats.

"See?" she said, coming to a stop a few feet from
where we stood. "How hard was that? Now we can all
get what we want." Hand thrust out, she wiggled her
fingers greedily. "Where's my flash drive?"

Dylan shook his head. "Yeah. Like I'm *that* stupid?"
He nudged Karl with the tip of his boot. "Here's your
traitor. Give us what we want, and then I'll fork over
the drive."

Cora laughed. Behind her, Yancy kept a straight
face, but it was impossible not to notice the way his
gaze raked over the scene, searching for...what? A
betrayal? The others? Did she know this was a trap, or
was the guy just paranoid? "Do I detect mistrust?"

"Damn right you do." Dylan jabbed a finger in my
direction. "Fix the chip in her head."

"Gladly. Simply hand over my flash drive." When
Dylan didn't move, Cora sighed. "You realize I can

make this extremely difficult."

"Dylan, just give her the drive," I snapped. Then, to her, I said, "After everything that you've done to me, you better keep your word…"

Dylan hesitated. I had to give him credit. His acting chops were dead-on. His face was the perfect mix of anger and frustration mingled with distrust and impatience. He dug the drive from his pocket, then rolled it around in his fingers for a minute.

He made a move to hand it to her, then jerked back at the last moment, grinning. Gripping it between both hands, he said, "Second thought, hold up your end. You fix her chip, and I'll hand it over. If not, I'll snap it in half."

Yancy made a move to come forward, but Cora held him back, face pale. "Fine. I will deactivate the chip. Then you will give me my flash drive."

"And you'll send me to Ava."

"That's what I promised." There was something about the way she said it that sent goose bumps popping up all over my skin. She pulled something from her pocket—a small black rod with a flashing red light—and motioned for me to come forward.

Closer to Cora Anderson was the last place I wanted to be—especially since I knew there was no chip in my head—but I had to play along to keep this thing going. It had to seem like we still needed her. She braced her hand against my head, and I suppressed a shudder as, with the other, she pressed the metal tube against my temple. "Stand very still, dear. One sudden move and it's an instant lobotomy."

I so badly wanted to call bullshit, but instead bit

down hard on the inside of my cheek. She kept it going for a few minutes, pressing the thing painfully into the side of my head. When she was done, she was grinning.

I tentatively touched my temples. "It's deactivated?"

"You won't die from a chip in the brain," she replied, a little too cheerfully.

"Now me," Dylan said, snapping his fingers in front of her face. He held out the flash drive and she took it. "You promised you'd bring me back to Ava."

Cora's grin grew wider. "I'm a woman of my word." She stepped aside and Yancy came forward, gun trained on him.

"What the hell is this?"

"I'm reuniting you with Ava, of course," she said with a snicker. "You really thought I could send you *back in time*?"

Dylan stared at her.

"The pretty ones aren't always the sharpest, are they? There's no such thing as time travel." She waved a hand in the air above her head. "At least not yet. Give me time, though."

Dylan seethed. I knew that look all too well. "Yeah? *I'm* the idiot? I'm not the one walking around with an empty flash drive."

Her amusement lingered for a moment, just until what he'd said sank in. She looked down at the small chunk of plastic in her hand, then turned her head up to glare at him. "What are you saying?"

Dylan laughed. "Your flash drive is long gone. Destroyed. Tiny bits and pieces."

Damn it! We should have planned for this. A Dylan contingency. Maybe we should have filled him in completely. If we'd told him what had been on the flash, then maybe he wouldn't have poked her. Or, maybe he would. This was Dylan we were talking about. She'd crushed him by telling him there was no way to get back to Ava, and he'd reciprocated by telling her she couldn't have what she wanted. Plan be damned.

Cora let out a howl, and Yancy bounded forward. I heard the snap as he released the safety, and I just reacted. Forget that if I'd had time to think about it, I probably wouldn't have tried to save him. Despite the reasons behind his pain, he was still a murderer. But he was also a human. Another version of G.

I stepped sideways and brought my arm up as hard as I could. It connected with the barrel of Yancy's gun just as he fired, and the shot deflected and bounced off the nearby trees with a horrible wail.

I made a move to scamper away, but Cora was faster than I was. She grabbed a handful of my hair and yanked back hard. The move disrupted my balance and sent me teetering backward until gravity won and I landed on a heap in the grass.

From there everything got a little hazy. I heard him before I saw anything—the distinct roar I knew had to come from G as he launched himself from his hiding spot and into the fray. I saw what I assumed was his blur fly by, straight for Yancy, as Cora barked out orders to the re-maining guards. Karl was on his feet and swinging as well, and from the corner of my eye, I saw more movement from the tree line as the others rushed in to help.

Two sets of arms hauled me to my feet, one on either side, and before I could scream, before I could cry out for G, everything went dark.

Chapter Twenty-Eight

The blows kept coming. From my right. My left. The soldiers launched themselves at me, one grabbing hold from behind and pulling backward. My momentum shifted, and I flailed, but I caught myself by grabbing the guy in front of me. I brought his head down as my knee came up. There was a sickening—yet satisfying—crack, and his body went limp.

One by one they came. One by one they fell. Knowing what their weakness was—and where it was located—was the only thing that spared us from massive casualties. I'd made sure to go over it with the others, and Karl proved to be a quick study. He took down two of his own by delivering a perfectly aimed punch at the center of their breastbone. Pods broken, they fell like dead weight. Several got away, not counting the few that dragged Sera off. But I'd deal with them. First, I had to deal with *him*.

"Have to be honest," Yancy said as we circled each

other. Karl and Cade both made a move to come forward, but I held up a hand to stop them. This was my fight. Win or lose, I swore I'd have my day with this bastard. "I was hoping it would come down to this."

"Makes two of us," I replied, feeling my lips tilt upward with an involuntary smile. The others had gathered around the edge of the fray.

"We've had a lot of fun, you and I."

"I owe you for each and every bit of *fun*."

"Think you can take me?" The bastard laughed. "You've had ample opportunity. What makes you think this will be any different?"

I could feel myself inching toward the line. That invisible fence I'd been trying so hard not to cross. I wasn't sure what would happen if I did. Cora had pushed me without mercy, desperate for me to give in. I used to be scared of it. I'd lay awake at night after they'd dropped me back in my cell and worry what I would become if I finally let go, if I finally gave in.

Time after time and test after test, I'd managed to keep myself grounded. In the beginning, it was stubbornness. She wanted me to lose control, so I refused, if only to piss her the hell off. Then later, it was Sera who kept me rooted. The idea that I'd turn into something else, something darker than the person I already was, terrified me. I couldn't let that happen. Not when I was the only one she had. But she wasn't alone now. She had people who would help her—and defeating Yancy wasn't going to happen unless I gave it my all. How many times had Cora locked me in a room with him in hopes that the serum would activate? Each time the beating got more violent until I could no longer retain consciousness.

That all ended now.

"You're wrong," I said. "It was never about not being able to beat you. It was about me choosing not to. I've had a change of heart."

I closed my eyes and inhaled deeply, searching for that spark, that fire Cora lit when she injected me with the Alpha serum. It was always there, always singeing my nerve endings and begging to be set free. It wasn't hard to find. In my mind's eye it was like a tiny black bubble. Over time the walls of that bubble had gotten thinner and thinner, and to break through now, all I would have to do was…

I opened my eyes, and everything was sharper. Colors were more vivid, details were more focused. I heard my own breath echoing as it moved in and out of my lungs, heard the faint rustle of the nearby trees and the soft whistle of the breeze as it blew. I was still dying. I felt the virus from my dissolving pod still moving through my body. But the activation of the serum deadened most of the pain. It jacked up my senses and offered an edge I wouldn't have had.

"Well, well, well. Looks like someone has joined the party." Yancy laughed. "How's it feel?"

"Feels like I'm gonna kick your ass."

His brow quirked, and he waggled his index finger at me. Just once. It was all I needed. With a howl, I launched myself at him, swinging. The first blow landed hard and connected with the side of his face. The momentum knocked him back—but he didn't topple. Not really.

Thrusting his arm back, Yancy caught himself just

before hitting the ground. With a single, massive heave, he was back on his feet and throwing a punch of his own. "My turn."

The blow struck my shoulder, the force of it spinning my entire body. Like Yancy, I was able to catch myself before going down. I didn't think it was possible, with the damage he'd done, but he'd held back during our sessions at Infinity.

"Good morning, G." Cora's obnoxiously chipper voice was like a foghorn in my ear. She rounded my chair and positioned herself in front of me. "How did you sleep? Well?"

They'd injected me with something every morning for the last ten days. Since then, I'd been restless all the time. Fidgety and raw. "Oh, yeah. Those five-star, roach-infested accommodations you've given us are sweet."

She smiled and took a step back. "I have something very exciting in store for you today." She motioned to someone standing by the door. "Someone I've been waiting to introduce you to."

A man entered the room. Broad shoulders and a neck like a tree trunk, he towered over Cora like she was toddler. "This is Yancy Haven."

I snorted. "Why am I not surprised to see you here, Haven."

Cora seemed confused. "Did you have a Yancy on your world?"

"Sure did. And he was a dick." I looked the guy up and down, then snorted again. "Also a damn pansy-ass."

She clapped her hand down on Yancy's shoulder. "Not my Yancy. Like I said, he's got that little something extra… He's going to be overseeing your training."

"I've told you a million times, lady. I'm not training for shit."

She just kept right on smiling. "He's very special. He's skilled in Krav Maga, Silat, and an assortment of torture methods." She jabbed a finger in his direction. "I'm just going to leave you two alone to get acquainted."

Cora breezed out the door, and Yancy took her place. He hadn't spoken, which for some reason was unnerving. "So, you're the resident badass, eh?" Sure, he was a big guy. One who supposedly knew how to fight. But so what? "I gotta say, she talks you up a big game, but you don't look like much to me."

He grabbed a handful of my shirt and hefted upward. The solid ground beneath the chair I was shackled to disappeared. My heart thumped inside my chest, but I gave nothing away. For the longest moment, he just stayed like that, suspending me in the air as though I weighed no more than a feather. Then, without a word, he threw me across the room. I crashed into the wall. It felt like hyperspeed. The chair shattered on impact—I was sure some of my bones did, too…

The pain in my shoulder was unlike anything I'd felt; it was like getting slammed by a truck. My mind and body registered the pain, but unlike our previous times together, I was able to ignore it. To stand my ground and push forward. No. "Able" wasn't the right word.

Motivated. Needed to. In that moment there was nothing I wanted more than to inflict pain. The target didn't matter. Thankfully, Yancy was standing by to accommodate my heightened craving for violence.

My reflexes were sharper now that the serum had activated. More honed. Hearing a disturbance in the air, I was able to duck and pivot as his next blow came. It sailed harmlessly by. For a moment we stopped and stared at each other.

"You're not the first, you know," he said with a wicked grin. "There were others before. Multiple versions of you—and *her*."

I didn't respond. Couldn't. I knew what he was doing, and it wasn't necessary. I was over the line already and about as amped as I could get.

"We met once, you and me."

"We met more than once," I said with a growl. Though this version of Yancy Haven was ten times worse than the one on my world, I would never forget him. Our rivalry probably would have gotten us both killed if Cora hadn't stolen me away. "You were a dick on my world, too."

He laughed. "No, I mean me. This me. I met you before Cora brought you back to our world."

"Bullshit." There was no way I wouldn't remember.

He held up both hands in mock surrender. "Hand to God. You were fifteen at the time, just out of basic and on your first raid."

He was insane. Of all the memories I had, the first raid they'd sent me on was the most vivid. It would stay with me until the moment I died. We'd gotten wind of a safe house and were instructed to kill all the male occupants. We were to bring all the women back to our camp. I'd seen violence at a young age, my parents having given me over to the army program when I was just four. But I hadn't been prepared for the brutality that went down that day.

"Don't remember? I'll give you a hint. I was there to make my first pickup."

Pickup? "You took someone?"

His grin widened. "From that very house. You almost walked in on me—remember?"

It took a moment, but suddenly I knew exactly what he was talking about. I'd managed to avoid most of the chaos, then during the last sweep of the house, I tried to enter a room as Yancy was coming out—only it hadn't been my world's version of him, had it? "You didn't take me, though."

"Never intended to."

A sick feeling bubbled in my gut and the spark in my chest burned a little hotter.

"Got my hands on our first version of Ava that day."

"Ava—she was there?" A voice in the back of my mind roared for me to finish this. We were supposed to be in the middle of a battle to the death, after all. But I was rooted in place. Stunned into silence. She had been there. The universe *had* given me my own version.

Yancy snickered. He held up his hand and pinched his fingers together until they were almost touching. "Just think about it. You were *this* close to meeting her." He threw his head back and laughed even louder. "I did you a favor, though. That version of her? Whiney as fuck. She lasted about a week before Cora had me take her out back and drown the little bitch just to shut her up."

The spark in my chest ignited into an inferno. Whether it was the poison making one final push, or the serum kicking in, everything turned red. I let out an unholy howl and flew at him. We crashed to the ground, both swinging. He growled and took aim for the spot my pod was, but I shifted. The blow grazed my side. In turn, I took aim at his. The punch collided with his chest, the force behind it sending him to his back, but it missed its mark. Still, it hurt him.

He coughed and tried to roll onto his side, but I was faster. I brought my foot back and let loose, brutally kicking his torso. He curled, spitting a mouthful of blood and coughing even harder.

Part of me wanted to drag this out. To make him suffer for all he'd done to me. For taking away my chance to meet Ava… I'd missed my world's version of Ava—but I'd found the one who was meant for me. And right now, she was in trouble.

I positioned my foot just beneath his neck, and he froze. Our gazes met. "You can't do it," he croaked. "How many times did you insist that you weren't a murderer anymore?"

I had said that. Every time he'd tried to get me to fight back, to rage hard enough to activate the serum, I'd told him my bloody days were over. "I was wrong." I lifted my foot high, holding it above him for a second, just long enough for him to register what I intended to do, before slamming it down on his chest. That time my aim was perfect. My boot crushed the pod. I imagined the sound it might make. Not a booming explosion, but a barely-there pop. Small and insignificant, yet deadly enough to fell a beast like Yancy.

His face contorted, and his hands went for his neck, clawing and scratching at something I couldn't see. His body stiffened and twitched, and in seconds went completely still. A thin trickle of blood trailed from his nose and right ear.

In that moment, the damage rushed back to me. The pain from physical injuries—and the reality of the fact that the serum was now active—all crushing me. My knees buckled, and I collapsed to the ground beside Yancy's body, struggling to push the air in and out of my lungs.

"Can you stand?" Cade's voice floated from somewhere behind me. At least I thought it was him. I could hardly hear it through the thundering of my pulse and the raging of my breath. A set of hands clamped on to my shoulders. Deep down I knew it was to help me up, to see if anything was ruptured or broken or hemorrhaging, but Cora's monster didn't care about things like that. I bucked off whoever it was and leaped to my feet.

"Whoa there, son." Anderson. That'd been him.

"G, take a deep breath. We're here to help you." Kori… She came around to stand in front of me. Her gaze flickered to something on my right, then back to me. "We're your friends."

Someone beyond my field of vision snorted. Had to be Noah. "Friends? Not sure I'd go *that* far," he said. "But we won't set you on fire or anything."

There was an echoing *thwap*—probably from Ash smacking the shit out of him—and a hiss.

"G, come back down, man." Cade again. He moved

to stand beside Kori. "We need you here. Sera—"

"Sera." I breathed the name as though it was the air and I was suffocating. Sera was the reason for all this. The reason I fought to keep my head above water. The reason I rebelled against the serum. She was the one good thing in my life. "Where—"

"Cora," he said. "She slipped away during the chaos of the fight. Dylan's gone, too. We think he went after her."

Noah snorted again. "Bullshit. That bastard cut out. I say zap his ass with the cuff you put on, and we'll go pick up his corpse."

Violent images of what I intended to do to Cora flashed through my mind, so fast, it made my head spin and my gut roil. Every instinct told me to lash out. Even though she wasn't here. Even though these people were my...friends.

Sera...

I squeezed my eyes closed. No.

This was what I'd been fighting so hard against. I'd dug my heels in and fought like the devil himself was breathing down my neck, all to be the person she deserved.

Deep breaths. In. Out. In. Out. I opened my eyes, surprised by my continued restraint. I'd done it. Pulled myself back from the edge. For her. In that moment, I knew I could do this, could be the person she deserved. The one she needed. I could be the man I wanted to be for *her*.

"Where?" I exhaled the word while my hands shook with a residual tremor. "Where would she take Sera?"

"We're going to find out." Anderson's large hand clamped down against my shoulder. This time when I went to shrug it off, he was ready for me. His grip tightened, and he turned me so that we were eye to eye. "We're going to get her back."

Chapter Twenty-Nine

Sera

I forced my eyes open, but the room didn't quite take shape. There was a bright light and watery outlines, but there was no detail. I closed my eyes again and inhaled. The air smelled sweet, like overripe fruit or strong flowers. There was something else, too. A subtler aroma beneath the sweet. An almost metallic smell. My stomach turned over, and I swallowed back the rising bile in my throat. The acidic taste was almost enough to make me gag. There was a sound… Like water dripping from a pipe, falling into a bucket or pot or something. *Plunk. Plunk. Plunk.*

"Hello?" I managed weakly. I felt like I hadn't slept in weeks, and it was an effort to hold my head up. "Anyone here?" I tried again.

There was no answer, and a part of me was thankful. I might not know where I was—but I knew *who* I was with. Cora. Cora Anderson had dragged me out of the park. While G fought an onslaught of her amped-up guards, while he'd taken on *Yancy*, I'd been carted away like luggage.

Again.

God. Was he okay? Had he pushed himself too far? Crossed a line he wouldn't be able to come back from? No. I refused to believe that was even possible. She'd done something horrible to him—to all of them—but there was no part of me that believed G to be weak. Whatever he'd done, wherever he'd gone, he would find his way back…to me.

When I opened my eyes again, things were less hazy. I surveyed the room. Satiny curtains did little to block the harsh sunlight streaming through two large glass doors directly in front of me. When my eyes adjusted to the brightness, I saw they led out to a balcony that overlooked water of some kind. I was strapped to a chair, my arms pulled tight behind my back and my legs…each ankle was secured to one of the front legs.

I should have panicked. I should have been terrified. But I wasn't. I was calm, and I was determined. I would not die in this room. I would not leave this world before I had the chance to make G see what kind of person he really was. He'd done this for me. Made me strong. Made me a fighter. So, for him, I would fight.

Every inch of me was stiff. I wiggled my fingers. They were numb but felt oddly slick, like they were coated in something slimy. I twisted to try and see what was behind me, but the bindings were too tight, and I couldn't move. Instead, I flicked my fingers. When I caught sight of the bright red splash against the stark white carpet, my heart stuttered. "Oh my God…"

"Wonderful," a hauntingly familiar voice said,

followed by a very unladylike snort. "Now I'm going to lose my damn deposit." Cora was in front of me, razor sharp nails digging into my chin as she forced my face forward. "Stop flailing around."

"I'm bleeding." It was all I could think of to say.

Her lip twitched, bending upward with a grin. "I should hope so. I cut one of your wrists."

The air in the room turned arctic. "You—"

"Oh, relax. Should be old hat to you. Besides, I didn't go deep enough to hit any major arteries. I couldn't have you bleeding out too fast." She bent down and picked up what looked like a coffee pot. "I'm working with less than ideal tools here, and space is limited. I can't risk losing any of that liquid gold you have in those veins."

"That's your plan? Bleed me dry and what?—you've got nothing to work with, Cora. The drive is destroyed."

Irritation flashed in her eyes. "So you found out what was on the drive, eh? Betting my husband was the one who spilled the beans." She sighed and picked at a small bit of lint on the front of her shirt. "That man is a royal pain in my ass."

"Was," I said. "He's dead."

Another flash of emotion—the quickest spike of remorse—and she had my face in her hands again. "You know what they say, it's all about sacrifice…"

"You're sick—and insane." I jerked from her grasp and spit at her. "Go ahead. Bleed me dry. You've still got nothing."

"Is that what you think? That just because I've lost the recipe on the flash drive that I'm dead in the water?" She straightened and spread her arms. "There are infinite worlds out there. Infinite possibilities. Just because I don't have it anymore doesn't mean someone else will be impeded by the same problem."

"Bullshit," I said. "The poison needs my blood. I'm a *rarity*, remember? Since the other versions of me haven't been tampered with, their blood is different from mine."

She shrugged. "This is true. That's why I'm going to keep you on ice." She leaned in close, fingers digging into my forearms. Her nails were sharp, and they pierced my skin in several places, causing small trickles of blood to leak. "I am *going* to go home—I simply need to find someone to recreate that recipe for me. Since I have no place to store you while I search, I'm going to freeze your blood. Before I came to this little slice of heaven, I was on a world where they freeze biological material. I'll simply tuck what I need away and come back at a later date."

I opened my mouth then closed it, at a loss. I knew G and the others would try to find me, but I doubted they'd make it in time. By then, Cora would have me dry, the entirety of my blood stashed away in everything from paper cups to the ice cube bucket. I was about to resort to begging, when I remembered something.

Something that made me laugh uncontrollably.

Cora didn't understand. She either thought I'd lost too much blood—or my mind. "What could you possibly find amusing about all this?"

"Your—your—" I coughed and caught my breath. G might not find me in time, but Cora still wouldn't get her way. "Your plan is seriously flawed, Cora. In fact, it's flat-out broken."

She gave me an offhanded wave and shrugged. "I assure you that I've thought it all out. Don't you worry your—"

"You're stuck here, you stupid bitch!" I couldn't help it. I started laughing again, this time so hard that the chair wobbled a little. Maybe I *had* lost too much blood. There was a very real possibility that I had lost my *mind*, too. I'd been through more hell than most people ever saw in a lifetime. I'd been sold to pay off my parents' debt, then abducted by a madwoman obsessed with teenagers. I'd been locked in her basement, becoming just shy of a science class dissection frog, and met G. I fell for him, was torn away from him, and now she planned to suck me dry like some freaky vampire. If that wasn't enough to make someone lose their marbles, then I had no idea what would do it.

I watched her lose her grin, then drop her attention to the inside of her forearm. With jerky motions, she poked at it—and nothing happened. Over and over she did this, expecting a different result each time. But the chip remained dormant, fried by Rabbit's beautiful device.

I was still laughing when she came at me. She grabbed a handful of my hair and yanked, while at the same time kicking out at the legs on my chair. The whole thing toppled sideways, and I hit the floor hard enough to clamp my teeth into my tongue. I tasted blood—but better than that? I *saw* blood.

The bucket she'd been collecting my blood in was a few inches from my head.

I jerked my body forward once. Twice. On the third try I managed to head-butt it, tilting the thing until it spilled. My stomach churned, acid rising in my throat as I watched the red liquid rush from the container and onto the carpet. The contrast in color was shocking, and when Cora let out a blood-boiling wail.

I had to do something. Stall her or distract her— otherwise she was going to kill me right then and there. I saw it in her eyes. I'd been a witness to her losing it many times before: she'd be fine one minute, then totally unhinged the next. Most of the times it happened, there was no real catalyst. Nothing obvious had set it off. Unfortunately, this time? There was a reason.

"Before you do whatever it is you're debating, think about this—you kill me, and you're stuck here. They'll never fix your chip."

She snorted and crossed the room, hauling me up and righting the chair. "I'm smarter than all of them put together. What makes you think I'd need them to fix my chip?"

I glanced around the room, then back to her. "Then go for it. I'm sure you'll be able to scrounge up all the resources you need right here in this *hotel room*."

She let out a frustrated growl and began pacing again. Like before, she was jabbing at her arm, hoping that whatever the problem was, it was only temporary.

"Phil MaKaden designed the device that fried your chip." That small bit of truth wouldn't hurt. I didn't worry he was in danger. He was under the protection of the government. She couldn't touch him on this world. Plus, the mention of his name turned her a little green. Her own world's version of him had betrayed her by helping Ash. "I'm willing to bet an arm that they'll be willing to make a deal."

Her lips tilted upward, and she shook her head slowly. "You for my chip, right?"

It was my turn to shrug. Not an easy task considering my bindings. I saw the fury in her eyes, and the way she stood, rigid and coiled—ready to strike like a cobra. The fact that she hadn't yet was encouraging. "Can't get something for nothing." I fought—and lost— the urge to smile. "What did you say before? About sacrifice?"

Chapter Thirty

They'd brought me back to Fort Hannity and had me wait in a room. That was the nice way of putting it. In reality, it took Cade, Noah, and Anderson to physically force me to go—cuff me and stuff me into the back of Anderson's jeep—then lock me in a cell. All because I wanted to go after Sera.

I hadn't stopped moving since they'd locked the door. Back and forth, end to end, I stalked the confines of my cell with just one thing on my mind.

Murdering Cora Anderson.

A deeply rooted part of me knew they were right. We needed a plan. We had to find her first. But the part that was in control, the monster Cora made...he didn't need a plan. He would scour the city, ripping it to shreds and uprooting everything until he found his prey.

Yep. It was probably a really good thing they'd locked me up.

"How you doing in there?" Cade appeared on the

other side of the bars.

I glared at him and swallowed my first response—a colorful combination of telling him to fuck off and die. After I'd tamped it down, I said, "Places I'd rather be."

"I know. And I'm sorry…" He tapped the bars. "About this. I know it must be hard being back in a cell after everything you went through."

"What's hard is being stuck here while she's doing God knows what to Sera," I ground out.

"Well, then you're in luck." He stepped back and produced a set of keys, hesitating just shy of inserting them into the lock. "You won't understand this, but this whole situation—me letting you out—is creepy and ironic."

I waited for a moment after he opened the door. I couldn't help being suspicious. "What gives?"

"I told you we just needed to formulate a plan. We've done that."

"We know where she is?"

I followed him down the hall. "Actually, we do. In a shocking turn of events, Dylan came back." He stopped in front of a door leading outside. On the other side, I saw Dylan standing between Anderson and Noah. "He's—"

The rest of whatever it was he planned to say was lost when I slammed out the door and barreled straight for Dylan. "Where the hell is she?" I grabbed him by the front of the shirt and spun him toward the hood of the nearby jeep.

Credit where credit was due—he kept his shit together. That sane part of me knew I was flying off the ledge, but stopping myself wasn't an option. "We're going to meet her now. Cora called me. Wants to trade Sera for her chip."

I let go of him. "Her chip?"

"She thinks we can fix it so she can skip out," Noah said. His lips twisted into a scowl. "Because we'd let her walk away…"

"So, what's the play?" Standing around was just pissing me off.

"She gave us her hotel and room number. Rabbit and Dylan are going up."

"And me," I said. If they really thought I was leaving Sera's life in Dylan's hands, they were fucking delusional. Anderson opened his mouth, but I held up my hand. "Don't. This isn't up for negotiation. Nothing short of you putting a bullet between my eyes is going to keep me from going."

"He's right," Dylan said. "Cora didn't say it, but I'd bet my hand that she expects G to come. If he's not there, she might spook. Think it's a trap or something."

It should have concerned me that he was so agreeable, but at that point I was going to take what I could get. "Settled, then." Without another word from anyone, I climbed into the back of the jeep and waited. A moment later, the rest of them joined me, and we were on our way.

"Pretty pricey for someone who has no resources," Anderson said as he slid from behind the wheel. We'd parked the jeep in the front lot, close to the building. Cora was on the top floor. The penthouse. She wouldn't be able to see us from there.

"Don't fool yourself," I said, taking a nice long look over the building. Brick. Each room had a balcony, and as far as I could tell, the back of the hotel faced out over a massive lake. "Just because she's a visitor here doesn't mean she can't fend for herself. Don't expect some pushover like your wife."

Anderson laughed. "Son, my Cora is anything but a pushover, trust me."

Rabbit came up beside me, flanked by Dylan. Cade and Noah joined Anderson on the other side of the jeep. "I think I can fake it and get her to believe that I've fixed the chip."

"How the hell are you going to do that?" Dylan snapped. Of all the people along for this ride, aside from me, he seemed to have the most trouble with Rabbit. Every time I looked his way, the guy was staring at him. The kind of look you give someone right before knocking his damn teeth out and feeding them to him.

Rabbit grinned, oblivious to Dylan's ire, and held up his arm. He gave his wrist a wiggle—I assume to showcase the weird-looking watch there. "Cade let me poke around his chip a bit. Run some diagnostics. My watch will project a perfectly replicated hologram of the chip's waking screen. She'll think it's up and running."

It was more than I'd hoped for—but not enough. "And what are you going to do when she tries to grab Sera and skip out?"

Rabbit flushed. "Well, I mean, we'll have to grab her first."

"Because that will work," Dylan muttered, not quite

under his breath.

"A lot of this is going to be improvising," Anderson said. "You up for that, son?"

"I'm up for it."

Ten minutes later, Rabbit, Dylan, and I were standing in front of room number 342. Rabbit knocked, and a few moments later, one of Cora's monkeys appeared. He stepped aside and gestured us in.

Rabbit let out a whistle. "Swank-kay."

"I distinctly recall this being a party of three—not four." Cora glared at me from across the room.

I returned her grin and jabbed a finger to the right, toward the three guards standing in the corner like statues. "Looks like seven to me."

She sighed and rolled her eyes. "I suppose I expected you to show." A wicked grin spread across her lips, and she winked at me. "You know, being the good little doggie you are."

"Where's Sera?"

"Right through here." She snapped her fingers at the men in the corner. "Do pay attention, boys. We'll be in the other room discussing business."

They didn't so much as flinch.

She led us through the hall and around the corner to the master bedroom suite. Sera was bound to a chair in front of an open glass door that led out to a small balcony. That alone brought a rumble to my throat. But add to it the fact that she looked ready to pass out, was pale as snow, and obviously hurt—there was an alarming amount of blood on the carpet—and the monster inside tore free.

"What the hell did you do?" I stalked forward,

ignoring the protests and curses from Rabbit and
Dylan, and made a move to grab Cora by the throat.
A move I aborted when she smiled wider and held
up what looked like a smaller version of a television
remote.

"I would put it on ice, little doggie." She waved the
thing around and sauntered a step closer, leaning in to
get a better look. "Well, color me surprised. Looks like
I won after all."

"If you think that, then you aren't familiar with your
own work. There's very little keeping me from tearing
you apart, Cora."

She shrugged. "Oh, I believe it. But something
to consider before you go on that self-destructive
rampage…" She waved the remote again.

"What the fuck is that?" Dylan snapped. He had just
as much patience for her show as I did.

"Oh, this? Nothing much. Nothing much…" She
tossed it into the air then caught it again. "It's just the
little gadget that controls the bomb I had my boys
plant."

"Bomb," I said. "And where is this bomb? Someplace
populated? A nunnery or orphanage?"

"Like you would care. Of course not." She nodded
to a black box on the bed, and the air in my lungs
turned to concrete. "Go on. Have a look-see. This world
is amazing."

"We're just here to keep our end of the deal," Rabbit
said. He sucked in a breath and came forward, giving
his bag of tools a subtle shake. I had no idea what was
in there, but it sounded like it was heavy. "I fix what I
did to your chip, and we get Sera back. You skip off on

your merry way, and no one needs to go boom."

"Let's get on with it, then," she said happily. "Oh. One sec. Need to do one thing first…" She aimed the remote at the box and pushed one of the buttons. A small digital panel on the thing flashed to life, reading seven minutes.

Dylan took a step toward the box then backed away. His mouth hung open. "You crazy bitch! What the hell did you just do?"

Cora's expression was the polar opposite. She was beaming like the fucking sun. "I'm motivating Mr. MaKaden."

Rabbit wore a similar expression to Dylan, except he was much paler. "Lady, you need to work on your motivational skills…"

"I was assured that you could fix my chip."

He dropped his bag to the ground. "I can!"

"Then get to it. You have"—she nodded toward the timer—"six minutes and change to get the job done."

"And what if it takes longer than that?" He swallowed. "This stuff isn't an exact science. You work the tech. You've gotta know that."

She shrugged like it was no big thing. "Then we're all going to die."

Chapter Thirty-One

Sera

Rabbit bent over Cora's arm in an attempt to make the chip work again. At least, that's what they told her. I couldn't believe that was true. She was dangerous to each and every human in the multiverse. Letting someone like her walk free would be like damning countless people to death.

"Tick tock," Cora said with a cluck of her tongue.

The timer on her bomb had just flipped to the three-minute mark.

Rabbit looked ready to vomit. He was pale and sweating, and I wasn't sure if he'd hurt his right hand, because he was holding it at an odd angle. "Done." He tapped her chip, and I couldn't believe my eyes when the main screen appeared on her skin in translucent blue light. "Now please kill the bomb before I shit myself, 'kay?"

She pried her hand from his grip and rolled her eyes. With a swipe of her back pocket, she had the remote out and aimed at the box, the button pushed. Thank God, right? Wrong.

Nothing happened.

"You got what you wanted. Stop the damn timer and hand her over," Dylan hollered.

She mumbled something and pushed the button again, this time harder. The timer still continued to tick off. "Well, I take it back. The craftsmanship on this world leaves much to be desired." She crossed to where I was, then poked at her forearm to wake the chip.

Nothing happened with that, either.

"What did you do?" she roared.

Rabbit raced to the box and gingerly lifted the lid. A quick inspection had him shaking his head. "Nothing I can do. It's *gonna* blow."

"Go!" G bellowed. He jabbed his finger at the door.

Rabbit hesitated for a moment, then took off. A few seconds later, the fire alarm sounded.

"Typical MaKaden," Dylan grumbled.

Despite my shaky feelings about him, I couldn't blame Rabbit for bolting. There was no reason for all of us to die. And he'd alerted the entire building by hitting the alarm. At least now, no matter what happened, fewer people would die. "Get out," I cried. "Please."

G took a step toward Cora and me. "Hand her over, and we'll all get the hell out of here."

"I'd rather die." Cora laughed. "You know, I did you both a favor." She jabbed a finger at G and said, "When I found you, you were bleeding out on the battlefield. Your team had left you for dead. And you..." She turned to me with a scowl. "You were pathetic. So close to death that I almost didn't bother. I saved both your miserable lives. I saved them—and now I'm choosing to end them!"

Dylan sighed. He turned to me and smiled. "Remember what I said about him." Then, without warning, he charged across the room, straight for Cora. She screamed and tried to move, but he was too fast. He crashed into her, then barreled them both through the balcony's screen doors and over the railing.

Oh my God… Gone. They were gone. Dylan had sacrificed himself for us.

Sixty seconds…

G raced to the edge, staring down. "Hundred or so feet…"

Forty-five seconds…

"G…" I whimpered. I'd escaped that hellhole only to die by Cora's hand anyway—but I refused to drag him along with me. He'd been through enough and deserved to be free. "Please go!"

There wasn't enough time for him to mess around with my bindings and nowhere near enough time to get the both of us out of the blast range.

Thirty seconds…

He went back to the railing and kicked at it with violent force. The whole thing came away from the balcony with ease, and he managed to catch it just before it fell. Setting it up against the side railing, he raced back to me.

"You're gonna hate this," he said, bracing a hand on either armrest of the chair.

Fifteen seconds…

"G…what are you—"

Ten seconds…

"And there's a good chance we won't survive it."

Six seconds...

"But I'd rather take a chance than stand here and blow up."

He dragged my chair to the back of the room, as far away from the balcony as he could get. "Count to four then hold your breath." With a jerky motion, we shot through the room and out to the balcony—then over the edge just as the explosion rocked the top floor.

Time's up...

I was weightless and falling, plummeting toward the lake. I hit the water, the force of the impact jarring every bone in my body and knocking the air from my lungs. Out of instinct, I tried to take a deep breath. I got a mouthful of water.

I forced my eyes open. It was murky and dark, and there was a pressure in my chest threatening to crush me. I was disoriented, but sure that I was moving in the wrong direction. The surface—the air—was up. I was sinking into the abyss.

I was going to drown.

Chapter Thirty-Two

My head broke the surface, and I gasped, greedily sucking down as much air as I could get. Intense pain told me I'd dislocated my left shoulder. I'd done it twice in basic training and was morbidly familiar with the sensation. "Sera!" I roared. Above us, the faint whine of sirens filled the distance, complemented by people's concerned cries. Frantic, I searched the surface. It was calm. She was nowhere to be seen.

That's when I remembered that she'd still been bound to the chair.

I tucked my injured arm close and took another deep breath, then dove. The water was icy, but thankfully clearer than it was on my world. I caught sight of her a few yards from where I'd landed. The chair had splintered. The left leg was gone and most of the back was missing, but there was enough left to keep her confined. She was sinking. Kicking hard, I fought my way to her and grabbed the chair with my good arm. She was struggling with the bindings and having no luck.

No matter how hard I kicked, though, we weren't making any progress. The chair was bulky and made from heavy wood, and I only had one arm to work with. That, in combination with the lack of actual gravity, crippled me. I let out a frustrated howl, bubbles exploding from my mouth, and let go. I kicked hard for the surface, so much farther away than it had been moments ago. Another lungful of air. Another dive.

This time I focused on freeing her. Pulling her from the water had proved impossible. If I could separate her from the chair… But that was no use, either. Her hands were cuffed behind her, the chain threaded through the back rung of the actual chair. If I hadn't been in the water, I probably could have broken it. But with the lack of force behind my movements, I couldn't snap the fucking thing.

Sera's eyes were wide. She was shaking her head slowly and had given up trying to rip her limbs free from the bonds. "Go," she mouthed. Her hair floated around, an eerie, swaying halo. She lifted her head so that we were face to face just as a small burst of bubbles trickled from her lips. The chair hit the bottom of the lake, giving me the opportunity to grab the back and push off hard.

It still wasn't enough.

The pressure in my chest was painful, and the effects of the pod still lingered, though thankfully dulled by the rush of adrenaline. I had to kick for air or we'd both drown. There was no way for me to save her.

In my gut I knew that—but I couldn't force myself to swim to the surface. I couldn't leave her behind.

Another burst of bubbles, this time larger, and her eyes closed. I was about to scream, to open my mouth and let death in, when I realized that there was someone above me. Someone diving to us. At first, I thought it was Cade, but as the form got closer, I realized it was Dylan.

It was in that moment that I understood how deeply rooted his feelings for Ava were. Cade had insisted repeatedly that he'd never have hurt Sera. I didn't believe it then, but I believed it now. He'd risked his life to give us a chance to survive. Like me, he'd managed to survive the fall. He could have swum for the surface and run again. Kept his freedom. Yet here he was. Here to save her again.

He grabbed the arm of the chair, hands next to mine, and together we pushed hard off the ground. It wasn't easy, and several times I thought we lost some ground, but with the two of us, we managed to get Sera and ourselves to the surface. To the air.

I sucked in a greedy breath and instantly began kicking for the shore. There was a crowd gathered—the hotel had been evacuated—and wading into the water to meet us were Cade and Noah.

"Up here," Cade said as he grabbed my arm to help drag me from the drink. "How long was she under?"

Anderson appeared behind him. He had the cuff keys in his hand and already had Sera off the chair and flat on the ground. She was so still. So pale. I dropped to my knees and started CPR.

One. Two. Three. Breathe.

"Anything?" Dylan asked. He was standing behind me.

One. Two. Three. Breathe...

I dropped my head to her chest. Nothing.

One. Two. Three. Breathe...

Something started to pull at my insides. A pressure different from anything I'd ever felt. It was like drowning and being torn to shreds all at the same time.

One. Two Three. Breathe...

"Sera," I said, keeping my compressions steady and my breathing even. Focused. I had to stay focused. The worst thing a soldier could do in a crisis was lose his shit. That's how people died. "Don't you fucking dare, Sera."

One. Two. Three. Breathe...

One. Two. Three. Breathe...

One. Two. Three. Breathe...

One. Two. Three—

A spout of water erupted from her mouth, and Sera began to cough and gag. The weight around my throat and in my chest lifted, and I could breathe again. It was the most amazing sound I'd ever heard. The most beautiful sight. With Cade's help, we rolled her onto her side, where she continued to expel what seemed like the entire lake.

"Cora?" Anderson knelt beside us, brushing a chunk of sopping hair from Sera's face.

Dylan pointed across the water. It took a minute, but I finally saw what he was gesturing to. Not far from where we'd been, a white form bobbed across the surface. "I got in one hell of a blow when we hit. Turns out you can't breathe underwater while unconscious."

He stepped in front of me and held out his hand. In his palm was a small glass vial filled halfway with a light blue liquid. "Take it."

"The antidote…" I couldn't believe it. In the chaos, I'd forgotten all about the poison. "Thank you," I said. I took the vial from him, uncorked the thing, and downed the contents. I probably should have used caution. Dylan could have given me anything. But, desperate times and all. A few moments ticked by. I was still here.

Out across the water, Cora's form bobbed languidly. I waited for her to move. To kick or flail or cry out for help. It didn't happen.

Cora Anderson was dead.

Sera and I were finally free.

I hadn't let her out of my sight since we reached the shore. There was a good chance I never would. Standing with her now, just inside the gates of Fort Hannity, it seemed like insanity that I'd even consider walking away from her. When I thought I'd lost her, back at the lake when I was sure she'd drowned, all I'd felt was black. There was a heaviness that tugged at me, and in those moments, I was able to understand Dylan better than anyone else ever could.

He was a monster. The things he'd done were horrible, and there would never be redemption. There was no coming back from the places he'd gone. No act of heroism or sacrifice would ever erase the horrors that he'd committed.

But he was also human. Flawed in so many ways,

but human. The connection he'd had to Ava had been everything. When it was severed, *he'd* been severed. It'd ripped his soul out and scattered it into so many pieces that it was impossible to put back together again.

He was me.

And if Sera had died, then I would have become him.

It was her presence in my life that held me back from that edge. She was my conscience, both the angel and the devil sitting on my shoulder, and my reason for wanting to resist my dark nature. To walk away from her would be giving up—and I was a stubborn son of a bitch.

The serum was active now, and there was no turning back. Anderson sat me down when we'd gotten back. He'd been cautious, but optimistic. I realized that I liked the old guy. I respected him. Cade and Noah were lucky, and as far as he was concerned, I could be, too. He'd offered Sera and me a place here. I had my choice of serving an honorable general who believed in doing real good for his world—and others—or leading a civilian life.

Sera... That one was going to be a bit more complicated. She was dead here. Well known and loved. Her parents still lived in town, but Anderson offered to talk to them. To bring them into the fold, so to speak. He would give them the choice he'd give his own wife once she returned—he'd called and told her about Kori, and she had jumped on the first plane back to the States. Her choice was easy. She would see her daughter again.

"What are you thinking right now?" Sera wrapped her arms around me and rested her head against my chest. It was amazing. There was a time, not long ago, that I didn't believe myself worthy of such contentment. But who was I to judge? Sera had deemed me worthy—and we both knew that girl was much smarter than I was.

"I just didn't think we'd get here, ya know?"

"Here…?"

"Six months ago, we were in hell. There was no light at the end of the tunnel. I was sure we'd both die in there. Now here we are. Evil Cora is gone, and we're free. Like, *free*. From Cora, from our old lives… I guess I never gave the future much thought."

"So…?"

"Do you want to stay? I still have the chip. Anderson promised they wouldn't remove it right away. I think they're at kind of a loss. If they take the chips out, then Kori will be stranded. She'd have to choose one world or the other. I don't think the general will be able to accept that. Not after getting to know her."

"From what Cade's told me, I don't think Cora will allow that," she said with a grin. "One thing that's the same here is that Cora Anderson rules the roost. Karl is like putty in her hands."

I laughed. I could see that. Just watching the guy as he spoke about his wife was intense. The other Cora had been passionate about her Karl, but she'd never been *in love* with him. Not the same kind of love that this Cora and Karl had for each other. It gave me hope.

"I think we should stick around. For a while, at least. Anderson is going to keep me monitored. We're still not sure what the long-term effects of the serum will be—if anything. I think I'm more comfortable staying close to people who might have a handle on controlling me if I go south."

"You won't." She was so sure, so confident. It was impossible not to share her opinion. "I'm okay with staying. I think I even like the idea of getting to know Ava's parents. Rabbit says they're really great..."

"What about him? You good with that? We stay here, and we're stuck with these people. Hell, I think wherever we go we'll be stuck with them. Doesn't seem to matter what versions of us are out there, we all seem to find each other. Over and over."

She nodded. "I'm good with it. They're our family, G."

She was right. They were. Sera couldn't remember, but I could. Neither one of us had ever had that. A family. I kind of liked the sound of it.

Epilogue

Two weeks later

Sera

The decision to stay on Cade's world had been fairly easy to make. Here, we had support. Here, we had family.

Speaking of the latter...

The general had left the ultimate decision up to me. He'd contacted Ava's family, had brought them to the base for a sit-down. From what I'd heard, they were in his office for almost four hours. Cade said he'd gone to check on them three times, worried that the conversation had taken a turn for the worse.

It hadn't.

They were understandably confused at first. I knew how they felt. The concept of multiple worlds? That was one hell of a pill to swallow. But they had swallowed. Swallowed *and* embraced. With about as much joy as this world's Cora Anderson—but that's a different story altogether, and not mine to tell.

I'd met them yesterday. Patrick and Mona Fielding. It'd gone pretty much as I'd expected. There were lots of tears and even more fears. Mona hadn't been familiar at all, but Patrick's face had tugged at something deep and unsettling. They were dark memories, unfortunately. My home hadn't been anything like the one we were in. But this version of him was brightness and love. In time, I knew he'd overwrite all the shady memories and uneasy feelings.

We'd talked for hours about everything under the sun. I told them a little bit—though, admittedly, not much—about my time at Infinity and the few things I remembered about my home. I found myself confessing the small truths I knew, about how my parents had used me to pay off their debt. How I'd been forced into an arranged marriage. That brought another round of tears and a whole lot of hugging. At the end of the day when I left them, I liked them. A lot. In fact, I could easily see myself falling in love with them—with everyone here.

After all, I was off to a great start.

I slipped my hand into G's. The guy I *loved*. We had walked through hell together and come out on the other side in one piece. My heart was his for as long as he wanted it. G had his good days and his bad. The serum hadn't shown any severe side effects, but we were still on guard. With Cora gone, we had no one to ask.

Since activating the serum to defeat Yancy, G had been a bit moodier. It took less to piss him off or, as Karl liked to say, rattle his cage. But Cade was determined to help with that. He'd been forcing G to meditate with him at least an hour every day. G grumbled that he hated it, but the truth was, he was growing attached to Cade—and the feeling was mutual.

As for me, I'd grown close to Kori. She'd never known me where she'd come from, and I didn't remember if I'd met her on my world, but here on this one, we'd been close. Related, actually. Kori Anderson was my cousin.

She and Cade had made it their personal mission to make us feel at home. They'd go out of their way to include us, and create opportunities for all of us to be together. It was a slow process, but we were starting to mesh. Some days it felt like we'd always been this way. Always together. Always there for one another...

"You ready for this?"

He mumbled something and tightened his hold on my hand. I'd had to beg and plead to get him here, and it wasn't until I agreed to take daily self-defense lessons on the base that he'd conceded. Our nightmare version of Cora and Karl Anderson might be gone, but he didn't want to take any chances. God knew with multiple worlds having the ability to skip, anything was possible.

I'd also told my parents—Ava's parents—about G. They knew he was another version of Dylan, who they'd known before, and they'd liked him. Well, at least they had before he'd turned into a raving lunatic in their daughter's memory. They'd made me promise to bring him back the next night for dinner. I had a feeling that it would be one of many, and I was more than okay with that. They wanted to get to know me, and I felt the same way. They even offered me a room in their house. Not Ava's, thank God, but the guest bedroom. I said I'd think about it.

Epilogue Part Two

One month later

Z

Dylan Granger had been slated for death when Cade broke him from jail more than a year ago. Upon recapture, Anderson had intended to pick right up where he left off. But I'd stepped up. The guy was a monster. There was no denying it. But I understood him in a way no one else could—or ever would. And he'd helped me save Sera. In the end, I felt like that at least warranted me taking a stab at it.

Anderson agreed to spare his life. Dylan would live out the rest of his days behind bars but would be permitted one visit a week. Since I was sure no one else wanted anything to do with him, I wagered that it would be Sera or me. But, like I said, I owed him her life. Without his help, we both would have died in that lake. It wasn't something I could—or would—ever forget.

Noah's opinion of me hadn't changed much. In the month we'd been here, he still avoided me. On the occasion he couldn't, he was sharp and cold as ice. Ash always apologized for him. They'd gotten an apartment together just outside the base, and he was starting medical school in a few months. Cade kept saying that he'd come around, but I think we both knew that was just his overly optimistic way of looking at things. Noah wouldn't come around—and I didn't hate or blame him for it. He'd fought me on recanting Dylan's death sentence. From what I'd heard, it'd created quite a rift between him and Anderson.

Things with Cade were…weird. There was no other way to put it, really. Unlike his best friend, his demeanor toward me had changed. While it wasn't a shitshow of sunshine and roses, I hadn't caught him glaring at me in weeks. He confessed once, at the end of the mandatory meditation sessions I'd been forced into, that he didn't see Dylan anymore when he looked at me. He saw a brother—just, a different one. Kind of like the way Noah viewed Kori. I was okay with that, too. I liked the guy.

Most of the time.

The town wasn't as accepting. I spent most of my time on the base and did whatever I could to make myself look as little like Dylan as I could. I'd dyed my hair a lighter shade of brown and started using contacts. Green was Sera's favorite color… And Anderson told people that I was a relative. A cousin of Cade's from South Florida. For the most part, people seemed to accept it, but that didn't change the way they all looked at me. It probably never would.

I slipped my hand into my jacket pocket, fingering the small, cool thing at the bottom. Sera was happy here, so here is where we'd stay until the day it changed. When—if—that happened, I would take her wherever she wanted to go. Out of state, country—or world. I would follow her anywhere, and if I had my way—and something told me I would—then she would do the same for me.

I'd taken a paying job on base as a combat instructor. My world's style of fighting was vastly different from the one they used here, and Anderson had been so intrigued that he'd insisted I come work for Fort Hannity.

The ring in the bottom of my pocket was a gift from Dylan. He'd given it to me moments before they took him away, after we'd pulled Sera from the water. He'd gotten it to give to Ava. Until this morning, I hadn't been sure I'd use it. I debated getting one of my own, but the more I looked at it, the surer I became that it was exactly what I would have picked out myself. Plus, there was an odd kind of symmetry to it. These different versions of us, all floating around out there doing their own thing, were unique in many ways. But we were also the same. We were tied together in a manner none of us would ever quite grasp.

The ring symbolized more than just a promise to Sera. I wanted to tie myself to her for as long as we both lived, but it also represented how far I'd come. On my world, rings were a symbol of service. I'd been forced to wear one from the time I was a young child. A token of my *pledge* to the government. They weren't something you wanted. Yet now it represented the potential of happiness. Of a future I never imagined was possible, with a person almost too good to be true. The serum would always be a dark cloud over my head, as would my time at Infinity, but I was determined to keep it at bay for her. Sera deserved to be happy, and I wanted to be the one to give her that.

I closed the car door and sucked in a breath. Sera had accepted a room with Ava's parents. At first, I found the whole thing weird. The way they'd looked at her made me uncomfortable. I knew they saw their daughter. But it'd gotten better over the last few weeks. In fact, I hadn't heard them slip, accidentally calling her Ava, in a while now.

I shuffled up the walk, down the small path lined with bright red bushes and small white flowers, and up the three stairs to the redwood porch.

This was the night my future began.

Noah and Ash

Noah

Six months after the events of Alpha...

"Is that the last one?" I set the box down and took a look around the room. The place was a disaster. Boxes from floor to ceiling, random piles of clothing, and bins of food stuffed anywhere there was room—which wasn't much. If Cade could see it, he'd have a massive coronary. Thankfully, he was off-world at the moment. He got three days leave every month to go with Kori so she could visit her father. I'd gone to visit him, too. He hadn't said it outright, but he wanted to get to know me. His own son, Kori's world's version of me, died before he'd gotten the chance. I told Cade I was doing it for the old man. The guy deserved an opportunity to get to know his son. But the truth? I liked the guy. Since coming home six months ago, our family had expanded. In four months' time, the plan was to get everyone together. Kori's father, my parents, Ava's family. Yep. We had everything covered except one person…

Ash pushed through the door and slumped against the wall. We'd rented a place about a mile from Fort Hannity. It was small and smelled like old cheese, but it was ours. I'd enrolled in school and was set to start in two months. Everything was right on track.

"So, um, we need to have that conversation you've been avoiding."

She dropped her gaze to the ground, suddenly fascinated by the loose thread in the carpet at her feet. She rolled it around beneath the toe of her sneaker, bringing her foot back and forth several times before sighing. "Gotta give you credit. You kept your word." She lifted her head and spread her arms.

I'd made her promise to discuss going back to her home world to meet her family. She'd made me promise not to bring it up again until we'd moved our stuff into the new place.

"You saw how things worked out for Kori. What are you afraid of?"

"My situation is different from hers."

Ash had been taken from her family as a child, stolen by an evil version of my own mother, and given to her world's version of Rebecca Calvert as a way to keep the woman focused on her work. During our escape from that world, Ash had skipped to her home world, but had chosen to stay with us until Dylan—and Cora—had been stopped.

Once things had settled, I'd worried she'd leave— but she'd been putting it off, even going as far as suggesting we get a place together…*for a while*.

I leaned back against the table and ran a hand

through my hair. "Ya gotta make a choice, Ash." I was treading on thin ice. I knew we'd needed to have this conversation, but I'd been dreading it. Before Cade and I skipped off to follow Dylan? Yeah. The me I'd been then would have simply ignored the issue. Let her settle in and get comfortable, because I wanted her here. That me was selfish.

I was still that same guy, but I'd changed, too. I wanted what was best for her. And what was best was for her to do the thing that would make her ultimately happy in the end.

"So you're asking me to choose? Between you and home?"

I crossed the room and took her hand—the one that housed the chip allowing us to travel between parallel versions of Earth. "You don't need to choose. Kori didn't. You can come and go. Get to know your family and your home, and still be with me." I gestured to the small, cluttered apartment. "This doesn't have to be for now. It can be home. It can be *home* without sacrificing everything else."

"What if she doesn't believe me? She won't recognize me…"

I tugged her forward and gently nudged her down on the only chair in the apartment. "I never told you about when we got to Kori's world, did I?"

She shook her head slowly.

"We changed tactics that time. Used to be that we just jumped into it. Started hunting Dylan, following the trail of bodies, yada, yada. That time, though, we took a big chance. Walked ourselves right into Fort Hannity and requested an audience with Anderson." I pulled over a stack of boxes and sat down across from her. "Cade did all the talking. Had some weird opinions about how I jammed my foot down my throat every time I opened my mouth."

She snickered. "Go figure."

"He told him the truth about everything—except me. All he said about me was that I was a fellow soldier on a mission to apprehend a criminal. Do you know what Karl said?"

She shook her head.

"He called Cade on his bullshit. Said that he'd know his own son no matter what. Didn't matter that he'd technically never met me. Made no difference that we'd never said a word to each other. He just *knew*."

"And you think they'll just know? My parents?" She rolled her eyes, but the action lacked her usual sarcasm. There was hope in her eyes, barely distinguishable beneath the layers and layers of walls she'd built up over the years. I'd broken through—like she'd broken, *smashed* through mine—but the rest of the world still had a ways to go.

"I think they'll feel it in here." I lifted her hand and placed it on my chest, across my heart. "I feel it…when I look at you. You belong with me. We just… We're supposed to be in each other's lives. I think they'll feel that, too."

"Why, Noah Anderson, that was uncharacteristically deep of you." She grinned and pressed the back of her hand against my forehead. "Feeling all right? Need a glass of water? Maybe an aspirin?"

I smacked her hand away but returned the grin. "I'm serious, Ash. I know things between us… Well, a lot of shit is kind of left unsaid, and I think we both like it that way. But…"

She leaned in a little closer. "But…?"

"But, I mean…" Shit. Why the hell was it so hard? She knew how I felt. This wasn't anything new. Not like it was news falling from the sky or anything. But we'd never said it. Made it all official and shit.

"But you love me?" she supplied.

"And you love me," I replied. "We can do anything together. Take down evil mad scientists—or go meet long-lost family."

"That doesn't sound horrible to me. And, the future…?"

"I'm not, like, suggesting we run out and get rings and a dog and matching tattoos or anything, but I want you to know. You're it. For me. You, Ashlyn Calvert, are the only girl for *this* Noah Anderson."

Reunion

Kori

Three days after the events of Alpha...

When I lost my mother, I would have given anything to see her again. A month, two weeks, five days...two minutes. Any small snippet of time. It was a dream, though. A fantasy. Science and medicine had made huge advances in my lifetime alone, but we couldn't bring people back from the grave. No one could do that.

Then I met Cade. Dedicated soldier, total hottie, sometimes too serious, and resident of a parallel version of my Earth. And Noah... Unrivaled pain-in-my-ass, secret softy, and the brother who'd died before I was born. I'd traveled the multiverse with them. Seen countless wonders and horrific atrocities. Found adventure and the fulfillment of a promise I'd made to my mom. *Living my life in vivid color.* They made it all possible.

They'd made today possible...

I crossed my ankles, shifted in my seat, then un-crossed them. I threaded my hands together, then set my own digits against each other in a rousing game of thumb wars. When that didn't calm my nerves, I jumped up and started to pace.

"Figured I'd find you in here." Cade poked his head through the door. His lopsided grin was a sight for sore eyes, and I grabbed his wrist and dragged him into the room.

"Oh my God. What took you so long? What if she'd gotten here before you did?"

He snickered and slung his free arm around my shoulder, pulling me close. Planting a kiss atop my head, he said, "The most badass version of Kori Anderson in the multiverse is afraid of a one-on-one?"

I pulled away and waggled a finger at him. "Nope. Not the most badass. Remember that wrestler version of me? She wins. Hands down."

"Huh. Good point."

"I don't know if I can do this." I'd said this to him a thousand times in the last twenty-four hours. His surrogate mother, this world's version of my mom, Cora Anderson, was due to arrive any minute.

She'd been out of the country when Noah, his girlfriend Ash, and I had arrived here. One call and she immediately hopped a plane to the States.

He placed a hand on either side of my face and tilted my head up so that we were eye to eye. "Cora could not get here fast enough, Kori. She's as eager to see you as you are to see her."

"But what if she—"

A knock at the door.

The bottom dropped from my stomach. "Oh my God…"

He kissed my forehead and stepped away. "You will be fine."

Before I could reply, he'd slipped out the door, leaving it open a crack.

A moment passed. Then another. In reality it was probably only a few seconds. But to me? It felt like hours. Days. An eternity…

She slipped into the room, closed the door behind her, and smiled. "Kori."

"*Mom*." The word slipped out, strangled and hoarse, before I could stop myself. "God, I'm so sorry. Cora."

She came a little closer. "I am to you whoever you would like me to be, Kori." She closed the distance, then, almost hesitantly, and brushed the back of her hand across my cheek. "You will never replace the Kori I lost, and I will never take the place of your mother. But you *are* my daughter. I will love you, and Noah, in any reality."

She backed away and settled in the chair across the room. There was one beside it, but I couldn't bring myself to sit. My heart hammered, and it felt like at any moment it would burst from my chest, leave a nice gaping hole for the world to see.

"Tell me about her. Your mother. What was she like?"

"She was funny and kind. She loved bad movies and animals." I snickered. "She made me pull over once in rush hour traffic to move a turtle from the road."

Cora laughed. "Don't judge. Noah will never admit it, but he does the same thing!"

"Oh my God, and junk food? She was frantic about junk food. Like, we kept a stash of it under the floorboard in my closet because it drove my dad insane."

"I knew a Cora once like that. She always had chocolate in her pockets. I used to tease her about it mercilessly."

Before I realized what I was doing, I'd taken the seat next to her. "Do you know a lot of, well, yous?"

"Quite a few, actually." She pulled up the hem of her skirt and stretched out her leg. On her ankle was the same kind of cuff that Cade and Noah had originally worn. She held up a finger to her lips, glanced to the left, and then the right and said, "I've been skipping since I was pregnant with Noah."

"So, you…what? Go in search of yourself?"

"I'm a scientist, Kori." She smiled. "My curiosity is never-ending. There are an infinite number of Earths out there, and I was rabid to know how they differed, how *I* differed."

"And what did you find?"

She leaned back. "Well, it wasn't always good. There are a few bad apples out there."

I snorted. "Yeah. Ran into one of them."

"She wasn't even the worst. But there are good, too. I've made some amazing friends."

"Friends? As in, you still have contact with them?"

"Of course! When you can travel across the multiverse, you're only a skip away. Look at you. You've been bouncing back and forth, right? Between here and your home?"

"I have," I admitted. "I wanted to meet you, and…" God. This was awkward. By the way, *I'm in love with your daughter's boyfriend…*

"If that hesitation is about Cade, you stop it right now. That boy is another son to me, and to see him happy, finally, is just about the greatest joy a mother can have."

"You don't mind?"

"How could I possibly mind? I love you both, and you're finally happy. My Kori, she was amazing. So bright and beautiful and kind… But she and Cade? They weren't the best thing for each other. You… I can see the changes in him since he's met you."

"Really?"

"Really," she said. "Now. Tell me about your father. Is he at all like my Karl?"

"He's a general, like your husband. He's harder, though. Sadder, ya know?"

"I cannot imagine how he must feel. I honestly don't know if I could survive losing him." She tilted her head back and sighed. "I almost did, once."

"Your husband almost died?"

"Well, not mine. Another version." She laughed. "It was the first and only time another Cora found me. She came here looking for help. Her husband was sick. Dying from a disease— Kori? Are you all right?"

I was just about the farthest thing from all right. In fact, I was ready to lose my mind. My final moments with my father, when I'd first left my own world, echoed in my head. "I… Yes. Sorry. So, another Karl Anderson was sick?"

"With something called Intracranial Dysplasia. The disease had yet to be discovered on her world, but on mine, we had a cure."

"And you helped them?"

She nodded. "I did. We were both pregnant with Noah at the time. The idea of him growing up without Karl…" She shuddered. "I couldn't fathom it."

"And that Cora? Is she one of the ones you keep in touch with? Your friend?"

A wistful look flickered in her eyes. "I would have loved that. Unfortunately, my cuff malfunctioned after that skip. All my data was lost. Her version of the tech was far less advanced than my own. I assume she couldn't find me again, either. I didn't skip again for a year and a half. I've always wondered about them. I hope they're happy."

"They're not." I said it low, under my breath and not really intending her to hear, but she did.

"Not happy?"

"Well, I mean they were. I suppose are, in most ways. Noah didn't grow up without Karl, but Kori grew up without Noah."

She was totally confused. "I don't understand."

"Noah. That Noah. He was never born. She lost him. He died."

"How could you know that…?"

I swallowed, and it took several tries to get the words out. "She's gone, too."

"She's—that Karl, that Cora, it was your—"

"My mother. He told me about it right before I left my world with Cade and Noah. He remembered seeing you that night. Standing over his bed… He knew you weren't her. That you'd come from someplace else to save his life."

She was off the chair and throwing her arms around

me before I could blink. I returned the embrace, clinging to her as though she was the only thing anchoring me to this world. She wasn't my Cora Anderson, but she was right—she was still my mother. Mom would have been happy I was here. She'd be thrilled that *this* particular version of Cora Anderson was now in my life. She'd find it poetic. Cosmic. Mom would swear that it was fate.

That it was living my life in vivid color…

Acknowledgments

On one hand, I'm so excited to have been able to give these characters their happy ending. They went through a lot and deserve it! On the other, I'm sad that the journey is over. This series was a blast and I'll miss it. Thank you to my editor, Liz Pelletier, and my agent, Nicole Resciniti, for believing in these books and helping me share them with the world. I'm grateful and blessed to have you guys in my corner.

A huge thank you to everyone who helped get this little book into the world. Stacy Abrams, Rosemary Clement, Melissa Montovani, Lisa Knapp, and to L.J. Anderson and Toni Kerr for making both the inside and outside of the book look so awesome!

Big thanks to Gia Mallory and Baker Hartford for the multiple read-throughs. Without you two, G's shirt probably would have changed color in every chapter. For all the midnight plotting sessions and encouragement—you guys rock my socks and this book is as awesome as it is because of you!

To all the readers who took this journey with me,

thank you. Without you, there wouldn't be a series. Without you, I wouldn't get to live my dream. I am grateful to each and every one of you!

As always, eternal thanks to my family, especially my husband. My rock, my sanity, and occasionally, the housekeeper/dog walker/chef/chauffer/everything else needed to function. You are my heart and soul.

Finally, my mom. When this series started, she was battling cancer. Now, as the series ends, she's fighting again. Words cannot express the love and respect I have for this woman. She is the definition of determination, of standing tall, and continues to be a source of true inspiration.

Thank you, Mom, for teaching me how to fight.

Grab the Entangled Teen releases readers are talking about!

True Storm
by L.E. Sterling

All is not well in Plague-ravaged Dominion City. The Watchers have come out of hiding, spreading chaos and death throughout the city, and suddenly Lucy finds herself torn between three men with secrets of their own. Betrayal is a cruel lesson, and to survive this deadly game of politics, Lucy is forced into agreeing to a marriage of convenience. But DNA isn't the only thing they want from Lucy...or her sister.

Unraveled
by Kate Jarvik Birch

Ella isn't anyone's pet anymore, but she's certainly not free. Turns out the government isn't planning mass rehabilitation... they're planning a mass *extermination*. With the help of a small group of rebels, Ella and Penn set out to end this for good. But when they're implicated in a string of bombings, no one is safe. If she can't untangle the web of blackmail and lies, she won't just lose her chance at freedom, she'll lose everyone she loves.

Zombie Abbey
by Lauren Baratz-Logsted

1920, England

And the three teenage Clarke sisters thought what they'd wear to dinner was their biggest problem...

Lady Kate, the entitled eldest.

Lady Grace, lost in the middle and wishing she were braver.

Lady Lizzy, so endlessly sunny, it's easy to underestimate her.

Then there's Will Harvey, the proud, to-die-for—and possibly die with!—stable boy; Daniel Murray, the resourceful second footman with a secret; Raymond Allen, the unfortunate-looking young duke; and Fanny Rogers, the unsinkable kitchen maid.

Upstairs! Downstairs! Toss in some farmers and villagers!

None of them ever expected to work together for any reason.

But none of them had ever seen anything like this.

Bring Me Their Hearts
by Sara Wolf

Zera is a Heartless—the immortal, unaging soldier of the witch Nightsinger. With her heart in a jar under Nightsinger's control, she serves the witch unquestioningly. Until Nightsinger asks Zera for a prince's heart in exchange for her own.

No one can challenge Crown Prince Lucien d'Malvane... until the arrival of Lady Zera. She's inelegant, smart-mouthed, carefree, and out for his blood. The prince's honor has him quickly aiming for her throat.

So begins a game of cat and mouse between a girl with nothing to lose and a boy who has it all.

Winner takes the loser's heart.

Literally.

THE NOVEMBER GIRL
BY LYDIA KANG

I'm Anda, and the lake is my mother. I am the November storms that terrify sailors, and with their deaths, I keep the island alive.

Hector has come to Isle Royale to hide. My little island on Lake Superior is shut down for the winter, and there's no one here but me. And now him.

Hector is running from the violence in his life, but violence runs through my veins. I should send him away. But I'm half-human, too, and Hector makes me want to listen to my foolish, half-human heart. And if do, I can't protect him from the storms coming for us.

SEIZE TODAY
BY PINTIP DUNN

Seventeen-year-old Olivia Dresden is a precognitive. Since different versions of people's futures flicker before her eyes, she doesn't have to believe in human decency. She can see the way for everyone to be their best self-if only they would make the right decisions. No one is more conflicted than her mother, and Olivia can only watch as Chairwoman Dresden chooses the dark, destructive course every time. Yet Olivia remains fiercely loyal to the woman her mother could be.

But when the chairwoman captures Ryder Russell, the striking and strong-willed boy from the rebel Underground, Olivia sees a vision of her own imminent death...at Ryder's hand. Despite her bleak fate, she rescues Ryder and flees with him, drawing her mother's fury and sparking a romance as doomed as Olivia herself. As the full extent of Chairwoman Dresden's gruesome plan is revealed, Olivia must find the courage to live in the present-and stop her mother before she destroys the world.

entangled teen

an imprint of Entangled Publishing LLC